All rights reserved.

Dedicated to all the men and women who have fought for our freedom.

1.

Hugh Smith came to attention outside the Captain's door and then knocked. He wondered what he could have done wrong for a lowly private to be summoned to the Captain's Office. Fear also struck him. Had something happened to Terri or one of the girls?

"Yes?" The Captain did not recognize the private at his door. There were so many recruits as they tried to ramp up for the coming threat.

"Private Smith reporting as ordered sir." Hugh answered as he entered the office then came to attention in front of the Captain's desk.

Ah yes, the Officer remembered. The private that all the DIs had been telling him about. The guy who might be teaching his recruit class more than the DIs were. "At ease Private."

Hugh took the proper pose.

The officer was addressing the lowest of low. He took his time, finishing the paperwork he had been doing. Finally, he looked up and considered the man in front of his desk. "The Drill Instructors are impressed with you, Private."

Hugh did not know quite what to say. He knew he was different than the average recruit that the DIs were used to. He was several years older and much more experienced than most others. He was twice the age of the average prewar recruit.

"That's good, sir." He could think to say. He thought that lame wondering if he just blew the first impression.

"The DI's think your officer material." For the first time the Captain took a hard look at Hugh. Just looking he was impressed. The man was squared away as few officers were. He looked like a DI. Maybe there was something here. "What do you think?"

"Believe I might make a decent officer, sir." After all he had been a Lieutenant on the Sheriff's Department.

"I'll schedule you to leave for O.T.S. at the end of the week." The Captain had expected the recruit to smile but noticed that the private was not thrilled. "Problem Private?"

Hugh was obviously troubled as he thought of the men, he had become close to and stammered into his reply. "Sir, don't officers need the respect of their men?"

The Captain smiled. Where was the guy going with this? Most recruits would be happy to cut even a day off basic. "Good thing to have."

"If, Captain, this is a one-time offer, I'll leave Friday," Hugh conceded, "but I believe that I'll have more respect from my men if I stick basic out with them and then go to OTS."

"You've got three more weeks of basic, and then ninety days of OTS," the Officer said. "You can cut out three weeks of basic. That's cutting out three weeks of torture. There's no need to put yourself through extra when you don't have to. No one expects that."

Hugh nodded as his mind raced. "Yes sir. I just don't think its right to leave my guys behind. If I can exercise the option, I'll go to OTS after basic, sir, if its o.k."

The DIs had been right. The best officers looked after the welfare and morale of their men. Doing that just gained you respect among the ranks. This man would make the best kind of officer. "I'll schedule you for three weeks from Monday. I admire what you're doing but think it unnecessary. The DI's say the men respect you more than they do the DI's. You've already got the men's respect."

"Maybe, sir," Smith nodded, "but I think it's something I should do."

The Captain's admiration continued to grow. "Have it your way, private. Just know you will only get the weekend off between basic and OTS, dismissed."

"Thank you, sir!" Hugh performed a smart military about face. He wondered what he had just gotten himself into. Not just the six weeks of basic but now almost five months when you add on OTS.

The Joint Chiefs were grim. From the looks of things, they would soon be only thing standing against the Chinese. No, the British Isles had not fallen but they could not muster an offensive. They were barely hanging on the way it was. Israel had not fallen but they were surrounded. Australia had not yet been attacked but that was a matter of time. Only four islands of democracy were left in the world, and they had no way of combining forces.

"Sir, the Chinese rolled over Europe like a steamroller only the U.K. has any chance of holding out. Many countries in Europe had good armies. There's not a quality army in Africa." General Sabota was speaking. He was the new Chief of Staff of the Marines.

"How fast are they moving?" Scott Douglas asked the question while fearing the answer.

"A good day for them they make a hundred miles," Wilcox answered. "On a good day for us they only make twenty-five."

Douglas knew that as Chairman of the Joint Chief's it was his responsibility to tell the President the truth as he perceived it. "Looks like the Americas will soon stand alone."

"That would be my assessment, General," Admiral Tingle agreed. "Given the situation I would say we already do stand alone. There is simply no military force of any significance that can come to our aid."

Will listened to this. What happened to that life of a simple farm boy. The weight of the world was pressing down on his shoulders.

The private looked a bit worse for the wear. Apparently, he had been traveling for some time. Still, there was something about his demeanor.

"Just who might you be," the Major asked.

"Private First-Class Hugh Smith, sir." Hugh saluted, and then handed the officer his orders.

The Major glanced over the orders. Yep, this puke was to report on this date to O.T.S. The Army must be getting hard up for officers. This guy did not look like much to him. "You're assigned to the Patton barracks, candidate. Go find you a bunk."

Hugh saluted and turned left to carry out the order he had just been given.

"What are you thinkin'?" Howard Sevrin was visiting the residence of the New White House. He no longer farmed, nor did he rent the place out. With the money they made from MEC he had turned the farm into a preserve and expanded it by several hundred acres. "You look troubled, son."

"It's hard not to be troubled in times like these. It's like waiting for the other shoe to drop." The President looked directly at his dad. "The Chinese have invaded every other continent in the world except the Americas and Australia."

"Maybe the supply lines too long," Howard offered. "They could be waitin' to solidify their gains in Europe and Africa before they come here."

"They've got the troops to do both," Will countered. "I think they will be here sooner rather than later."

"We gonna be ready, son?"

"No, dad." Will had been looking out the window at the Capitol city of Lincoln. Now he turned to look at his dad. "We are not."

"Then we leave the battle to the Lord" Howard said. "He can win even when we can't."

Admiral Lee had been on the supersub for four hours. He was not at all sure how to get out, or how long it would take him to get out if he wished to leave. This was like Beijing but under water. The men would have luxuries here that they would not have in the field. The food would be the best; there were various rec areas and so forth. You had to keep them occupied for the journey of a week or more. Such large vessels did not travel at high speeds.

"Sir, we are coming to your quarters if you would wish to freshen up and rest," the Captain said. "We will be having lunch soon, and then we can resume your inspection."

"And where are you planning on serving me my lunch, Captain," Lee asked.

"Why, the officer's mess, of course, sir." The Captain smiled and bowed slightly.

Lee frowned. "What is good enough for the men is good enough for me. I will eat with the enlisted men."

Now the Captain looked apprehensive. "But, sir, the Chef has gone to great lengths to provide a special meal for you. He would…"

"Let him eat it then," Lee barked, "I will eat with the men."

The junior officer snapped to attention and bowed. "Yes sir."

Lee went into his quarters. He would lie down until lunch. In truth he was getting a bit long in the tooth for this. Still, he would not miss the conquest of the world. All that really stood in the way was America and they were too fat to fight. He drifted a moment and then came back to himself. Lee had never been a true believer in Communism. The Party was a means to an end. Their system instilled discipline and silenced those that would buck the system. This had led to the greatest military machine that the world had ever known. Lee knew his health was failing. Age did that to any man no matter how great. He would die with his boots on, not in battle, but celebrating victory. Then would come the long night.

"Progress report on the IPF fighters." Frank moved onto the next item of business on the agenda for the MEC board of directors. The meeting was already into its third hour.

"To bring her up to the specs the government has put forth, to have her fully tested, developed and ready to fight will take another year." Lance, the engineer in charge of the project, said smugly.

"Did you see what they did today?" Frank was instantly out of his seat shouting while he leaned on the table toward the engineer. "The Chinese are moving through Africa. Who knows how long it will be until they're to our very shores? A year is not good enough! If you guys can't build this war bird, I'll fire the whole lot of you and find engineers that can build it!"

"You know there is no one in the world that knows these systems better than I do." Lance was out of his seat leaning on the table toward Frank. He was red-faced and full of self-importance. "We simply cannot perform miracles."

"You're working what, eight or nine hours a day?" Frank was still angry. He stood straight but his volume was still up.

"Sometimes ten," Lance shouted back leaning harder on the table.

"Not good enough," Frank shouted.

"I will not work my people into the ground!" Lance shouted back knowing he was milking the project to stay in his position as long as possible. He straightened up. "We'll get it done when it's right."

"I expect it in no more than six months," Frank said it calmly as he looked Lance in the eye and sat down. "The world simply doesn't have longer than that."

"An unrealistic expectation!" Lance was still a little loud. He knew that they could have it done by then but liked the perks one got heading up an important project. He retook his seat.

Frank called the next thing on the agenda. He was not yet going to push this any farther today. Lance did know these systems best; he had designed half of them. Still, America could not wait much longer.

The Chinese Lieutenant saw the lone figure at the end of the long wooden pier in what was once known as Saigon. Viet Nam had now become a province of China. The small, thin man stood ramrod straight in an impeccable naval uniform. As he approached the face of the Admiral Hu became clear.

"What are you doing, sir?" The Lieutenant asked the question as they exchanged salutes.

The Admiral smiled as he recognized one of his up-and-coming junior officers. "All my life I have dreamed of worlds to conquer. All my life I have trained for this moment." He pointed out to sea. "The world is ours for the taking. It will be nobly won by a people always destined to rule the world. The Chinese people know no peer in this world. We have the longest, richest history of any race. The future is unlimited."

The explosion rocked the entire port. The Admiral and Lieutenant, standing directly above the charge were vaporized. A dozen nearby ships were damaged. One of the smaller frigates was sunk and a battleship listed badly. The Chinese would blame the local resistance. The Vietnamese were a stubborn people. The Chinese had helped them throw off the French and then the Americans. The Chinese thought the people of Viet Nam should have been grateful for the Chinese intervention in their country.

No one saw the frogman slip below the waves after the explosion. He dove fifty feet or so to the waiting submarine with the silent engine from MEC. It was quite luxurious for a sub, carpeted floors and a full kitchen. She was fully automated and acted on her master's voice commands. The computer controls were imprinted on his voice and his alone. She was the size of a small house. The little boat could literally stay submerged for months as much of its capacity was taken with food, water and oxygen. She was also more silent than any sub in any military command. The frogman entered the air lock and pressurized it. Wilson took off his wet suit, walked through drying blowers and strolled toward the bridge.

"Control." Wilson spoke in a normal voice. He was not bothered that he had just killed multiple enemy combatants. He was especially not bothered that one of the enemy uniformed personnel was Admiral Hu. Wilson knew Hu. He had studied the man and his tactics. Hu was the best naval commander the Chinese had, maybe the best naval strategist in the world. The odds were not yet even, and he would not be able to even them alone, but he could help even them up for America. He would make strategic strikes where and when he could.

"Awaiting your command." The automated voice answered.

"Set course and engage for the United Kingdom," Wilson ordered.

"Parameters," the computer asked.

"Combat mode," Wilson stopped for a moment, thinking, "stealth approach."

"No active threats currently detected. There are many vessels operating in the area, but none appear to have a lock on to this vessel. Also, none are in an attitude bearing toward this vessel." The computer informed him of the tactical situation. There was a pause. "Ready to activate program."

"Activate." Wilson felt the boat move under his feet. He would get some sleep. When he had this rig built, they wondered why he had put a recliner and bed right next to the operations board. This was why. The little sub would run independently until it perceived a threat, and then ask him what to do. Hopefully it would be a smooth voyage. He could use the sleep.

Premier Ho decided that his army simply could not be spread too thin. Anything to enhance his glory. The men who died did so to further his power. No sacrifice was too great for that. As they wrapped up Europe and Africa, he watched the fully loaded super submarine slip below the water in a building larger than any he knew of anywhere else in the world. The sub could slip under water inside and then leave undetected beneath the water. A quarter of a million men were aboard her along with dozens of combat aircraft, armor, and everything they would need for two weeks of combat. When it surfaced the top three decks could be used as an aircraft carrier. Soon the Americas would come under the wrath of the Chinese Army. Soon The Party would prevail worldwide. The Russians had once been their allies in this fight. Now the Russians would also feel the wrath of his power. They would see now how true believers could get things done.

He remembered watching the American movie about their General Patton from the Second World War. Such a man would not have lasted in the Communist system, but he had lessons to teach. 'All glory is fleeting,' he said. Ho guessed that was probably true. He knew that as he got older, a younger man would eventually wrestle control of the Party from him. By that time wrestling control of the party away would mean to wrestle control of the world away. Glory might be fleeting, but few would know the glory he would know in his time. He felt a strange kinship with Alexander the Great. They would both know what it was like to rule the entire world.

A few days later a young Argentinean ensign manning the watch on the Argentinean naval frigate thought he was seeing things. An island was rising from the ocean off the coast of Santa Cruz. He had seen it as it started to first break the surface, but still had not sounded the alarm. His cousin had told him that aliens had bases on the ocean floor near there. He had not believed him until now. Surely this was otherworldly. No government on Earth could build anything this size. The technology would have to be so advanced that it was beyond human comprehension. When the Chinese supersub was halfway out of the water, the

Ensign finally found his wits and sounded the alarm.

The senior officers were enjoying a dinner prepared by the Chef wondering what the young one was shouting about. They got up from the captain's private dining room and looked in the direction that he was pointing. They stood slack-jawed for a long moment. None of the ranking officers could believe what they were seeing. The captain was the first to regain his senses. He ran to the bridge where he ordered the ship to come about, away from the behemoth and all engines to full. Immediate and full throttle retreat was the only option that crossed anyone's mind.

Admiral Lee had taken complete control of this first mission to the Americas. His command of the sub was not in keeping with naval etiquette, but rank had its privileges. The huge submarine was just breaking the surface when he ordered the outer doors of the upper decks opened. As soon as the flight decks cleared the water each one opened and prepared for launch. Ho did not bring the boat completely to surface when he leveled her out and ordered the launch of all aircraft. Two dozen fighters screamed into the sky. Each aircraft had a target to hit and went to their assigned duties. When all aircraft were away Lee brought the great boat to full surface and steamed for port so that they might dock and unload their human cargo.

The Argentine Ensign was transfixed. He would be part of first contact with an alien species. Were they hostile or friendly? He hoped friendly because how could he live to write a best-selling book about it if they killed him? The U.F.O. had launched smaller craft. He wondered if this was how they were going to attempt to contact humans for the first time. Would it not be wild to be one of the first to touch an alien? Several were now closing on their ship. What if they were hostile? How do you fight aliens? They had come across thousands of light years to get here. Their technology was certainly beyond anything humans understood. He was expecting a death ray to lash out at them any second.

The Chinese Flight Commander leading the first air strike bore down on the military surface ship. Yang's squadron was to seek targets of opportunity, preferably military. He thought it nice that such a target should present itself in the first moments of their operation. It looked like an older U.S. frigate. Probably one that Argentina had bought when the U.S. decommissioned it. That was a thought! Would it still be called the United States after they had conquered it? Who knew what The Party would do? Yang dove his plane at the front of his squadron and loosed a missile. Per his orders two other pilots also targeted the ship.

The Argentine Ensign thought that the UFO's were shaped strangely like human aircraft. Of course, aerodynamics was basic, so they might look the same on another world. The puff from the wing of the craft looked like a missile firing from one of the Argentine fighters he had seen during war games. Just before the missile hit, the defensive guns of the frigate began to fire on the aircraft. He saw no effect. It was then that the aircraft was close enough that he could see the red Chinese star on the side and wings. He was disappointed that he would be killed by the imperial Chinese, not an alien.

Commander Yang watched with satisfaction as the frigate exploded. All three missiles had found their mark. The first battle of the Americas, however small, was won.

At almost the same moment that the Argentineans died, the entire Chilean Navy went on full alert. Something huge was approaching their coast and launching aircraft. They had no warning. How could something so huge get in so close without being seen? As they fired their engines of their ships that had lay dormant in port, the Chinese aircraft bore in. Soon the tiny navy was afire. Within a half-hour almost every ship in the Chilean Navy was on the bottom of the harbor floor.

Admiral Lee got the reports of the Chilean action that evening. He was angry that his forces had been so inefficient. They had sunk several ships at the mouth of one of the best harbors along the Chilean coast. Now they would have to clean out the harbor before they could use it. Wasted time and wasted resources. At least they could have let the Chileans think they were making a run for it. They could have let them get out of the harbor before they sunk them. He commanded the Chinese Navy he did have resources to waste, but he hated waste. He would discipline the commanders of the Chilean operation.

For hours the port had been secure. Troops continued to pour into Argentina. The city beyond was nearly secure, only sporadic gunfire could still be heard. The small military force that had confronted them had fought bravely but had no chance against such overwhelming forces. Much of the city burned, fouling the air.

General Chan now stepped ashore. He would lead the conquering of the Americas. He turned to those surrounding him and spoke. "Americans have always thought themselves so superior. They are about to find out who really is the super race."

"So much land with so few living on it," Agreed Colonel Ye. "Their arrogance knows no bounds. They use much of the world's resources for their own glutinous habits. They will learn the right way, the Chinese way!"

"They shall find temperance under the rule of the Party." Chan smiled with satisfaction at the thought of the arrogant Americans under his thumb.

His was a simple equation. He had many times the number of men of any army he would face. You throw overwhelming numbers at them, and they fall from attrition. He wished he could match wits with a worthy opponent who had a like number of forces. Alas, there was no army on Earth that could begin to match the manpower and no commander that could match his intellect.

There were refugees as far as he could see. Some were in vehicles, some in horse drawn carriages and many walked. They easily numbered in the tens of thousands. Gary set the camera up so that it had the longest shot of the road, literally thousands of people in the camera view. He was in southern Brazil, the war was still in southern Argentina, the land of Evita, and already the people were panicking, fleeing. Where did you flee to from this? What was now officially called World War Three had engulfed all the world except North America and it was headed there. Gary flipped on the camera, stepped in front of it and pressed his ear- piece further in so he could hear his cue from WNN.

"This is Gary Patton." Everyone watched WNN now. They had the most reporters in the most places of interest. Gary was becoming the voice of the war in America. The jungle road that was packed with people heading north was clearly visible behind him. "The roads into Brazil are so crowded that they are nearly at a standstill. The Third World War has come to the America's. People are fleeing north as the Red Army floods into Argentina and Chile. They are sweeping all resistance before them. No one on any continent has stood before them and now the armies of South America prove to be no different. The forces here are not well trained or equipped and other armies that have been beaten were much more formidable. Ominously, they are moving north. This is Gary Patton signing off."

Safety was north. When Gary finished his report, he headed south.

General Chan had found an office with a satellite dish. He had the best technical guys in the country. They would put the dish to good use. The office appeared to have had some military application, but what that was he could not tell. They had left in such a hurry that they had left the television and coffeepot on. He poured himself a cup of coffee and found the blend rich. That would be something to enjoy in this area now that he had decided to move his headquarters on shore. Much of the world's coffee was grown in southern American continent.

Chan noticed the picture change on the television and could tell it was a report on the war. He ordered a Lieutenant on his staff to interpret for him. Patton's report was gratifying. People well away from the fighting were already panicking. This could only help the war effort. He decided to leave the news on. This was a good way to gather intelligence. The General issued an order that the broadcasts would be monitored around the clock. He was sure that the U.S. President would soon speak, and he wanted to see what he had to say. With his forces pressing this close he expected the inexperienced American to panic. Panic in your enemies was a good thing. Panic usually caused bad decisions. Maybe they would sue for peace. Chan knew that anything less than unconditional surrender would never be accepted. The Americans must be beaten for the world to truly be conquered.

Sandy watched as her husband prepared for his fireside chat. This war was not really engaged, and she could already see the wear on him. Crow's feet were starting to grow around his eyes, she saw gray around his temples and bags beneath his eyes. Men were about to die on his orders. As she rubbed her protruding belly she prayed, *'Dear God, give him strength. Sustain him.'*

"My fellow citizens of this great land." Will started his fireside chat. "Today we have learned that the Chinese invasion of the America's has started. This is not something unexpected. The question is not if we will stop them, but where. We can accept no other outcome. They are yet a long way from our home soil, yet they are in our back yard. We will fight for the Americas as a whole, but if they dare to set foot on our land, we will wage a war more terrible than they can imagine. I warn the Chinese to think before they try to invade the nation called 'One Nation under God.'

"To paraphrase Winston Churchill, we will fight them in the air, we will fight them on the sea, we will fight them on the land, we will fight them in space if necessary and we will never give up. To take a page from Franklin Roosevelt, the only thing we have to fear is fear itself. We have no reason to be afraid. God will sustain us if only we, as a nation, will beseech him in prayer and fasting while obeying his commands. If He be with us, then numbers do not matter. The peoples that inhabited the Promised Land were bigger and stronger than the Children of Israel and yet Israel was victorious. I point to what they do now as an example, they continue to push the enemy backward and even win large tracts of land. Weapons do not matter. The battle belongs to the Lord. We must again pay for our country in blood because we, for a time, turned away from Him. We thought we were self-sufficient and no longer needed God. Now we must make this ground holy again. The Bible says that if we humble ourselves before God and pray, he will heal our land. I call our nation to humble prayer. This must be our most urgent priority."

Chan smiled at the translation. Let the President depend on some unseen Being, he would trust his guns. Mao said that power comes from the barrel of a gun. The Party was his god. The Party was power. The gun was his god's tool.

The Chinese Ensign took off in his bomber. His co-pilot, a Lieutenant, was nocuous. This was not fit duty for a military pilot. This time they had drawn the grim assignment. It was not the first time. The smell was already intense even though the fighting was only hours old. They would clean the plane when they landed, but the smell would persist for days. Once several miles out to sea he opened the bomb bay doors and released the cargo. Hundreds of bodies of dead Chinese soldiers and Argentines fell from the plane and splashed into the ocean. Even as they hit the water was so clear he could see the sharks starting to gather for their feast.

The brass said it was simply too expensive to ship the soldier's bodies home, so their bodies were stripped of useful items and loaded aboard planes. If they had studied the currents right the bodies would be taken out to sea, those that sea creatures did not claim. The Ensign turned the bomber toward the base.

"There is good news tonight.' Jim Arvin wrote the major story of the day that was above the fold on the front page. "Yes, the Chinese have landed in South America. No, no one seems to be able to stand before them. Even as each army in turn crumbles before the relentless war machine of the Asian juggernaut, good things happen.

"The President of the United States and the First Lady today have welcomed their seventh child into the world. With Will Jr., Ester, Matt, Mary, Mark and Luke to help her mother, Ruth Ann Sevrin will have plenty of people to look after her. Not to mention, of course, her grandparents.

"The seven-pound eight-ounce bundle of joy arrived just before five a.m. The President was at the First Lady's bedside through the entire birthing process. So, miracles still happen. The world has not yet come to an end. There is one more precious life to fight for, one more reason to believe that God is still in control. There is one more reason to have hope."

Pictures of the newborn and the entire Sevrin family were on front pages everywhere.

2.

General Webster always liked doing this. It was always a privilege to welcome these bright young faces into the officer corps. Right now, all the faces were not so young. All comers were welcome if they could pass the test. He wondered how many of these, America's best, would even be alive one or two years hence. This was a war of survival. Lose and life as you have come to know it would cease to exist. Life would never be the same regardless of the outcome. Large wars had a way of changing life permanently. World wars changed the whole world. Win and you get to do much to reshape the world, make it better or worse as is your ilk. There would have to be well thought out steps if things were to be properly executed in the peace that would follow. Nobody thought of such things when they were fighting for their very existence. That's why things were never done quite right after the war.

Of course, he could not wait to go south, east, or west, and engage the enemy. He had trained his whole being for such a time as this. There was no greater test of a man than outfoxing the enemy when everything is on the line. Win and live. Lose and die. The enemy was in all directions. Still, he had been assigned to train the new recruits and that was a daunting task, as so many took their first turn at military service. At last, he had shaken all but three graduating hands. The captain vacated the microphone where he had been calling off the names of candidates that had become Second Lieutenants and the General stepped up to it again. There were three men that had earned special recognition from this class.

"Under normal conditions everyone to graduate from Officer's Candidate School graduates as a Second Lieutenant. These are not normal conditions. At the order of the President of the United States we are expanding the United States Army so fast that we need some higher-ranking officers. They must be men well-chosen with the ability to lead men in desperate times. They simply do not have time to come up through the ranks. Due to this the rules have changed so that any Candidate who graduates number one either physically or academically in his class shall graduate as a First Lieutenant. Any Candidate who graduates number one in his class both physically and academically will graduate as a Captain."

Now Hugh was sure that they had simply forgotten him. He knew that he had not graduated number one in either case. Oh well, he knew he had graduated. He would simply point out their mistake quietly after the ceremony. Terri and the girls would be disappointed that they had not seen him cross the stage. Things like this happen.

"Further" the General continued "the five Drill Instructors that have dealings with this class have voted by secret ballot on who is the best Candidate in this class. If any three vote for the same Candidate he will graduate a First Lieutenant. If all five vote for the same Candidate he will graduate a Captain."

Yep, Hugh thought. They had forgotten him.

"Would Candidate Mitchell E. Standmore step forward." The Candidate strode across the stage, his uniform tailored to his body builder frame. The General continued as he pinned the silver bars on Mitch's collar. "Mitch was basically uncontested in the physical aspects of this training. He has earned the rank of First Lieutenant."

Mitch saluted and held it until the General had returned it, then made his way back to his place into formation to the polite applause of the crowd.

"Now would Candidate Angelo V. Lopez step forward?"

Lopez was a smaller man who simply looked smart. His decorum was not lost on the more than casual observer. He was born for the uniform. His stride was purposeful as he made his way to the podium.

"This is the brain of this class." Those gathered laughed politely. "In fact, Candidate Lopez has scored one of the highest scores ever recorded in these academic rigors." The crowd applauded. "Therefore he graduates a First Lieutenant."

Lopez faltered for a moment, his knees giving slightly, when the General announced that he had scored one of the highest scores ever. No one had told him this. He accepted his handshake, gave his salute, the General returned it, and then Lopez found his way back to the formation.

Terri could not imagine what had happened. She could see Hugh in the formation, but they had not called his name. Had he failed something and so not graduated? Tears started to fill her eyes.

"Now I have the pleasure to introduce to you the first of his kind," the General said. "Since we are in such great need of good men, let us hope that he is not the last of his kind."

The General would later say that while others graduated Captain, there was never another like Smith.

"As I stated and you have seen, graduating first in your class has its rewards. So, it has been in every class. In two other classes three Drill Instructors agreed on the best candidate and we had a third First Lieutenant. Never has any man been able to graduate first both physically and academically or garner all five votes of the Drill Instructors. As you know, two men graduated first in a discipline and so were awarded the silver bars of a First Lieutenant. For the first time a man has received all five votes of the Drill Instructors as the best Officer's Candidate in the class."

There was a gasp from the crowd. All the Candidates started to glance in the direction of Hugh Smith. Those near him started slapping him on the back.

"Would Officer's Candidate Hugh Wallace Smith please step forward?"

A huge cheer went up from the newly promoted Lieutenants. Even the Drill

Instructors, who usually made it mantra to show no emotion clapped. Hugh was frozen in place. He had to be prodded from his place by his classmates. He thought his knees would fail him as he ascended the stairs.

As General Webster pinned the double bars of a Captain on Hugh's collar he spoke quietly to Hugh. "Would you have time to come by my office later, Captain?"

The General was clearly impressed by the man before him.

"Sir, my family is here," Hugh boldly stated, "I haven't seen them for almost five months."

The General smiled. He was a family man too. This impressed him even more. "See you in my office at 0900 tomorrow. You have free time until then. With what I've got in mind for you, you should be able to see a lot of your family."

Hugh saluted. "That would be wonderful, sir."

Webster returned the salute. "Take it while you can, son. This war will get a whole lot uglier before it's over."

Hugh descended the stage and took his place with the rest of his class. Soon the General dismissed the class to liberty. Most were now on a week's leave, Will had about sixteen hours. The girls rushed into their Daddy's arms. They did not quite understand what had happened; they just knew that Daddy had done well. What was more important was that they could finally get a hug from him.

Terri stood a short distance away. "I'm so proud of you."

Hugh let go of the girls and she rushed to his arms. He lifted his college sweetheart off the ground, swinging her in an arch. They had not been apart this long since he was a senior and she a sophomore at Indiana State. He marveled that she still seemed to have the same figure she had then, only better. Their eyes said more in seconds than most people could say in days. The love and desire were still there after nearly fifteen years together, the last thirteen as man and wife.

Terri held the little one's hand, Hugh the older girl's hand and their arms were tightly around one another as they walked from the field and headed for the motel where Terri had rented a room for them.

An afternoon in the motel's pool had worn the children out. They were fast asleep.

"Did you get enough of the girls today" Terri asked.

Hugh had spent the day playing with them in the water.

"Could I ever get enough of them? The reason I volunteered to fight is for them." He ran his fingers through her long, brown hair. "Nor could I ever get enough of you. As much as I want to be with them, I wish we could be alone for a few hours."

She playfully punched him, taking his meaning. Still, she had the same desires and laid her head on his chest with a sigh.

"After all, I waited more than two years to make love to the woman I love." They both smiled with the knowledge that they had waited to have sex until their wedding night. Waiting for each other, controlling their lust had been worth it. She had made up her mind that even if this war took him, she never would never know another.

"Thirteen years of getting to was not enough," she teased.

"I could never have enough of you." They involuntarily smiled, then kissed deeply and passionately.

"You'll be happy to know, sir," Admiral Tingle reported to Will, "carrier groups five and six have been commissioned. They put to sea this week. The coasts should be well covered."

Will nodded with satisfaction the industrial complex had geared up and was doing work at a rate that bent the mind. Still, he had to wonder if this was too little too late. "Even if we have every able-bodied man in uniform and turn out the equipment they need will it be enough, Admiral?"

Tingle hesitated to answer. "Sir, I forget who said it, they called China a sleeping giant. That was meant in an economic sense. They said that if the giant ever awoke it would be a juggernaut. Well, the giant awoke and it's a beast. It's kinda like hunting a bear with a flintlock musket, sir. Sometimes you get the bear, sometimes the bear gets you."

"Well, Admiral, I believe that God will protect us but I'm tasking you to be His hands and feet," the President said.

The Admiral face showed the question in his mind. "Sir?"

Will turned to the Joint Chiefs. "While always seeking the guidance of the Almighty go win the war."

The Generals and Admirals recognized the President's dismissal, rose from their feet, saluted, and left the room to be about their grim task. Gordon started to leave as well.

"Wait a minute, Gordo," Will said.

Gordon stopped and turned. "What can I do for you, Mr. President?"

Will waited for the last person to clear the room before he spoke. "I'm going to assign you a task that is even harder than the one I just gave them."

Kirk could not imagine what task that might be. "What could harder than winning a war against impossible odds, Will?"

"I want you to lay out a plan for winning the peace after the war," Will told him.

Gordon Kirk thought on this. The actual shooting war had not even begun, and Will wanted to plan for peace. "Isn't that a bit premature or are we going to sue for peace?"

Will slumped in his chair. "I will not surrender to the Chinese as long as I am free and alive."

Gordon made his way back to the table and took a seat across from Will. "That's what I thought so why plan for something that is not a certainty?"

Will straightened in his chair, "I believe that God will see us through this. There will be more dark times before we can walk in the light again, but it will shine, and we must be prepared for it."

"Go on," Gordo encouraged.

"In my study of history, the one failure I have seen in all the great statesmen and generals was that once they won the war, they had no plan for the peace. Once the war was over things in every country went back to pretty much the way they had been before the war. The same form of government, the same corrupt ways, and sooner or later history repeats itself. Invariably there is another war to fight."

"What can we do about that?" Gordo still was not seeing Will's point.

"We must see that this war changes the world for all time."

"How do we do that?"

"We root out corruption. We put democracies in place where they do not exist now. We make sure that all persons on Earth have opportunity to make something of their lives." Will was thoughtful for a moment. "It will be a much more difficult to change the world once it is liberated from tyranny then it will be to simply win the war. If we do not bring reform to all corners of the Earth, then we will leave the same conditions to fester that brought on this war and our children or grandchildren will have to do this all over again."

Kirk was beginning to see what Will was getting at. "I can put together a commission to study the problem and lay out a plan."

Will nodded. "You can start with a smaller commission for now but as we win countries, we can add members. We must put this plan in place as we liberate each country and place a governor there or an overseer to at least try very hard to make the world democratic."

"I'll get on it." Gordo rose and left the room.

Will bowed his head. *"Give them your wisdom Lord. Help me banish war from this world for generations to come. Help me show the world your love in this time of great tragedy."*

The morning after graduation Hugh stood before Webster's desk.

"I've read your resume," Webster said, "you have extensive training as a police officer and many certifications as a trainer of police."

"Yes sir," Hugh acknowledged.

"Do you think you could teach MP's?" The General stunned him with the question.

Hugh hesitated for a moment. "Sir, Military and civilian police are quite different animals."

"I'm aware of that. You've actually written curricula for police officers." Webster looked Hugh in the eye. "How long would you need to study the difference and write curriculum?"

"Several months at least sir." Hugh was taken aback.

"We don't have several months. At the rate the Chinese are moving north they'll be here in six months. We need MP's trained and ready to go by then. We need them not to just be police officers on base but to secure the area around the bases so that the troops can relax while they are on base. You have two months," Webster said flatly. "I expect the curriculum on my desk in eight weeks. I expect you to start teaching it then. You can requisition staff and equipment you need and base housing, keep your family here if you wish. At least you'll get to see something of them. With the hours you'll be putting in I doubt you'll be seeing a lot of them. Some is better than none. The country needs this. The country requires your best effort, dismissed."

Two months was simply not time enough. Hugh started to object, but just snapped off a sharp salute and about face then left to start his new assignment. An office, a secretary and base housing was more than most got. The girls would have their own room. He and Terri would have theirs. The war could wait for one night. Maybe two.

Colonel Ye was all smiles as he strode into General Chan's office. The junior officer snapped to attention before his superior's desk.

The General looked up from the paperwork that he was engaged in. "Yes Colonel?"

The younger man's smile grew wider. "I have good news, sir."

"This is something I would like to hear." Chan sat back in his chair. The day had not been one of good news. Supply shortages, production delays. He had argued against mounting so many fronts at once. A few more months and they could have had many more armored vehicles. His troops were almost exclusively infantry, but their overwhelming numbers had carried the day to this point.

"Our glorious troops in South America have crossed over into Brazil, the last stop in South America."

"And soon we push into Central America," Chan added.

"Yes sir!" The Colonel had a grave look on his face. "Then only the United States will stand between us and world domination."

"You are forgetting Mexico." The General countered as he looked at a map and pointed.

"They should be of little consequence." Ye was unconcerned.

"True, their army is weak." Chan leaned on a table map and looked at the strategic situation. "Their deserts will be formidable for troops who have spent so many months in tropical forests. The Mexicans are well armed. We will get a taste there of what the United States will be like. In the United States most citizens have arms, and many will snipe our troops from every angle, lone wolves acting on their own. We will see some of this in Mexico. There are many criminals in Mexico that have state of the art weaponry and will not give up their territory willingly. We must be careful not to allow this to harm the moral of our troops."

"Sir, we have fought in deserts before and won handily. We have fought under most every condition and won. We will carry the day."

"Yes Colonel, but these troops have not fought in this desert." Chan was grim. "We will prevail, but the desert will slow us."

Hugh could not believe he had done it. Barely six weeks had passed since the General had given him the order. The first curriculum was finished. True, he had seen little of the family with them so close, but he had slept with his wife each night. The army was not all bad. There were some good jobs in the Army. He happened to have one of them. If this is how God chose to use him during this conflict, so be it. If he was sent to the front, so be it. Still, a bed for two that was full was much more pleasing than a single bed that was also to capacity.

Even more surprising his second course was well on its way to completion. The time was only 1621 on a Friday. He could drop this at General Webster's office and be home in time to play with the girls before supper. He would even give himself the weekend off for the first time since he entered the Army.

Will Sevrin was never ashamed of prayer. He often prayed in public. Funny how, when the Red Chinese were bearing down on them, the Supreme Court and A.C.L.U. did not mind public prayer. Prayer on his knees, however, he reserved for private.

'Lord my God You are my God. Please, in the name of Christ hear my prayer now. I am still just a simple country boy, but I need the Wisdom of Solomon that I might lead my people in your ways. Give wisdom also to the Generals that will lead the fight against our enemies and vanquish them. Surely there are Godly men among them, and I ask you to raise them up. Lord God, as a nation our sins have been grievous. We have turned from you, oh Lord. We have killed babies for our own convenience. We have killed the elderly and disabled for the same reason. We have denied You and our Christian heritage. Now we must cleanse our land in our own blood as we did with the sin of slavery. Redeem us to the country that we were meant to be. Make us a country that is pleasing in your eyes, One Nation under God. May this become more than a motto, One Nation with You as our King. We cannot do this on human strength alone. Guide us. Fight for us. The battle belongs to you, oh Lord. Raise up Godly men who put on your full armor before they do battle. Deliver us from our enemies. Give us strength that we might run and not grow weary, that we might walk and not faint. Lord, on my orders, millions of my fellow countrymen will fight. Help us to keep our country free. Help us to liberate those that have fallen under tyranny. Loose the fateful lightening of your terrible swift sword upon our enemies. Soften the hearts of my countrymen that they might turn to you again. Strengthen us that we stand before our enemies. Help us to become a nation of prayer. Help us to truly be One Nation under God."

As Will Sevrin rose from his knees, Philippians 1:21 kept running through his mind. "For to me, to live is Christ, to die is gain." Again, he saw no reason to fear.

Hugh was surprised at the work he had been able to get done that day. He had done right in taking the weekend off, precious time with his daughters and wife had revived him. His intercom buzzed, "Captain Smith."

"The General requests your presence in his office sir." He recognized the voice of the General's secretary.

"Be right there." Hugh disconnected the call then moved immediately. One did not keep a General waiting.

"You may go right in." Webster's secretary just glanced up from her work as Hugh entered the outer office. For some reason, even though he had gotten used to the ways of the military he still took a deep breath before entering a General's office.

Hugh snapped to attention before the General's desk his hat tucked neatly beneath his arm. "Captain Smith reporting, sir."

The older man was busy with paperwork. With him bent over his reading Hugh realized that he had never seen the General from this angle. He had not realized the man was so gray, nor had he noticed the bald spot near the crown. Finally, the superior officer looked up.

"Captain, I want to compliment you on your work." The General had a look of sincerity.

"Thank you, sir!" Hugh continued at strict attention.

"Relax, Hugh, have a seat." The General waived him to a chair on the other side of his desk.

Webster had never called Smith by his first name before. This signaled a new respect in their relationship. Hugh took the offered chair but continued to sit at attention.

"Captain, I've run this curriculum past several career MP's," the General started, "they think it's brilliant. They say it is especially good for training new MP's in short order. Some have said that it's the best they've ever seen especially with the new protocols I gave you."

Hugh was a bit flabbergasted. "Would you thank them for me for saying that sir?"

"Don't go modest on me Hugh," Webster smiled, "you're good. I intend to use that to its best. Your course is best taught to trainers so that they can duplicate your efforts. In the next few weeks, you will be all over the country training DI's. I know you have another course in the works. I expect it as soon as you can possibly get it done. That's why God invented laptops, so you can work on the road. We need to get our people the best training we can as quickly as we can. I'm depending on you to see that they get it. My secretary has your next month's schedule."

Hugh stood. "Yes sir,"

So much for his seeing the wife and kids every night. Still, he would keep them as close as possible. Hugh had started toward the door when the General called him back.

"Oh Hugh?" Smith turned back to the General. "There's something you ought to take with you on this training tour."

"Sir?" The Captain was confused.

General Webster came around his desk with a small box in his hand. "While the rank of Captain is actual because it was earned in O.T.S., this is not." He opened the box to reveal oak leaves. "This will be a brevet rank. You will have all the rights and privileges of a Major, even get Major's pay, but won't really be a Major yet. I'll see to it as soon as you are time in rank eligible."

Webster pinned the new rank on Hugh and then saluted.

Smith returned the salute.

"Congratulations, Major," the General said. "Also, you'll be leaving for a different base each Sunday. You'll return Friday night or Saturday morning depending on what flight you can catch. You should have at least twenty-four hours at home each week as long as you continue in this assignment. Get as much time with the family as you can. This is the calm before the storm."

"Thank you, sir." Hugh turned on his heel and left. His grin was too big to hide. He had risen so far so quickly. Surely this would be the end of his promotions, but who cared. Major pay was better than private pay. Getting to see the family at least one day a week was better than most military men would ever dream of in time of war. He thanked God for all the blessings.

Hugh rounded the corner of the hall as he returned to his office. There was a private from maintenance changing the sign on his door to show his new rank. Hugh thought of how efficient the General was. He also noticed that Terri was standing watching the change. Since the girls were in school, she had been coming in and helping him on a voluntary basis. Her smile grew as he approached.

"What do you think," Hugh said as he pointed at the sign.

"At the rate you're going you'll be a ten-star general before the war's over," she teased.

He came up to her and draped his arm around her waist. "Don't expect any more promotions. I'm probably in my niche now. I'll probably be here for the entire war."

Hugh Smith paced back and forth in front of a classroom of squared away drill instructors. He wondered what he was doing there. He was not Army. He was only playing Army. These guys in this class were the heroes. They had to take what he taught them and teach it to others. The chance of the front-line guys coming home alive depended on them teaching the troops how to stay alive. He was teaching the instructors how to teach the troops. He had to get it right.

"The whole idea of this approach is that combat troops can feel secure when in a base camp. Sure, they may have to respond to their own defense at a moment's notice, but we must give them the warning. They must trust that early warning will be given.

"Military Police have always patrolled the interior of the base. They have performed the police function. Police function is still needed. This is the inner ring. Someone may slip past the first two rings. The inner ring must not ever let its guard down." Hugh slapped the diagram on the board with his pointer. "The inner circle can't afford to let its guard down. Everyone they deal with will be armed, whether American or Chinese."

"The second ring must be tight. We will be the perimeter defense of the base. No, this is not new either. This is just greatly tightened. This must stop anyone that the outer ring does not detect. This will be the front line on base. I cannot stress enough that we must make the base safe for front line troops to blow off steam. They must have a time to simply relax if they are to remain an effective fighting force.

"The most important ring is the outer ring. If we can find enemy troops before they can get in position to open fire, we have secured the system. These patrols should range for miles and perform the function of recon patrols. This should be done with all possible stealth. We can secure our bases if we can find the enemy as he is on his way, sound the alarm, and open with our artillery before he does. These patrols should not only be numerous, but repetitive. If you have not guessed we will be greatly expanding the Military Police so this plan, which has been approved by the General Staff, can be implemented. You have a lot of men to train and not much time to do it in. Your best recruits for this outer ring duty are the kids that grew up in the woods, someone that spent his youth hunting and playing paint ball. They already have the basic skills from hunting animals, now we teach them to hunt the enemy. Studying recruit information data sheets is a way to find out what recruits best fit the job. If you will notice, we have a questionnaire. You can determine through this what men will take to this like a duck to water. We are basically developing a division of scouts. These scouts must be better than the enemy scouts. If we can find small units of Chinese and destroy them apart from the main body, then they cannot throw such overwhelming forces at us."

For the fifth time in the last seven weekends thousands of women and older men crowded into a large sports stadium. This time it was the football stadium in Indianapolis. No there was no sporting event about to take place; all professional sports except Baseball had been suspended because the athletes were off to the war. Most baseball players were also gone, but Sevrin and Congress thought it important that the National Pastime continue as it had done in the Second World War. The place was sold out, but thousands more clamored for tickets. All proceeds went to organizations that served the enlisted men. The citizen's prayer movement, as it was called, was growing geometrically. All shapes, sizes, ages, and classes came.

The Emcee, a national news anchor, was finishing up announcements when the featured speaker of the Prayer Conference slipped on stage and took a seat. Despite her slight frame and her normal, understated attire, she was dressed in a gingham jumper, she did not go unnoticed. The women near that side of the stage began to cheer. Slowly the murmur rippled through the crowd and each person, one at a time or in small groups, began to clap and cheer. Before long the crowd drowned out the Emcee.

"O.K." The Emcee, Galena Gomez, motioned for the crowd to quiet. "O.K. I can see we have to get on with it."

The crowd quieted. Galena was a tall, strikingly beautiful Latina and was wearing **the** red dress. When she wore that dress, she knew that she easily held the attention of most persons. This time, however, the First Lady had trumped her in a simple jumper. Sandy Sevrin had become an icon on the American scene. Always humble and reserved she radiated a quiet power. Poll after poll showed her to be the most respected woman in America. "Ladies and gentlemen, the featured speaker of this weekend," the cheer started low, "the First Lady of the United States," now a roar was growing, "Sandy Sevrin!"

No one could hear themselves think. She was the symbol of present-day American women. She was also the most popular woman in America, a woman of considerable talent and means that chose to stay home and raise kids. Even if home was presently White House II, as it was now being called. What had become clear was that she could have been anything but chose to be a wife and mother. Sandy waved to the crowd several times, but they refused to retake their chairs. They cheered on and on.

"Oh my" Sandy said after the crowd finally began to wind down. "I thank you for cheering me but we must turn to our Lord Jesus Christ."

The cacophony rose again. This one did not last as long. It took energy to cheer at that level for that length of time. "Our prayers can do more to win this war than any weapon. Remember the armies of Israel in the Old Testament. Look at what Israel is doing now! They are gaining territory against the Chinese. They do not win by their own strength, but rather God fights their battles for them. This would not have happened if they had not called on God. This will not happen for our husbands, brothers, sister, daughters and sons unless we call on the name of God."

Those present began to sit. "We must pray. To guide our soldiers through this fight we must remember Psalm 23 and pray it's blessing on them. Pray our soldiers are kept safe from harm, their rifles shoot straight and true, their bullets work every time, their grenades are thrown on target, their body armor deflects the bullets and shrapnel, and their boots are comfortable for their feet. For them to be shielded we must put on the full armor of God as in Ephesians 6:10-18."

"We must pray for the commanders. Pray that the Lord will give our commanders the Wisdom of Solomon. Pray that the Lord will help our commanders to outthink the enemy commanders every time. Pray that our industries will provide everything our soldiers need and then some.

"Pray for each state by name every night, all fifty states. Pray that none of our states ever fully fall to the Chinese."

People were scribbling furiously.

"We as people cannot keep our country free. We as prayer warriors can keep liberty alive. God can do anything. As the Bible says in Matthew 19:26 all things are possible to God. My husband has always said that if you pray about something before it happens it always seems to go better. I guess he must have prayed before he took off for Mars!"

The crowd erupted as one in cheers and laughter.

"We must pray that the bullets of our enemies do not find their mark while our bullets do. We can pray that each injured American soldier recovers from any wounds. We can pray that Chinese anti-aircraft missiles miss our aircraft. We can pray that each of our missiles fired from our aircraft finds its mark. Our soldiers are already living out Ephesians 5:25, we can pray that they do not make the ultimate sacrifice."

Sandy went on about each specific item that attendees should pray for. Nothing that she could think of was left out. The list seemed to expand every day.

"Prayer for our Government leaders is also a must. Right now, my husband needs all the prayer he can get. Not only do you need to pray for wisdom, but for health. If you know history, the great American leader of World War Two, Franklin Delano Roosevelt, died before he could see our troops to victory. The care of it all simply wore him down. If you look at pictures of him as he progresses through the war you see his health declining at a steady rate. We must pray that this does not happen to our present leaders.

"And it's not just the President. Your local officials will be called on to be leaders as they have never been. To organize material drives, to calm panicky town folks. If the Chinese get to your town, they may have to lead under the most difficult and dangerous conditions. As far as the Chinese go remember Matthew 10:28

"Let us not forget to pray for ourselves. We must keep the home fires burning. Living out the war on the home front can be almost as difficult as living it out on the front line. We cannot be idle while a soldier's every waking minute is involved. Waiting is sometimes worse than placing one's life on the line. While our loved ones go off to war, we must not only manufacture what they need to keep fighting, but we must also keep our homes in such a manner that they will be proud not only to fight for, but to return to. Nothing ends a war more quickly than the soldier's anxious quest to get home to a place he fondly remembers and a family he dearly loves."

Sandy spoke without ceasing for two hours. Remarkably, no one left their seat in that entire time, not even for a bathroom break. As she mentioned each scripture, they busied themselves with looking up each verse, "In closing, lean on God. Lean on Christ Jesus. Let the Spirit fill you that you might be one with God. Until we meet again may He bless and keep you. May He make His countenance to shine upon you and bring you peace? Good night."

The crowd erupted. Sandy did not wait around and bask in it. She waved as she left the stage but walked steadily to the exit. The First Lady was already in her limo and the motorcade was speeding away long before the crowd stopped cheering, applauding, whistling, and stomping. The nation was truly turning back to God, led by the First Couple.

When the cheering died down the praise group started. They would go on for two more hours.

There was one slightly ugly incident in Indianapolis. A small group of atheists were protesting outside the convention center. When the crowd had let out, the protestor's signs were literally ripped away from them and shredded by the crowd. The people who had been carrying the signs were bodily picked up and carried blocks from the stadium before being released unharmed. They were, however, sternly warned not to return or their fortunes might not be as good the next time.

The same group had filed a lawsuit weeks earlier. As groups like this tend to do, they had searched out the judge with the most liberal reputation. A judge that had decided things in their favor before was sought out and the group filed the action in his court. The suit alleged that it was improper for the First Lady to speak publicly of prayer, that such violated the separation of church and state.

They could not have known that world events had made the Judge re-examine his life. The conversion of his teenage son to Christianity also had much to do with his new faith. His son had been a problem child with a drug habit and now he could see the glow that his boy's face and wanted it for himself.

Upon reading the suit, the Judge grew red in the face. He called the litigants before him and dismissed the case with prejudice. In chiding the plaintiffs, he stated that the founding fathers had guaranteed us freedom of religion, not freedom from religion.

3.

"My suggestion would be that we send First Army to Central America to slow the Chinese." General Scott Douglas, the Army Chief of Staff was speaking. "Have them fight a delaying action. A single army cannot stand against the numbers we're facing, but the landmass is narrow down there. We can ball them up for some time. We need more time to prepare our other forces. If we can hold them there for a while the time would be invaluable."

"Admiral Tingle," Will turned to the Navy Chief.

"Our hold on Central America's waters is shaky at this point," the Admiral admitted. "We are out-manned and out-gunned. I do believe that the General has a good idea. If we can pull it off it might be the difference in the war. If we lose at sea, though, the Chinese could get troops in behind our ground pounders and destroy them in detail. That would be a disaster beyond the obvious cost in men."

"General Douglas do you think it's worth the risk," the President asked.

"I do." Douglas knew that he was taking an awful chance, but they needed time to build their forces.

Will turned to the Secretary of Defense. "What do you have to say?"

"No one ever won a war by playing it safe," Secdef nodded agreement; "we might surprise them and throw them off balance. They've never been truly challenged. It could be a huge coup. It could be disaster. It will probably fall somewhere in-between."

Will was silent for a moment as he prayed that God would protect the troops. "Send First Army south."

Admiral Sheets knew that his assignment was to hold the Chinese Navy south of Costa Rica. His ships, skippers and seamen had fought valiantly, but they simply did not have the resources. While they sunk two Chinese ships for every one they lost that did not even the odds. The move had been premature he saw that now. A few more months and he would have had the sea power to pull off such an action, but not now. Of course, if they had waited those few months, the move would have been worthless because the Chinese were moving too quickly. He had lost half the ships in the task force fifteen percent more were badly damaged. The main fight was now going on about fifty miles south of his flagship and was not going well. If he did not call retreat soon, he would lose a dozen more vessels. They could not afford the losses they had already taken. One carrier was sinking. Live to fight another day. "Signal Admiral Jackson to disengage."

"Aye aye, sir." The Ensign turned to the radio.

"We've lost the waters of Central America," Sheets said.

Captain Stevens looked at the Admiral. "We didn't have what we needed to keep it. Their numbers are too superior."

"I know." The Admiral was melancholy. "Now the ground troops have no offshore backup. I'll have to tell Admiral Tingle. He'll have to tell the President. We may have to withdraw the ground pounders."

"How would we do that," the Captain asked.

"They'll have to run," Sheets answered.

"At least they should still have air support," Steven offered.

Sheets harrumphed. The American fighter jocks were also spread too thin. China now had hundreds of planes in the Americas and was bringing more and more to fight in the northern actions. The possibility that the skies would soon be cleared of American air power was also a very real one.

General Chan was not far behind the front lines. The Premier might not like his top General being so close to the front, but he reveled in the real-time reports. No one could plan a battle like he could. The simple savagery of his battle plans destroyed most enemies mentally before they were destroyed physically. The Nicaraguan Army was fighting bravely, but that was of no consequence. They had neither the numbers nor the weaponry to sustain a fight against his forces and were being summarily slaughtered. He would take up residence in Managua in the next day or two, but even then, he would not be there long. Moving north always moving north.

Paul Green's black skin glistened with sweat in the hot and humid weather of the Honduran mountains. He had pushed his troops into the southern part of Honduras, as far south as he dared.

"Sir, latest satellite recon," a Captain told him.

The Commanding General of First Army took the photos. "So, they are in Nicaragua?"

"Yes sir," the Captain replied.

Paul turned to his Chief of Staff. "No support out on the water, precious little air support. We've pushed as far as we dare."

"Maybe too far, sir." Colonel Livingstone was hoping that the General would order the troops to pull back. "We should fight here these mountains, such good ground."

Green nodded, he had made his decision. "Order the men to dig in where they're at. Get good ground. Good killing fields. We stand here."

"Yes, sir." The Colonel moved off to set the lines.

The extra-large man that stood before the President of the United States wore three stars. General Glenn saluted his Commander in Chief.

"You have a weighty mission, General," Will said. "You must take the Second

Army of the United States and defeat any and all threats to the United States."

"We'll be movin' south directly, sir," Glenn said. "The Chinese will wish they had never taken on the United States."

"God go with you and your troops, General."

The General saluted and left for his command. The Second Army was now operational. Will knew that it was still not enough.

"Look, Frank, realistically we're still nine months away on the IPF," Lance Yale said.

Frank had always told Will that this man was incompetent in leading a rush project of any scale. This was one of the biggest in MEC history. This thing had to be done now. Will had always liked the careful engineer because he never risked lives to make a deadline. You can get things done safely and still get them done on time in this situation, he thought.

Frank had a downcast look. He always hated doing stuff like this. "I've studied our problems with the IPF 1 project. I've concluded that the problem is not systemic."

"So where do you think it lies?" Yale was already defensive.

"The problem is managerial and you're the manager." Thomas said that a bit more harshly than he had intended to.

"You firin' me, Frank?" A bit of fire was growing in Lance's eyes.

Frank looked him in the eye. "Your whole management team is gone, Lance."

The balding, portly man rolled back and roared with laughter. "There's no one else in this company, shoot, on this planet that can get this thing done. Not on your timetable or on mine. I'll get it done. I'll do it right."

Yale's arrogance always bothered Frank. No one was irreplaceable, but Lance made it a point to tell everyone that he was. Thomas pushed a button on his desk.

The engineer eyed the CEO angrily. "You're not just removing me from this project, you're firing me period."

Frank nodded as the security personnel came through the door. "Yes Lance. Clean out your personal items now. If you set foot on the property again, you'll be arrested for trespass."

The engineer started angrily for the door. "You ain't heard the last of me! You're gonna pay for this!"

Frank rolled his eyes. That was part of the problem. The guy was so much talk and so little action.

The next morning Frank arrived at MEC carrying not just his briefcase, but he also lugged in several suitcases. He guessed that this would be the end to his latest relationship. He never seemed to keep a relationship with a woman going for very long. Anna had lasted for almost eight months, a new record. Maybe after the war he could make something work. The conference room next to his office, some closets, and two more offices had been his personal living space until he had moved into Anna's. Frank would not be leaving the plant again until the Interplanetary Shuttle was ready for combat. Carryout, coffee, doughnuts and pizza would be his staples for some time to come.

General Lian stood on the bridge as the great boat emerged from beneath the waves. A quarter of a million men, all under his command, were surfacing near the northern east coast of Honduras, well behind the American lines. He had to give the Americans credit; they had stalled his armies. Taking up good ground in the Honduran Mountains, they had held off the Chinese advance for nearly a month. This was precious time lost for the Chinese army, precious time gained for the Americans to prepare. This delay had cost many Chinese lives. Oh, well, lives were one thing they had to spend.

The great boat disgorged its aircraft as soon as she was stable. They would pound the port and secure the area so that the ground troops could land with a minimum of opposition. He had expected there to be no resistance in Central or South America, but he had miscalculated. With the legendary corruption in Latino countries, he had expected the military to cut and run. They had fought bravely. They had stood their ground to the last man. They had died bravely. No armies in history had acquitted themselves better. You had to admire them. This was one of the ironies of war; you had to kill what you admired. Was it doublethink to kill what you admired and not flinch at the action, much less the thought?

Even now Lian could see Honduran fighters bearing down on the super boat. These planes were no match for any of the fighters that they were launching. He doubted that the pilots had the training to compete with his men even if they were in a comparable jet. The old Honduran Air Force jets bore in. The Honduran jets were swarmed by his fighters and flamed out each in turn. The General guessed that twenty had attacked his boat but doubted that any would get through the fighter shield.

One Honduran jet did not waiver from its course as Lian saw the strategy now. The other jets purposely punched a hole in his air cover for the one plane. The pilot flew it straight and true at the Chinese sub. The Chinese pilots were too busy with their dogfights to notice that one plane had gotten through.

Lian could hear the air boss calling off the plane but could see that none of his jets were close enough to intercept. The General saw the puffs that indicated that the pilot was firing on the boat. The first thing he could see was an Exocet. This was not a danger to sink a boat so large but would do great damage. The defensive systems of the boat activated to try to bring down the missile. Other missiles were firing from the jet.

Lian staggered as the boat bucked beneath his feet. The Exocet had struck home. The boat would have to be repaired before it could return to sea. Two other, smaller missiles also found their mark. Gatling guns destroyed the others before they could get to the Chinese boat.

The brave pilot was passing into guns range when a Chinese jet that had broken free from another engagement locked on. The General watched the missile fire and take off the rear of the enemy jet. He was gratified to see the pilot eject and float to earth. Such a brave man should have life.

Zira Lopez gathered her chute. She had precious little time to make her escape before an enemy jet found her and therefore enemy ground troops took her prisoner. She had gotten through and damaged the Chinese boat. Being the only woman pilot in the Honduran Air Force, she was glad that it was her that had managed to land such a blow. She would, surprisingly live to fight another day and fight she would.

"So, what you're saying is that because of greed the Magnetic Engine Corporation has fired you," Rock asked.

"It's all about greed." Lance said trying to appear sincere. "I was working on a top-secret project that is vital to the war effort, but they thought that they could get it done with younger engineers that would cost them less. So, they fired me."

"Just over money?" Rock tossed the Engineer another softball.

"I still have a number of contacts from inside MEC. From what they tell me that was the entire reason," Lance nodded. "Oh, they have their official reasons, but you can't believe that."

The Rock turned toward the camera. "Once again the greed of corporate America has jeopardized the safety of every American. What's worse is the President of the United States owns the corporation that is doing this. Maybe a Congressional committee should investigate this, Rock James, Around the Clock News."

The speaker of the house was watching The Rock. He had no idea why. A wall of his office was covered with TV's that were almost always on news channels. The man was simply becoming a farce. Frank Thomas was reporting directly to him on the IP Fighter project. There was no truth at all to the story. He was pretty sure America was tuning out The Rock.

The speaker got up and started down the hall. There was no one on earth that he trusted more than Frank Thomas except maybe Will Sevrin. He wondered if he could charge these guys with treason. No, freedom of speech and all that.

"Yeah Linda," Will acknowledged the buzz from his secretary.

"General Douglas and Admiral Tingle need to see you, sir."

Will did not like the interruption of his meeting with Vice President Charlie McCoy. Still, he knew that the Generals coming with no notice meant that it was urgent. "Send them in."

The two military men strode into the office with a purpose. Douglas thought that this was a remarkable recreation of the original Oval Office in the old White House. The entire Capitol on the outskirts of Lincoln, Nebraska was a remarkable achievement in such a short period of time especially considering the circumstances. Workmen too old for military service were building the new capitol, some of them well beyond retirement age. This new capitol would be more magnificent than the old one.

"Sir, we'd like your approval on something," Tingle said.

"What's that," the President asked.

Will, Charlie, and Tingle gathered around as Douglas laid some pictures on a table.

"Sir, more bad news," Douglas said.

"Now what," Will asked?

"The Chinese managed to dock a super boat in northern Honduras, behind First Armies lines. I'm afraid First Army is surrounded."

"Can we break through to them," Charlie asked.

"No, sir, Mr. Vice President," the General said. "We knew that the supply lines were way overextended when we sent them. We don't have the men or machinery in place to mount a breakthrough. Second Army is our only other operational army and right now we need to hold them back to defend the homeland. We can't get to them by air, sea or ground."

"That's our only effective fighting force in the area," the President observed.

"Yes, sir," Douglas agreed, "I'm afraid we've lost the entirety of First Army."

"We can't take any more blows like this," Will said. "If we do the people will lose their will if we don't start giving them good news."

"Then maybe we have something for you." The Admiral spoke now. "It might be slight next to the loss of First Army, but it is good news."

"What?"

"The Hondurans got lucky," Douglas said. "They hit a super boat with an Exocet. The boat is badly damaged. They won't be able to move it for some time."

"And" Will asked.

"Sir, if I launch an all-out strike on that boat from maximum range, we have a chance of sinking it," Tingle said. "It could be a great boost to moral if we could report that."

"What are your chances of pulling it off?"

"Sir, their air support is all off pounding First Army," Douglas said. "They have only a minimal fighter shield over the boat. We've got a good chance."

Will bowed his head in prayer, something he had also done prior to sending First

Army south and that had now come to disaster. Will felt his answer and said *thy will be done.* Will felt God's rebuke for his oversight in the matter of First Army and asked His forgiveness. He had tried to assert his will with First Army but now left it up to God. Now he felt God's leading in the matter at hand. "Launch the attack."

General Paul J. Green could tell things were falling apart. "Where did all those enemy troops come from and how did they get north of our positions?"

"Lincoln says the Chinese have landed a super boat north of here." Colonel Umberto Sanchez was the intelligence officer for First Army. "We've got two hundred thousand or so bad guys coming up behind us."

"You're full of good news," Green told his aide. "Can we get any help?"

The two men were shouting to be heard over the falling bombs and shells.

"No, sir." Sanchez shook his head. "Right now, the Chinese have total air and sea superiority in this area."

"This thing just gets worse and worse." Green thought for a moment. "Spread the word to our field commanders to watch their backside. Let's swing first and second corps around and make a circle. This may be a fight to the end."

"On it, sir." Sanchez saluted and turned to issue orders.

General Lian jumped as the air raid sirens sounded. He punched the intercom. "What is it?"

"Sir," an aide said, "American fighters and bombers coming from the northeast."

Lian threw down the phone and ran to the window of the high-rise building he had taken for his office. He could clearly see the dogfight develop over the bay. The door burst open behind him.

"Come, sir." A Major shouted urgently at him, waiving him to the door.

"Where to," Lian asked perturbed.

"To the shelter," the Major said.

"Why?" Lian had seen lots of combat. He saw no danger here.

"The air raid, sir!"

"They will not hit the city." Lian turned back to the window. "They are after the boat, brilliant, actually. It would be a major public relations coup if they can sink the boat just before they lose an army."

The Major walked over and joined the General at the window. They watched the dogfight for a short time. Lian realized that he had left too few fighters in reserve to protect the city and port in his zeal to crush the American First Army.

Now he watched as the bombers bore in. The fighters could not stop the American bombers, as they were too busy fighting for their lives with the American fighters. America's bombs were generally hi-tech and seldom missed their targets these were no different. Bomb after bomb slammed into the boat. The bulk of the boat withstood it for a while, but the attack was too much. Soon the ship was afire, then listing. As the attack wound down the bow disappeared beneath the water.

The American aircraft had been gone half an hour when the bottom of the boat came to rest on the bottom of the bay.

"Such a blow." The Major was obviously upset. The group of the window had grown to nearly twenty.

"A minor setback," Lian observed. "They have sunk one of four such boats. We are about to decimate their best army. We will either kill or capture General Green, their best commander. We come out the better."

"The Party will not be pleased to lose one of their prize boats," a Colonel observed.

This sounded like a threat to Lian. He had never liked the Colonel's attitude. The Colonel would die in the war, the General would see to that. "I must inform the Premier. He will not be pleased. Even the best incur casualties in war. Get me some news from the front so that I might give him some good news as well."

Patton lay quiet in the weeds just outside of Cedros. The Chinese had been passing for two hours without letup. If he were discovered he would be interred at best, execution was more likely. The camera might make them think he was a spy. In some ways he was. WNN might have to buy him new equipment because he would abandon it all to get out of this. They could bill him if he lived through it.

Patton had always made his living on the edge. He had started as a crime reporter that always seemed to be able to find his way into the middle of a shootout. When the network called, he was soon reporting overseas. First, he was reporting on coups and civil wars in Third World countries then came this war. He had wanted to report the war in Europe or Africa, but the network would never let him go. When the Chinese hit South America, they could not say no to him. He wished they had. If the Chinese won, the war he would never see home or family again.

"Sir, we're being squeezed pretty hard," Colonel Sanchez said. "Our lines to the north have been pushed back to within ten miles of our lines to the south. We can't seem to even slow them down."

"Tell our guys they have to do better!" General Green was adamant though thinking it was false bravado. "This is a fight to the death. We have nowhere to retreat to. There's no help coming."

"Yes, sir." Sanchez saluted and left the command bunker.

For the first time Green thought of surrender. This was becoming a more obvious probability every hour.

There had been no Chinese for several minutes. Gary wondered if they had passed or if this was just a break. He cautiously slipped out of his hiding spot and looked both ways, no sign of Chinese. Patton gathered his equipment and started up the road. He had gotten only a tenth of a mile when he heard the rumble of armor. Looking around frantically he realized he was too far from cover.

"Senior!" An older woman waived to him from the doorway of a nearby house. "Senior!"

Patton sprinted for the front door of her house as she held it open and frantically beaconed.

The woman managed to slam the door just before the first Chinese vehicle came into view. She hustled him to the basement. Pulling back a board she waived him into a crawlspace about four feet high and twenty by twenty. She slammed the board shut behind him. No light came into the hiding place. Gary could hear the heavy armor rolling by. It crossed his mind to turn on the light on the camera to have a look around, but he thought it might show through a crack alerting the Chinese. He would gladly sit in the dark for a while.

General Green's bunker was under constant pounding now. He knew he would soon lose the ability to contact Lincoln. "One Adam actual to John Charlie Actual."

Scott Douglas answered. "John Charlie Actual, go one Adam."

"Sir, it's just about over here," Green admitted. "We can't hold out much longer."'

"General, do you know who this is?"

"Yes, sir, Mr. President," the General answered, "I know the voice."

"General, you are authorized to take any action you deem necessary." Will was trying not to break down while he spoke. "Surrender is authorized."

"Are those your orders sir," Green asked.

"No, General." Will's eyes glistened with tears. He knew that surrendering to this enemy might be much worse than dying. "You have no orders, all action at your discretion. You'll know when it's time to quit or if it's right to fight on."

"Yes, sir," Green said, "understood."

"God go with you, General." Will was losing control of his emotions.

"Green out."

No one in the President's command bunker could look at anyone else. Tears ran down the cheeks of several men. No one cared. Many had friends or relatives in First Army. Everyone knew Green.

The General of the First Army of the United States had just signed off with the President when Sanchez ran down the stairs and into the bunker as shells continuously exploded outside.

"What's it looking like out there, Umberto?" Green had lost any need for formalities.

"Not good sir."

Green thought Sanchez did not look good. "Go on."

"Our position is now less than two miles wide," Sanchez swayed, "they'll break through today."

"You okay?" Paul started toward his aide.

Sanchez collapsed. Green rushed forward. Apparently, the shell that had exploded as he entered the bunker had found the mark. A large piece of metal was imbedded at the base of the Colonel's skull. Sanchez had no pulse.

Green said a quick prayer over his fallen comrade, and then walked to the radio. "To all commanders this is One Adam actual. I am ordering all forces to surrender. Get the best conditions you can if you can get any. Repeat all American forces are to surrender."

Green put down the microphone and spoke to himself. "God help us all."

All the aides in the bunker had stopped and looked at their commander.

Green switched frequencies then picked up the microphone again. "This is the Commander of the American First Army calling the commander of the Chinese Army."

Sandy had just gotten back from another prayer conference. She had been informed that the President was in the residence. She was surprised to find that he was not in the living room since he knew that she would be home that night. She checked the kids and found them all asleep. When she entered the bedroom, she saw her husband sitting on the edge of the bed with his back to her. His shoes were off, and his tie loosened.

"I'm home," she said. There was no reply.

Sandy walked around in front of Will; there were tears in his eyes. "What's wrong?"

"First Army surrendered." Will buried his face in her bosom. "They're all gone!"

The President cried for twenty minutes. She held him, his face against her chest. Her front was soaked when he fell asleep, exhausted both physically and emotionally.

4.

Gary Patton had spent two days in the dark and was starting to lose track of time before his hostess came for him. When the coast was clear the woman, he had found out her name was Maria, had let him into the light and fed him then sent him back to the hole. Suddenly the door opened once again.

"Come, you go!" Maria had a little English.

"Are they gone," Patton asked.

"You go" she said once again.

Patton thanked her and headed out into the night. The battery on his watch had died and so he had not known the time of day for some time. Moving for two hours along the road he did have to run for the bushes three times because of an approaching vehicle. Finally, as the sun started to peak over the horizon he headed for the heavy brush. He was exhausted, but thought he had better check in. He had not called in to WNN in more than a week. Pointing the satellite dish toward the sky he then pointed the camera at himself. "Anybody out there?"

Gary could hear what appeared to be a scramble on the other end through his earpiece. "That you Gary?"

"One and the same," Patton answered.

"Where have you been?" He recognized the voice of Wade Babinski, his boss.

"Good to hear from you too, Wade."

"We thought they got you."

"You mean the Chinese?" Patton stopped to listen to an armored vehicle rumble along somewhere out of sight. He decided it was not coming toward him. "The books still out on it."

"Where are you?"

"Let's not get too specific," Gary said, "I'm in Honduras."

"Can you get to safety," Wade asked.

"I don't know where that is," Gary admitted. "Where's First Army?"

There was a long pause. "Gary, First Army doesn't exist anymore."

Patton had been squatting now he fell on his rump. On his way south he had passed through first army then they had passed by him again. He had come to know a lot of people in First Army. "I'm in it deep."

"Get some place where we can send some people to come get you." Wade could not conceive how they could pull that one off but could think of no other advice.

"We'll see," Patton nodded, "I guess I'll get back in the war. Look for my reports."

"Gary! No!" Wade screamed at his reporter, but the screen had gone blank. "Doggonit!"

Gary Patton stepped from the brush with the tools of his trade on his back. He had no idea where he would find shelter or food. He would report the war from behind the lines or die trying. That is if he could find a place to plug his equipment in and keep it charged.

"They shall not have died in vain, but rather to buy time for the forces of freedom." Will's voice was steady as he spoke to the radio audience in his latest fireside chat, the near breakdown over the loss of First Army a memory because now he had to lead. While he looked collected on the outside he was still mush on the inside. "With the time bought with the lives of our brothers, dads, husbands and friends we shall build the arsenal of freedom. The Chinese are not invincible. With the help of God, we will prevail.

"If you do not believe that God can help, look at Israel. The tiny country of Israel has not fallen despite a great onslaught against them. On the contrary they have now taken all or parts of Turkey, Syria, Lebanon, Saudi Arabia, Iraq, Iran, Yemen, and Oman. They are now driving through Egypt and into the Sudan. This tiny army is beating the Chinese back, not just holding their own. We can do the same."

"And so the Americans see that they are nothing before the armed forces of China." Ho told the Chinese people the opposite story from what Will was saying on the other side of the Pacific. He saw what had happened to the United States Navy in the waters off America and First Army in Honduras so he thought they could wade through the rest of America's armed forces just as easily. "They now see who is destined to rule the world. Their imperial days are over and ours are just beginning. The glory of the Chinese Empire shall rival if not surpass the Roman Empire. Our reign shall be at least a thousand years. We have never been defeated in any significant battle throughout this war. We have just North America to conquer, and all the world will be ours."

"This is only as it should be." The Premier was almost in a trance. He was charismatic when he spoke. The man could give a speech with any man in history. "The Chinese people are the greatest people that have ever been. There is no one who can even claim parallel accomplishment. We shall dominate until only our own complacency brings us down"

The Premier had finished with a crescendo. He would not mention the Middle East because that might cause unrest among the people. He **would not** believe in the God of Israel. They would fall like everyone else. He could not conceive of how the Israeli's were doing what they were doing. In the end China would win. He had also not mentioned that their attempts to take England and Australia had failed. He would conquer America and then circle back to the Island nation and the Outback.

The picture showed American soldiers being marched down a road. These were obviously POW's.

"You're on, Gary, in four, three, two, one."

Gary whispered over the link. He was way too close. "This is Gary Patton reporting from somewhere in Central America. As you can see there are several thousand survivors from First Army. I don't know where they are marching our troops."

Just then a Chinese soldier veered off the roadway. He was coming right at Gary. The Reporter had managed to come into possession of a knife. He clutched the knife and remained silent.

The soldier apparently never saw the camera that was pointed right at him. He relieved himself in the bushes and headed back to the road.

Gary was glad that he was not on live. If he had been the entire audience would have just been flashed. When the soldier was far enough away Gary started talking again.

"The march has been both brutal and unrelenting. I will try to stay with this, if possible, Gary Patton signing off."

Just after Patton signed off he saw an American soldier stumble and fall. A Chinese soldier came up and started yelling at him. He was obviously ordering the American to get up. When the American did not the Chinese soldier fired one shot and walked away.

Patton had to wait for the whole group to pass. No one made an attempt to retrieve the body. What if the man were still alive? It took more than an hour for the last enemy troop to pass by far enough for Gary to come out of hiding. He rushed to the spot where the soldier had fallen.

There was no helping the man. There was a bullet hole in the middle of his forehead. He had no pulse. Gary took the chance and set up his camera pointed at the deceased soldier. He would document this if it killed him too.

Green wondered if this was just another town, another passing stop along the way. The men had come to call the march Bataan Two in reference to the Bataan death march in World War II. Over ten thousand American soldiers had surrendered. Beatings had claimed some. Unprovoked shootings had claimed others. The march had probably claimed over a thousand. If a soldier fell, he had to get up quickly or he would be shot where he lay. Green could not protect them all. They were his responsibility. Once there had been more than 100,000 men in his army. He should have fought to the death it would have been preferable.

The guards marched them into a walled complex. The place contained what were obviously a church and related buildings. The walls were new. There were other captured soldiers here, both from the United States and ones from other fallen armies. There were guard towers and newly built barracks. An older priest came toward them with water. He offered it to Green, but the General waived him off.

"My men first," Green croaked, so dry he could barely speak.

The Priest and other, younger priests passed water to the men.

"Where are we Father," Green asked.

"Please, call me Padre Marco." The man did not look at Green.

"What is this place Padre?"

"This is my church," the Priest said, "or used to be. It has been a POW camp since the Chinese passed through here. They allow me to minister to the prisoners."

Green nodded. "What town?"

"Chinandega."

"What country?"

"Nicaragua."

"What part of Nicaragua?"

"Northwest."

"A lost land." Green let himself fall to a seated position.

Padre Marco came and squatted before the General offering him a drink again, this time he did not refuse. "All is not lost General. God is still on his throne."

"Maybe He should get off his throne and come down here and whoop some butt," Green said.

"In His time General." The Padre moved off to refill his bucket. "He is in control."

'Hard to tell that,' Green thought. 'Doesn't look like anyone's in control right now but the Chinese?"

As Green contemplated the creator, the Chinese army crossed from Guatemala into Mexico.

Hugh was teaching at the base that he had come to call home, Fort Leonard Wood. Terri and the girls were close by in base housing. With the storm clouds to the south growing darker every day, he was thankful to the Lord for every second he could spend with them.

A young Lieutenant came striding quickly into the room. He recognized the boy as an aide on the General Staff. The Lieutenant handed him a note.

"Thank you, Lieutenant," Hugh said.

The Lieutenant saluted, "Yes sir."

As the butter bar left the room, Hugh opened the note.

Report to me as soon as your class is done.
    Webster. Cmdg. Leonard Wood

Hugh recognized the General's scribble. He wrapped the class early and went to see the General.

Major Smith entered the General's office at the Secretaries bidding. He found the General staring out the window. Hugh went to the front of the desk and snapped to attention, "Major Smith reporting, sir."

The General waited a moment before his gaze turned. "Hugh, have a seat."

Webster walked back and sat behind his desk. Smith took a chair across the desk.

"I guess you know about First Army," The General started.

"Who doesn't, sir?"

Webster nodded. "The President has asked me to reconstitute First Army. Build a new one from scratch with trainees."

"You're the one to do it, sir."

"It will be a daunting task."

"I know of no one better General." Hugh noticed for the first time that there was a new third star on Webster's shoulder.

"I'll need good officers to help me with the task." The General rose and paced toward the window again. "Your one of those officers."

"What would my new job be, sir?"

"Deputy Commander three hundred and first infantry regiment."

"Sir?" Hugh was on his feet. He strode over to the General. "I don't have any experience in the infantry. I've taught school, not fought."

The General looked at him and smiled. "Combat experience is at a premium right now. Most of our battle experienced troops died in Honduras. The job is yours. You'll be second to Colonel Johnson, he's a good man."

"Sir, that's a job for a Lieutenant Colonel," Hugh observed, "I'm just a Major."

"Your right about that," Webster nodded. He pulled a box from his pocket and tossed it to Hugh. "Congratulations on another brevet."

Hugh opened the box. He had just been promoted again.

The engine roared and he was slammed back in his seat. The pilot had warned him to have his back firmly against the seat when the jet started to hurtle down the runway. He would pay more attention to such instructions from now on. Operation Open Seas was under way. The United States was taking back the seas farther south. The Navy had been pushed back to the southern borders of the United States, now the Navy was doing the pushing. Other than Israel, this was the first aggressive move against the Chinese.

"Bogies at one niner zero, they're on course two seven five!" Colonel Mitch Renner, call sign Burner, was calling off the enemy fighters.

'What am I doin' here?' Jim asked himself. Reporters do most anything for a story. Maybe this was too much. He could die up here. He was not trained for flying back seat in a fighter jet.

"Roger on the bogies, I count eight," Lt. Jones, call sign Cowboy, responded.

"Let's bring it right," Burner said, "get on their six."

The nine US jets swung as one into pursuit of the Chinese. Jim knew enough about radar to know that when they turned west the enemy jets turned east.

"Closure of a thousand knots," Cowboy called to the others.

"Stick with your wingman and engage," Burner ordered.

A few seconds later the Chinese jets met the American jets and Cowboy broke high and right then brought the jet around on a dime. Jim wondered if he would ever see his stomach again. His head cleared enough to see that they were on the tail of a bogie.

"Tone, I got tone." Cowboy was excited.

The radar was screaming. "Firing!"

The enemy jet disappeared in a ball of flame. Suddenly the threat radar screamed. Cowboy looked in the rearview mirror and cranked the jet hard left. "Got one on our tail!"

"Oommpppphhh," Cowboy said as he cranked it back to the right.

Jim saw the Chinese missile fly by to his left. They had nearly been hit. Jim felt something sticky fill the seat of his pants. Now the enemy jet that had been on their tail was in front of them. Cowboy fired and the missile took off the right wing of the Chinese jet.

"Two buggin' out," someone called on the radio, "goin' after 'em."

"Negative Farmer," Burner called, "we're getting' too far into their territory. We splashed most of them let's head home."

The US jets swung back toward their base.

Cowboy made a sniffing sound. "Smells like a barn in here."

Jim was surprised that was all that was ever said. He had filled his pants like a six-month-old. He would write a long article from this one, maybe several. The reporter would later learn that six enemy jets had been 'splashed.' As they flew home, he looked around and counted only eight friendlies. He opened his mouth to question Cowboy but thought better of it and stared out the canopy. Who would not be at the debriefing?

The man who did not come home was Manfred "Tiny" Haggen. Haggen was only five foot three and no more than one-forty. He always smiled and joked with everyone. Jim asked the squadron members for their remembrances of Tiny. A picture of the man emerged. Tiny lived for his wife and son. His son was only two and simply would never remember a dad that had been gone on deployments for more than half his life. They said that if Tiny was not teasing you, he did not like you. Jim wished that he had gotten to know Tiny.

"We need one hundred and fifty planes in the air to support this operation," General Lian announced.

General Chen shook his head. "We no longer even have that many aircraft in theatre."

"What?" Lian was shocked.

"The Americans are good. We have suffered heavy losses here." The Air Marshal was grim. "We have lost more aircraft in the American campaign than all the other theatres of this war combined, except Israel."

"What do you suggest?"

"Bring one of the great boats over with a full load of aircraft." Chen was not sure they could win the air war no matter the number. He was aware that at the present loss rate they would soon run out of experienced pilots. You could turn out an infantryman in a month; a pilot took a year, a good pilot several years. "When America is defeated, we must study their training methods for their pilots. Even the conqueror can learn from the vanquished."

"I will suggest it to General Chan." Lian wondered how the Supreme Commander of the Chinese Military would say. They had two hundred million men under arms when they had started this and one hundred and fifty million on offensive operations. Even with all the numbers they were starting to get thin. Occupation took a lot of men. They had lost twenty million men before invading the Americas and were losing men at a much higher rate than ever before since engaging the United States. They had annihilated the American First Army but paid a huge price. He picked up the phone despite the apprehension he had at asking for more equipment. He knew that losing meant death. He needed the aircraft to win.

Sandy looked at the clock it was two a.m. She rolled over to find Will's side of the bed unused. She went in search of her man. He might be the President of the United States, but he had been her husband first. She found him in his study writing letters to the families of those who had fallen.

"When are you coming to bed?"

Will looked at the clock and was genuinely surprised. "I did not realize it was so late."

She squatted so that she could look him in the eyes. "You will do your country no good if you collapse. Come to bed."

Will realized that in some situations even the President of the United States was outranked. He held out his hand. She took it and led him to their bedroom. In two minutes, he was asleep.

Colonel Paul Johnson emerged from his parlay with General Webster. "Get them mounted Hugh. We're pulling out."

"Where we goin', sir." Sergeant Tex Saddler asked Hugh this from the driver's seat of Hugh's Humvee.

"West." That was all the Colonel would say.

Hugh walked back toward the soldiers that were gathered around the trucks. "Mount up! Prepare to move out!"

The men all started orderly loading of the trucks; their duffels were already aboard. He could see the fear in their eyes. The only man with combat experience in the entire three hundred and first was Paul Johnson. Hugh started back toward his ride.

"Watch for stragglers Colonel," Johnson called.

"Yes sir." Hugh saluted and took the passenger's seat in the Hummer.

"Where to sir," Tex asked.

"To the rear of our column," Hugh ordered.

Tex wheeled the successor to the jeep around headed for the rear.

"What part of Texas are you from?" Hugh had known a month but had never gotten to talk to on a personal level because of the intensive training that General Webster had put them through.

"Not from Texas, sir," Tex admitted, "I'm from Illinois."

Smith looked oddly at the man. "Why Tex, then?"

"Has a lot to do with my last name being Saddler, long story that goes back to grade school." The Sergeant smiled. "Anyway, they started callin' me Tex and then I got a pair of cowboy boots for Christmas. Until I signed up for this, I'd never worn anything but Cowboy boots ever again. Cowboy boots, blue jeans, western shirts, and a cowboy hat became my uniform."

The three hundred and first wore something akin to cowboy hats for standard uniform. "Guess that makes this the right outfit for you."

"Do kinda like the hat," Tex agreed.

The camera view showed that the cameraman was running for cover. Explosions were heard nearby.

"Swing the camera around to me," a female voice called.

The camera came around to focus on a reporter with a microphone in her hand. She spoke while breathing hard. The reporter had obviously been running. "This is Galena Gomez in Mexico City."

The camera swung around to show a wall crumble down the street as another explosion rocked the area.

"As the Chinese Army relentlessly moves north the capitol of Mexico becomes the latest world capitol to fall into their hands. The Mexican army is buying the

United States army precious preparation time with their guerilla action. They continue to hit and then fall back. The ranks of the Mexican armed forces are getting thin. From here it's simply not far to the United States. My cameraman and I will have to run north quickly to stay ahead of the advance. Still, we are occasionally run off the road by raiding aircraft. It is best to travel at night, but sometimes, like now, you don't have the luxury. Galena Gomez, WNN."

Admiral Lee looked over his fleet. A year ago, he could have mustered another twenty ships for such an expedition. Now he tried to drive the front lines back toward the United States with forty ships, counting the four carriers. It would have to do.

"Sir, enemy planes," Commander Yang shouted. Yang was quickly gone to try to get to his own plane.

"Why did we not see them coming," Lee barked. "Why did the radar not alert us?"

"Stealth technology," Captain Lok answered, "we can neither see nor hear them."

An American aircraft bore in on the carrier without sound, obviously fitted with magnetic engines. A whistle emanated from the bombs when the American craft dropped them. Two bombs landed in the middle of the deck where the jets catapulted into the sky.

Lee was thrown to the deck by the percussion of the bombs. When he could struggle to his feet, he saw that there was a gaping hole in the deck. This ship would launch no aircraft in this battle.

The next closest carrier attempted to launch her planes, but the two that started to climb from the deck were quickly shot from the sky, then bombs hit her deck also. Two of his four carriers were afire; he looked around to see five more ships on fire and one slipping beneath the waves. The Americans were all over the sky and were still attacking. What if he ran into the enemy ships now, he would be no match.

Lee strode over to Lok. "Turn the fleet about, order retreat."

"Yes, sir." The Captain gave the order.

He had too many loses. He could no longer hold a line north of Honduras. Southern Central America was getting tentative. Despite their great numbers things were being destroyed quicker than they could replace them. "How many enemy planes did we bring down?"

"None reported," Lok said.

"How many planes did we get launched?"

"Four."

"From four carriers?" The Admiral shouted the question.

"All four carriers were hit before they could launch their compliment."

Another bomb slammed the afterdeck of the carrier. Admiral Lee was thrown into the arms of Captain Lok. Captain Lok sat the older man back on his feet.

"Damage report," the Captain barked.

"Sir, that one was astern," a Lieutenant reported, "we're taking on a lot of water and the helm does not answer."

The Captain watched telemetry for a moment. "Admiral?"

"Yes?"

"I believe you need to transfer your flag."

"Why would I do that?"

"I'm not sure we can save this ship."

Lee had been staring out the window at now seven burning ships not counting the four damaged carriers. On a quick count, he could not account for four ships. At least the Americans had, at last, broken off the attack and were returning to their bases.

"Order my barge lowered," Lee said.

"Assessments," Will was meeting with his war council.

"We've pushed the Chinese Navy way back to about the Honduran-Nicaraguan border," Andy Tingle said. "We have sea superiority now. We have more ships coming online every week. We'll keep pushing the Chinese navy south and west. It will take some time, but we're starting to get the upper hand."

"That gives us an advantage," Scott Douglas pointed out. "To sustain any North American action, they'll have to bring their supplies from South America by land or air. Neither way can they haul the amount of supplies as they would have by sea?"

"We are starting to take control of the air. With the magnetic stealth birds, they can't see us coming and we jump them. We drop a couple of them before they know we're around. That means roads, or railroads." Tom Bennett was enthusiastic. "We can pound those from the air. Eventually their supply lines will crumble. When their supply lines crumble it won't be long until their armies in the field crumble."

"We still have the numbers to deal with." One could tell that Winston Sabota, the Commandant of the Marines was not as enthusiastic as Bennett. "If we can interdict the supply lines for long enough, they'll crumble. We have to hold on for a while."

"Yes," the President said, "looks like we've got them just where they want us."

No one laughed. Will chastised himself for letting some doubt in again, especially for letting others hear him express doubt. It was not a good witness.

In the night Gary Patton had managed to build a makeshift blind. The blind camouflaged him and his equipment. The Chinese had proven unable to pick up his signal and so he could broadcast with impunity behind their lines. Since broadcasting what he saw would have let them know where he was, he was now working with the US military as a surreptitious operative. The people of Nicaragua had shared their meager foodstuffs with him to keep him alive. They had also given him tips of where to look for things. The latest thing was a POW camp in a place called Chinandega. Gary's blind was built on a hill overlooking the complex where his camera could look down into it.

Gary activated the camera.

"Receiving." He heard the voice in his earpiece.

"Who am I talking to today," Patton asked.

"This is General Douglas."

"Chair of the Joint Chiefs." The reporter was impressed.

"Yes," the General acknowledged.

"Are you seeing this?"

"POW camp?"

"Right," Gary said.

"American troops?" The General was hopeful.

"Yes, sir, mostly." Gary panned the camera around and zoomed in on a group of men. "There are some from other armies, but mostly American."

"Stop there." The General thought he recognized the black man in the picture. "Zoom in."

"Better?"

"A little tighter," the General said. He knew that man! "That's Paul Green, isn't it?"

Another voice agreed. "Yep, that's General Green."

"At least we know that some survived and where they are," the General said. "I hope they can hold on until we get there. Green doesn't look too good, lost at least thirty pounds."

"The locals have told me that our guys were marched here from where they were captured, almost without rest. Some of 'em dropped on the way." There was a disturbance in the camp. Gary swung the camera toward it. Two Chinese soldiers dragged an American out of a building, across a lot and to a small metal structure. The soldiers opened a door on the metal box and looked inside, saying something. A man crawled from the box and the one that had been dragged there was thrown inside. The door was again locked. The man who had crawled from the box had collapsed only feet from it. The Chinese soldiers ignored the man and shared a laugh as they walked back toward the building.

When the Chinese were gone, Green and some other P.O.W.'s rushed to the man. They picked him up and carried him into the shade.

As Gary followed the scene, his camera crossed the sun and the lens reflected it. A guard from a tower started to shout and point.

"Gotta go, General." Patton shut off the camera and packed it in seconds. He slipped out the backside of the blind, down into a ravine. Running down the ravine he found a public transportation bus, an old school bus from the United States, idling and waiting for him. Some men waiting outside the bus pulled some items from the underneath luggage storage and Gary threw his equipment in a large trunk, which was closed, locked and placed in the back of the compartment. The other items were replaced to hide the camera equipment and satellite uplink. He jumped aboard the bus and the bus immediately surged down the road. Several people stood and lifted their seats that were hinged in the floor. A coffin-sized compartment opened up, Gary dove in, and the seats were replaced.

The bus had lumbered down the road for several minutes without incident. Then Gary heard the honking. He knew it was a Chinese patrol. The bus stopped. The Nicaraguan people were very angry with the invaders, and he had yet to find one sympathetic to the invaders. Still, it only took one and he was dead.

First, he heard the luggage compartment open. A short search and the compartment closed. Next there were footsteps down the aisle. This took several minutes. Time was running short for Gary. When the bus was rolling his compartment was well ventilated, now the air was already stale and the temperature rising each minute. The exhaust fumes leaking into the smuggling hold would asphyxiate him if the bus did not start to move again and soon. He choked back the urge to cough. The compartment had never been meant to haul a human being.

Gary coughed and a soldier looked around at that spot. A man sitting in a seat above where Gary was secreted coughed with a cough that sounded enough like Gary's cough to fool the soldier. He moved on down the aisle.

The soldiers seemed to be checking the papers of every person. As the soldiers worked their way back to the front, Gary's breath came harder. The temperature was at least one forty beneath the floor and oxygen was getting scarce. He knew he could not gasp for air.

Finally, he heard the door close, and the bus started rolling again. Patton heard the Chinese patrol pass the bus and continue on. After a moment, when the Chinese patrol was out of sight the seats came up and hands grabbed the reporter, pulling him from his hiding place. He had just started to lose consciousness. The Nicaraguans knew he would be in trouble but, if the Chinese had found him, they all would have died. They gave him water and let him ride in the passenger compartment for the remainder of the trip. Letting him ride in the open was taking a terrible chance. The Chinese could be around any corner.

Gary was growing to love the Nicaraguan people. They had little but would gladly share what they did have. They always had a smile on their faces despite their dire circumstance. There had been earthquakes, hurricanes, Sandinistas, dictators, volcanoes, and now the Chinese. Yet, they smiled.

Hugh and Colonel Johnson walked into the huge tent that was General Webster's headquarters while First Army was on the move. A map took up an entire large monitor showing the location of the First in the mountains of southwestern Colorado. Second Army was farther south, about halfway between the Mexican border and where First Army had stopped. The newly commissioned Third Army was mustering at Fort Leonard Wood in Missouri.

"Come in, Gentlemen," General Webster waived them to a chair, "have a seat."

There was pleasant conversation between the assembled officers until they were all gathered.

"Let's get started." The General was walking toward the map. "You can see here the relative positions of First, Second, and Third Armies. As you may know the Mexican Army has pretty much crumbled? We expect to have Chinese on our soil within the next day."

This caused a murmur from among the assembled warriors.

"We have intelligence that says the first priority of the Chinese is to seek out and destroy in detail any and all United States Armed Forces that they can contact." Webster started to pace. "Now, we have fed them false intelligence on our readiness levels. They believe that the only battle-ready force in the United States is Second Army. If they can force a retreat by Second Army, they have orders to pursue wherever that might take them. We're betting on them following that plan."

The General's aides changed the map as he had been using showing the way Webster thought the battle would develop. "Second Army will engage the Chinese in eastern New Mexico, hold for a time, then retreat to the northwest. That is why we are digging in here. Second Army is going to retreat right through our lines. They will fall back to roughly south of Grand Junction where they will regroup and again turn to face the enemy. They will form a line from Grand Junction projecting south. Third Army will move into Colorado, then form a north south line to the east and advance west from the Pueblo area. When we are pressed, we are to fall back to the north to form the third side of the box. Our fallback area will be roughly on a line from Grand Junction toward Pueblo. When we have formed a loose box, we can close the sides of this trap and crush the Chinese army from three sides."

Johnson raised his hand.

"Question Colonel?"

"How long do we hold," Johnson asked.

"Until you're told to retreat," Webster answered. "Gentlemen, the retreat must be done in orderly fashion, but must be made to look as much like a panic as possible, won't be easy. The more panicked we look, the harder they'll chase us. The harder they chase us the better the trap will work. Right now, the Chinese

Army is a very confident army. If we can give them a bloody nose and hopefully a couple of fat lips and maybe a few loose teeth to go with it, we can shake that confidence."

The men in the tent laughed at that.

"If we can shake their confidence maybe we can make them second-guess and even start doubting themselves. If we can do that, we've taken a giant step toward winning this war."

"But, sir, won't we still be outnumbered even with all three armies in the fight," another officer asked.

"Let's get off the number thing!" Webster was showing more confidence than he felt. "Our soldiers, even the green ones, and our weaponry are far superior to anything the Chinese have. I'd say ten to one odds to their favor is an even fight. With all three armies engaged our numbers will be better than that."

When Johnson and Smith were back in the Hummer Tex set it in motion toward their encampment and Hugh spoke. "The old rope-a-dope huh?"

"Sure, looks like it," Johnson said. "Worked for Ali, sure hope it works for us."

"What are you guys talkin' about," Tex asked.

Hugh clapped him on the shoulder. "Need to know, Sarge, need to know."

"I know," Tex agreed, "need to know and I don't."

"Good man," Johnson smiled a paternal smile.

5.

Admiral Wilcox relaxed in the captain's chair of the Houston, a fast attack sub. The five boats under his command were all of the fast attack variety, but of new design. The subs were quieter than the boomers of old since they had been fitted with the magnetic caterpillar engines. The Houston, Philadelphia, Jacksonville, Olympia, and Topeka were but five holes in the water to anyone who might be out there listening. Each American sub could track its own kind, but even other US craft could not track them. They were a very nasty wolf pack out hunting for prey.

"Sir?" There was a quaver in the voice of Specialist Philo Bachner.

The Admiral knew the quality of the sonar man. When the Admiral had made his way to the Specialist's console he spoke. "What do you have?"

"Sir, this new detection equipment is either working or showing a huge ghost." Bachner pointed to the screen.

There on the screen was what appeared to be the motherlode. At least it was the mother lode from a submariner's point of view. All the dimensions appeared correct from the new intelligence the Admiral had been made aware of. "That's one of those supersub, carrier, and transport jobbies?"

"That's my opinion sir."

"Battle stations." Wilcox said it calmly, almost coyly. "Get me the other boats."

"You're on tight band broadcast sir." The radioman informed him.

With the locator technology built into the new boats that meant that the American boats would link via a radio beam only a centimeter wide before they left dock. Every boat knew where the other was and they could communicate instantly, but no one else could locate them unless they drove right through the beam.

"Wilcox to Wolf Pack Charlie," the Admiral said, "enemy sighted course zero seven four at thirteen miles. Get in close and get hits. Make all your torpedoes count, turning on my mark, mark!"

The Admiral waited for a moment.

"Everybody following," he asked.

"All the boats but Topeka are turning," said Bachner. "Wait, turning now sir, all boats moving into attack speed and formation, Admiral."

Everyone on all five boats broke into a sweat despite the climate controls. The newest torpedoes were effective from as far away as ten thousand meters and were just as undetectable as the subs that carried them. The torpedo speeds had also increased. If they were within a mile the torpedoes would impact seconds after launch. The Admiral had already made his orders clear. Close within two thousand meters before firing. Make extra sure of hits. No one knew how the enemy vessels were armed. As big as they were, they might have armament everywhere. They had to get the enemy vessel in trouble from the get-go and sinking something so mammoth was going to take several hits.

"Seven thousand meters." The First Officer of the Philadelphia was glued to the instruments. You could have heard a pin drop on their deck. Would the enemy vessels suddenly start firing from fifty ports. Would there be any warning before they fired. They could have stolen magnetic technology and made weapons like the ones on the American sub.

"Four thousand meters." This was the sonar man on the Olympia a short time later. The breathing on Olympia almost came to a stop.

"Two thousand meters." Bachner was leaning over the sonar console as they closed in on their quarry.

"Weapons status," Wilcox asked.

"All tubes loaded and hot," the weapons officer said.

"Seventeen fifty!" Bachner was the only one speaking. The other subs were firing when Houston did. Everyone was wondering how close in the Old Man would push before he loosed the torps. "Fifteen hundred, twelve-fifty, eleven hundred, passing one thousand meters to target."

Wilcox was sweating profusely. "Tell me when the last boat passes one thousand."

"Now."

"Fire all tubes!"

The Houston shuddered noticeably as all eight forward torpedo tubes fired within seconds. Before Houston's last tube had fired, the other four boats were firing, and each finished within ten seconds of the lead boat.

True, the supersub should not be able to find the fast attack boats, but it could project trajectories and fire back along those lines. If they fired a lot of ordinance, they did not have to get that lucky to hit the American boats even when they could not see them. As soon as each sub had fired its last torpedo, they went into evasive maneuvers.

Admiral Lei was impressed with his new command. They had crossed the Pacific Ocean without a hiccup. As massive as his new boat was, no one could find it when it was submerged. He knew that the Americans were looking hard for his command, but there had been no hint of the Americans or any other hostile force. Three days hence, he would land his cargo on the shores of Mexico. A quarter million infantry, fifty planes, one hundred armored vehicles and fifty helicopters would join the conquest of the Americas. Working as a ferry Captain was not exactly his idea of a glamorous job, but he was a major part of the war effort, and he knew it.

"Sir," his sonar man called.

"What is it, Lieutenant." Lei did not even look his way. The man was too nervous and jumped at shadows.

"Something odd." The Lieutenant was not looking at his scope, but rather pressing his headphones to his ear. "Something I can't quite identify."

"Another whale," the Captain asked.

"I don't think so" the Lieutenant said, "not this time, sir."

The Admiral shook his head in disgust and was about to speak, but never got the words out.

The first torpedo struck the Chinese boat directly below the bridge. The sonar Lieutenant never would know what that sound was. In the next fifteen seconds, thirty-six more torpedoes would strike the boat from front to rear. The water in that part of the Pacific is especially deep. As the huge boat sunk, it fell apart and was shrunk. There would be no distress calls. Due to radio silence, the Chinese would not suspect anything for three days.

All five American boats cheered as they watched, via sonar, the enemy vessel break apart. The celebration was on that night. The Admiral even approved one beer per man.

"Get me Lincoln," Wilcox ordered, "the President has to know about this."

At that moment Will sat in the Oval Office with the Joint Chief's. "Have we overlooked anything at all, and will this rope-a-dope thing really work?"

"Sir, it's the best plan we have right now," General Douglas assured him.

"And if it doesn't work," asked the Commander in Chief.

"If this doesn't work, we are in position to retreat in three different directions. We'll be able to maintain an effective fighting force. The Chinese won't be able to pursue in just one direction with their entire force and engage all our troops. So, it's the best we have to fight them with the best contingencies built in."

"Might I also say that we're winning the air war now," Tom Bennett interjected. "We'll pound them the whole time."

"May God's banner go before us gentlemen." The President was wondering why he had not thought of that open-eyed beseeching prayer before the old First Army was destroyed.. "Whether with many or few the battle belongs to the Lord."

"I am standing here with the Second Army of the United States as we await the onslaught of the Chinese Army." Galena Gomez was reporting from New Mexico. "Sometime today we expect them to come over the horizon. All day long, our fighter jets have streaked overhead to pound the enemy before they can attack. The hardest part is waiting, waiting for a hostile force to invade your home."

"I must say that we have learned good news," she continued. "The Chinese fostered this invasion via huge submarines that can carry up to a quarter million soldiers and all their equipment. As you know, some time back, one was sunk in a

Central America harbor when it surfaced to unload. Now our submarine force has reported sinking one at sea. This is better than the first sinking since the first sub had already off loaded its cargo. This second sub was sent to the bottom fully loaded. Galena Gomez, somewhere in New Mexico."

As Galena wrapped up her story and prepared to move north Burner and Cowboy flashed by overhead on their way to the war. They did not disturb her report because no one heard them.

"This is still spooky to me," Cowboy called to Burner.

"What's that," the Colonel asked.

"No sound," Cowboy said. "I'm used to the thunder of a jet engine. I can hardly feel that this things on."

"Well, as long as you stay in the air with these magnetic things on and you'll be alright," Mitch grinned. "Let's get treetop."

The MEC jet engine had changed such warfare. Now, since the enemy could neither see nor hear you coming, you stayed low until you saw the enemy. Then you locked on a target and started your climb just before you dropped ordinance. If you did not climb you got hit by your own stuff bouncing off the ground or just the explosions of whatever you hit. The good thing was that you were only vulnerable to enemy fire for a short time. The bad thing was you had only seconds to find a target, lock on to it then release.

Mitch Renner suddenly realized that he was over the Chinese Army. He found a tank and locked on, then released and climbed. When he climbed there were suddenly shells popping around him. He was able to see the tank explode. He also saw a line of trucks flame out, he guessed that was the work of Cowboy. Mitch curled and dove back to the deck. A few seconds later, Cowboy settled in off his right wing.

"A few less bad guys for the ground pounders to worry about," Cowboy called over the radio.

Each plane held five such bombs. That meant they had four more trips to make.

"Ready for round two," Burner asked.

"You know it!" Cowboy answered enthusiastically as they turned back toward the enemy.

Hugh thought the engineers in the Three-Oh-First had done a great job. Part of the command bunker was built into solid rock. A little blasting had opened natural cavities in the rock. The rock could withstand more punishment. They would need that when the time came.

Hugh, Johnson, and the other officers had been listening to the battle south of them as it developed. The Second fought well. The enemy numbers were just too many. They held their ground for nearly forty hours as wave after wave of enemy troops came. When the fake retreat started, the radio frequencies that the US forces thought the Chinese would crack flowed with messages that showed abject panic. The frequencies that they thought were still secure, told a different story, one of an orderly redeployment of US troops.

On the second day of the redeployment things changed, Chinese were suddenly where no one expected them to be. They showed up in bad places in large numbers. The faked panic started to be a real panic. The real panic became a headlong flight. During this time, General Webster stopped by the Three-Oh-First for inspection. The General waived the Colonels into the CP for a conference.

"Gentlemen," the General was contemplative, "as you know the pretend panic has become a real one. Second Army has fallen apart. It will be some time before the troops can be rounded up and formed back into an effective fighting force. They should be falling through our lines any time. There goes the west side of the box."

"And the East Side, sir." Hugh asked the question sensing there was more to come.

"Major logistics snafu." The General turned to face them for the first time. "Most of the Third is not even out of Missouri."

"So, sir, we stand alone," Johnson asked.

"Yes, Colonel," the General acknowledged, "that is why I decided to personally inspect each unit, pep talk time. We have to hold on by our toes, fingernails, and whatever else you can use. If we don't stop them here who knows how far they can go. After the Rockies the Mississippi River is the next natural barrier."

"Not a wonderful prospect," the Colonel observed.

"Get your troops ready, Colonel Johnson!" Webster became official. "You are the far right of our line. If they get around you the whole flank will collapse."

Johnson drew himself up to his full five feet ten. "We'll hold the flank, sir. To the last man if need be."

Webster saluted; Paul and Hugh returned it, then the General left.

"Standing alone," Hugh observed, "not a pleasant prospect."

"Our chances aren't good," Paul agreed, "but we've got to sell it to the men. Our country depends on them. Let's hope the last man thing isn't necessary."

"People always said I was a pretty good salesman," Hugh grinned.

"When the battle starts you need to stay on the left. Watch to make sure that the line holds and there are no holes," the Colonel ordered, "I'll take the right. If you see my side start to falter, we'll have to swing back like a gate to the right so that First Army doesn't get flanked."

"Understood," Hugh was grim.

"The Chinese will be here within twelve hours." Paul looked into the eyes of the man he had come to like and respect. "Let's get the men ready. God go with you, buddy."

The men shook hands. "And with you, Paul."

Hugh exited the bunker, heading for the left side of the Three-Oh-First. He patted his breast pocket to make sure that his testament was there as he said a silent prayer. Tex fell in beside him.

"Got your radio, Sergeant," Hugh asked.

Saddler held up the cell phone sized device. "Yes, sir."

"O.K., Tex, take your scouts and get out there." Hugh pointed south. "I want to know exactly where the lead units of the Chinese are."

"On it, sir," Tex started away.

"Tex." Hugh called after him.

The Illinois cowboy turned back.

"We've got to hold this ground at all costs. Get me good intelligence. When you fall back into the lines, you find me and stick with me. You hear?"

Tex saluted. "Yes, sir."

"General, I want to know how this all fell apart!" This was the first time anyone in government had heard Will Sevrin yell.

"I don't know, sir." General Douglas answered truthfully. He was a little taken back by the red-faced man in front of him. "We're looking into it. General Glenn let things get out of hand. I can see some heads rolling over this."

"Heads have already rolled, literally!" The President's volume was still up. "We're going to lose more men than necessary in more battles than necessary because you did not pull this off. If we do that just two or three times, we lose the war."

"Yes, sir," was all the General could say.

"Now, First Army is gonna take the full brunt of the Chinese because of this fiasco. Let's light a fire under General Hauser and get Third Army up there to help."

"Striking the match as we speak, sir." The General was off to put his size twelve's up multiple rumps.

The artillery started a little before dawn. Some men had been dozing, but they knew that they would get no sleep for quite a while now. The Chinese were getting close.

Hugh took his radio off its belt clip and punched in a code.

On the other end he heard the whispered reply, "Saddler."

"Where they at Tex," Hugh asked.

"Four miles out sir," the Sergeant answered. "They aren't exactly in a hurry, but they ain't smellin' the roses either."

"O.K., Sergeant, when they get within a mile, you get your butt back here behind our lines, clear?"

"Yes, sir," Tex answered.

"Keep me informed." Hugh broke the connection, and then dialed another code. "Johnson."

"Sir, Tex says they're about four miles out."

"Get everybody in their holes."

"Yes sir." He clicked the radio off.

Just before 1100 hours Tex came sliding back into the lines.

"Report," Hugh ordered.

"Sir, they are less than a mile out," Tex said. "They are really pickin' up speed as they get closer. They're commin' hard."

Hugh clicked on his radio and punched Johnson's code. Johnson checked the ID then he answered. "What's up Colonel?"

"Here they come sir," Hugh said. "Probably half a mile or less could be any time."

"Roger, out."

It is a funny thing how when you do not want something to happen waiting for it to happen seems an eternity. When it does happen it almost seems a relief. The next fifteen minutes seemed forever. Then there was an awesome and intimidating sight. Chinese troops as far as the eye could see. Thousands of them and they all seemed to be coming toward Hugh.

The front row of the Chinese troops knelt and fired rockets. Everyone in the American lines ducked. The second line of the Chinese troops screamed and charged. Hugh did not see the rocket hit his CP.

Lieutenant Colonel Hugh Wallace Smith pulled a picture from his pocket. The picture was of Terri and the girls. He stared at it for a long moment, kissed it, and then placed it in the Testament that he placed over his heart. Hugh Smith did not believe that he would live out the day.

Quickly the Lieutenant Colonel made his way down the trench to the left of the command bunker. "Hold your fire."

The Chinese came closer.

"Don't fire till I give the order."

The Chinese moved from a trot into a dead sprint.

"We can't afford to miss!" Hugh stopped. "We've gotta make every bullet count."

Just then the enemy got within what Hugh considered killing range.

"Fire!"

The world seemed to be set ablaze. Everyone in First Army had opened up at virtually the same time. The first rank of Chinese fell. The second rank jumped over the first and continued the advance.

"Take careful aim and fire at will!"

Now another rank of Chinese fell, the next rank on top of them and the one after that on the first two. The chatter of machine guns was constant, cutting their deadly swath. Still, they came. There seemed to be no end of enemy soldiers willing to die for their cause. There was, so far, no shortage of American soldiers willing to oblige them.

As Hugh was passing down the line exhorting the men again, he was suddenly knocked from his feet, bounced off the back wall of the trench, and slammed to the ground. His head swam for a moment and then cleared. He had not been hit, but rather was hit by a man who had been hit. An RPG had landed just in front of the trench and taken a soldier's head off, then slammed his body backward against Hugh. The man's blood and brains were all over the Lieutenant Colonel. Tex, who was following his Colonel everywhere as ordered, rolled the body off of Hugh. Hugh tore the man's dog tag from what remained of his neck and placed it in his pocket. The Lieutenant Colonel and Sergeant exchanged a look, but no words. They did not read the dog tag. They did not want to know, not yet. Then, it was back to the war.

When the bodies were stacked five high the Chinese paused. Everyone knew it was a pause. They would come again.

A Sergeant stood up so that his head was above the trench, "Hey Colonel…"

Hugh opened his mouth to tell the man to get down. Tex dove for his feet to bring him down, neither was quick enough. The man was struck in the head by a bullet before Hugh could speak or Tex could get there and fell dead.

"Reload and check your weapons while there's time." Tex was barking orders. "Every third man, clean your weapon, when they're done the second guy and then the first."

The silence was eerie for about fifteen minutes. Since most of the Chinese armor had been destroyed by air on the way north the only sound was marching feet. Even those halted for a time.

With a war cry that sounded as if the entire world was screaming, the enemy came again. This time they came even faster and with greater numbers. The piles immediately started again, but they were pressing closer than before. Grenades were exploding in front of the trench, behind the trench and occasionally in the trench. Twice they were close enough that Hugh spat their dirt from his mouth. The whine of bullets passing overhead was constant. The sound of bullets striking the ground just short of the defensive trench was also without pause.

He could hear the far end of his line screaming for medics and sent Tex to check the situation. Upon inspecting the cause, the Sergeant found that an RPG had affected five men. Two were dead; one had lost the better part of an arm and two more had more minor wounds.

As Saddler started helping with the first aid the amputee looked at Tex' shoulder.

"Your hit, Sarge."

Saddler looked where the private pointed with his good arm. A piece of shrapnel had dug in under the skin of his right shoulder. He pulled it out. "Don't have time to deal with that now."

Up and down the lines, up and down the lines, up and down the lines Hugh continued, usually followed by Tex. Hugh was too busy seeing to the deportment and deployment of his men to watch for his own safety. Twice Tex had to shoot a Chinese soldier just before he shot the Colonel. They were occasionally breaking through now.

More and more Hugh and Tex would have to step over fallen men that would not rise again. The wounded were carried from the ditch; the dead lay where they fell. Occasionally they paused to give first aid to one still living. The piles of bodies on the other side of the line kept getting bigger and were forming a barrier for their comrades to snipe from behind. It was as if the grim reaper were stacking sheaves.

Suddenly the noise stopped. There was no firing from the other side.

"Cease fire," Smith ordered, "cease fire."

Tex looked at his watch, it was one a.m. Fourteen hours had passed in what seemed like five minutes. As best he could tell of the one thousand men that were under their command, roughly two hundred were dead or wounded.

Hugh peeked over the top of the trench. The battle continued to rage to the left but had ceased to their front. Most men would have been happy, but Hugh was suspicious. Hugh clicked on his radio and punched in the code for Johnson; 'Unable to connect' was shown on the display.

"Tex," Hugh called.

The Sergeant was instantly at his side. "Sir?"

"I suspect a ruse." Hugh kept looking toward the enemy. "Go find Johnson. I want to send out the scouts. Go."

Tex was off. Hugh busied himself seeing to the men. Guns were being cleaned and the wounded to be checked on, etc. Then Tex was back.

"Well," Hugh asked.

"Congratulations on your promotion to command of the three-oh-first, sir," Tex said.

"Paul," he asked of his commander.

"Dead sir," Tex said. "The Major says it was shortly after the fight started. He just didn't have time to come get you, sir."

The decision had been made by the circumstances. "Get the scouts out."

Tex and four other men were over the wall in less than a minute. The new commanding officer watched as they slithered on their bellies among the bodies and gore. They were soon swallowed by the darkness.

6.

Hugh busied himself for two hours seeing to the redeployment of the eight hundred men now left to him to command. A fifth of the Three-oh-First was down, but not a single man had run. Hugh was proud of their...his regiment.

Two hours after the scouts had slipped into the early morning darkness on their bellies, his radio buzzed.

"Sir, it's Tex." Even through the Sergeant drawl Hugh could sense the urgency.

"Where are you?" Hugh immediately regretted the question.

"Rather not say, sir." Tex corrected his superior. "I think I know what the bad guys are up to, though."

"And?"

"Ain't good sir," Tex understated, "look off to your right."

Enough of the smoke had cleared and the moon was full so that he was able to see the pass in the mountains. "The ravine?"

"Yes, sir," Tex said. "That valley curls around to the south. It starts out about four miles south of you, sir. It makes a curl and comes out where you see it. It's going to be about a ten hour walk for the Chinese infantry, but I'm guessin' they'll be pourin' outta that valley behind you by noon, sir. Guess they've got scouts too."

The end of the valley was maybe a half-mile behind First Army's lines. "How many bad guys?"

Hugh heard Tex talk it over with one of the other scouts. "About a hundred thousand, sir."

"Keep me informed." Hugh cut the connection with Tex and punched in the code that he never thought he would use. Every officer of command rank knew the code to General Webster for emergencies, but only Regiment or larger unit commanders used it.

The General answered. "This better be good, Smith."

"It is, sir," Smith was nervous.

"Where's Johnson?"

"Dead sir."

"What's the emergency?"

Hugh could still hear the constant fire to his left and over the phone wherever the General was. "The Chinese withdrew from our front about two hours ago, sir."

"And that's an emergency?'

"Hear me out, General," Hugh added quickly, "it all looked fishy to me. I sent out scouts. Sir, look on your map."

"Got it in front of me."

"Do you see the valley about a half mile to the northwest of my position?"

"Yes."

"Sir, follow it around."

There was a short silence. "If the Chinese send troops up that valley they'll come out behind our lines, right behind you."

"Yes sir."

"What about your scouts?"

"General they tell me that about a hundred thousand bad guys are going into that valley. They should be here for lunch. Think we're gonna need some help, sir."

"Sounds like it," the General gruffed, "only one problem."

"What would that be, sir?"

"We're fully engaged all along the remainder of the line, I've got no one to send you."

"Sir," Smith was desperate, "I've got about eight hundred men. That's not going to hold a hundred thousand."

"How far is the fighting from you?"

"A mile, maybe two," Hugh guessed.

"Move to your left," the General ordered, "take as many regiments out of the line as you safely can. Don't expose our flank. Plug that valley, Colonel."

"Yes, sir." The connection went dead.

Take from the regiments to the left. That, at least, would relieve him of command. He would turn the project over to a Full Bird or higher. Tex was still out. "Sergeant Owens!"

The man came running. "Sir?"

"Transportation," Smith said, "now."

"Major Dinkins!"

The Major came running.

"Major, do you see the valley there." He pointed.

"Yes sir."

"Gonna be a whole bunch of bad guys commin' outta that valley in a few hours. Get the men there and dig in at the end of the valley. We've gotta hold."

"Yes, sir." The Major started barking orders.

In three minutes, the Sergeant was back with a Hummer. The vehicle was some the worse for wear but ran.

Hugh jumped in. "Get me over to the Eightieth's CP."

Owens gave it a good amount of gas and was there in minutes. When Hugh pulled up, a skinny Captain that did not look old enough to be playing soldier met him. "Colonel am I glad to see you."

"Where's your commanding officer, Captain," Hugh asked.

"Sir, I am the commanding officer."

"No, I mean for the regiment."

"I mean for the regiment, sir."

Hugh stared at the pimple-faced kid. "Everyone above Captain is dead?"

"Sir, the CP was hit with an RPG when they were having a pow-wow" the Captain informed him. "No, they're not all dead, but they're all out of action."

"OK, Captain," Hugh was thinking on his feet, "I'm taking command of your regiment."

"Yes sir. Good, sir."

Hugh pointed to the pass. "You see that pass?"

The moon seemed brighter than ever. The Captain squinted through his thick glasses. "Yes, sir."

"You pull outta this line and redeploy at the end of that valley," Smith ordered. "The three-oh-first is already on their way. Take up a position next to them. There's a world of hurt coming down that valley, Captain. You've gotta plug that hole. What's your name, son?"

Hugh guessed that the man was at least ten years his junior.

"Captain Percy Hardwick, sir."

"Percy, how many men you got left?"

"About seven-fifty sir."

"Get 'em going. I'm going for more help. I'm leaving it up to you and Major Dinkins to place the Three-oh-First and your guys to plug that valley."

"Yes sir."

"Captain, if the bad guys get through, we lose this battle, maybe the war. You got that?"

"Yes, sir," Percy saluted, "hold to the last!'

"We cannot retreat," Hugh confirmed, "move out!"

Percy was off to gather and move his men.

Twenty minutes after sending Percy and his boys down the road, Hugh was at the CP of the One-Sixty-Forth. He asked a Major, "Where's your CO?"

"Sir, the Colonel and Lieutenant Colonel both bought it," the Major said, "fraid I'm the CO."

Hugh sighed. "How many men you got?"

"Just under nine hundred sir."

"What's your name, Major?" Hugh liked to know the names of men he was going to ask to commit suicide.

"Major Aaron Dian, sir."

"Aaron," Hugh pointed to the valley, "you see that pass?"

"Sir, yes, sir," Dian answered.

"There's a whole load of Chinese Infantry coming down that valley trying to flank us. That's why they gave up the frontal assault here. You pull your men out of this line and take them to that pass. As we're lookin' at it you deploy your regiment on the right promontory. Understood?"

"Sir, yes, sir," the Major said.

"Hide your men well Major," Hugh said. "We don't want the Chinese to see us until we open up on them. Move it."

Fifteen minutes after redeploying the One-Sixty-Fourth, Hugh's hummer pulled into the CP of the Sixty-Second. Hugh walked into the bunker to find it manned by a Captain and Major.

"Who's in command," Hugh's tone was resigned.

"That'd be me, sir," the higher-ranking man said, "Major Raul Domingo."

"Both Colonel's dead?"

"No, sir," the Captain spoke, "both were wounded and medevacked."

"Follow me, men."

The three officers walked out of the bunker. Hugh pointed once again at the valley. The moon was still glowing with cloud cover settling low over the mountains to the west. "You see that valley?"

"Yes sir," they choroused.

"The Chinese are coming down that valley in force," Hugh looked at his watch, "they should hit us before noon. You take your men out of the line here and dig them in on the left promontory. Use all the concealment you can find. Understood?"

"Yes, sir," Domingo acknowledged.

"Move."

Hugh was back in his Hummer and gone. "Who's next in line?"

"The two-fiftieth," Owens answered.

"Find their CP."

The Captain of the Sixty-Second was not so sure. "Sir, hadn't you better check with HQ before running off on a mission assigned by a Lieutenant Colonel we've never heard of?"

Domingo thought that was a good idea. He called the non-emergency frequency for HQ and was surprised when he was transferred to General Webster.

"Major, if Colonel Smith told you to do something you'd better be doing it post haste or I'll have your backside, understood?"

Major Domingo came to attention as he got the radio chewing. "Yes, sir, understood!"

The General broke the connection, and the Sixty-Second was on its way.

"Stop," Hugh said as the Humvee piloted by Sergeant Owen approached the emplacement of the Two-Fiftieth.

Owens braked the vehicle, but it took some time to stop, the brakes were nearly gone. "Sir, their CP is a mile or so yet."

"We can't use 'em, Sarge," Hugh could see that the battle was yet too close to pull another regiment out of the line.

Owens said nothing.

"How many men do we have with the four regiments I sent to the valley?"

"Near as I can tell, sir, about three thousand two hundred and fifty."

"Better than thirty to one odds."

"Yes, sir." The Sergeant agreed with the math. "Maybe you should call the General back."

Hugh pointed to the battlefield. War raged wherever you looked. "He still can't spare anyone. We're on our own."

"Well, they say ten to one is good odds," Owens observed. "Thirty to one sounds a bit steep."

"We'll just have to be three times as tough today, Sergeant." Hugh thumbed over his shoulder. "Get us back there."

The Sergeant turned the Hummer back toward the valley. Hugh pulled out his radio and punched in Saddler's code.

"Saddler." It was practically a whisper.

"How far are they away Tex?"

"Sir, about five hours give or take half an hour."

"Stay well ahead of them," Smith ordered. "Get in at least an hour before they hit us."

"Yes, sir," Tex said, "and sir?"

"Yes Sergeant?"

"We've counted several more times. A hundred thousand is pretty close."

Hugh had been hoping it was an overestimate, a wild overestimate. "We're working on pluggin' the hole, Sergeant. Check back in an hour or so."

"I just don't see how that's possible, Tony." Rock was skeptical of what the head of Around the Clock News had told him. "We are the voice of the common man. I am the voice of the unwashed masses."

"That's what the numbers say, Rock. Your ratings are dropping every month." Tony hated dealing with the big ego jerks.

"It must be a right-wing conspiracy to fake the ratings." Rock shook his head. "They'll stop at nothing to damage me."

"Maybe your coverage should be more balanced?"

The Rock was on his feet, feigning anger. At this point in his career, he had no real emotions, but could act any emotion at any time. "There's no one more balanced than ATCN. Everyone knows that the Rock tells them what they need to hear. I'm insulted that you could say such a thing. Besides, who cares what some church goin' NASCAR redneck with a shotgun in the back window of his pickup thinks?"

Wow! The guy had just actually referred to himself as 'The Rock.' "I'm just tellin' you what the ratings and surveys are tellin' me."

Rock started to the door. "I will save this country from itself. Right now, I may be the most important man in America."

With about two hours to go, Hugh had finished his inspection of the position of the more than three thousand men under his command. Under any other circumstance, three thousand might have seemed a huge number to command for someone so inexperienced. Right now, it seemed tiny. His radio buzzed; he was expecting Tex. "Smith."

"Colonel," the familiar voice growled, "General Webster."

"Hope you're sending me some help, Sir."

"How many troops do you have, Colonel?"

"A little over three thousand, sir." Smith's heart was pounding.

"What's the latest bad guy count?"

"Holdin' steady at a hundred thousand, sir."

"I'm sorry, Hugh," Webster was quieter than normal; "I've got no one to send you. The Chinese are still pressing us all along the remainder of the line. The Second is still reassembling and Third is a day away at best. If you noticed the cloud cover, we can't get any air support either. Maybe a few choppers, but that's it."

The clouds were lowering by the minute. "You're full of good news, sir."

"A final thing, Colonel." The General sounded depressed. "You are to hold your position to the last man. If you retreat, the whole flank caves in. You will not retreat. If you are about to be overrun you will radio me with that information, understood?"

"Yes sir."

"God's speed Colonel." The connection was broken. Webster was sure he had just ordered the death of one of the finest officers on the planet. Fate could be a cruel master.

Hugh went behind a nearby bolder and knelt in prayer. "Father if it be your will save us all from death. If you cannot save us from death, then give us victory over our enemy. If I must die today in defense of my country, please take care of Terri and the girls."

Lt. Colonel Smith emerged from behind the rock and gathered his command staff around him. "Let's pray."

Everyone bowed their head. There are no atheists at times like that.

"Lord our God," Hugh started, "we commend our lives to your hands. We do not know whether we will live or die this day, but it is all good if it is within your plan. For those of us who do not survive we ask that you personally look after the loved ones we leave behind. Now, Lord, go with us as we fight for freedom that includes the right to worship you as we please."

Everyone present said Amen at nearly the same instant.

Hugh stood on a boulder that allowed him to look over another bigger boulder. Tex stood on one side of the Colonel and Captain Hardwick on the other. With the help of binoculars, the Chinese were just barely visible. They were not exactly hiding, thinking they were moving with impunity. Hugh checked the Sixty-Second on the left promontory. He had trouble seeing them when he knew they were there. He was sure they would be a huge surprise to the Chinese. The same was true on the right with the One-Sixty-Fourth. The surprise would be terrible but would not last very long. Could they take out enough enemy soldiers with the surprise to win the engagement?

Hugh turned to Hardwick. "Captain, check our line. Make sure it's ready. It's almost show time."

"Yes, sir!" Percy was off at a trot to his assigned duty.

Tex offered his hand to Hugh. "Been a pleasure servin' with you, sir."

Hugh shook the offered appendage. "Likewise, Tex, likewise."

Hugh let the Chinese close within a hundred yards of his line without firing. The lead elements of the Chinese force were well into the crossfire of the Sixty-Second and One Sixty-Fourth. They obviously had not yet seen his positions. The Colonel's finger squeezed the trigger of the magnetically driven mini gun and thousands of rounds per minute spat at the enemy troops. The other three thousand plus Americans opened up on their CO's mark. Enemy soldiers caught death from three sides.

Once again bodies started piling in front of the Hugh's lines. This time the Chinese backed off more quickly than they had in the original attack. Or had they died more quickly. This time Hugh's forces had hit them from three sides instead of one. Their opponents had been used to armies crumbling before them and were not used to one's that stood their ground. The enemy troops went to slinking through the boulders that littered the battlefield. Soon the fighting in the front line was often hand to hand. The Colonel had run out of rounds for his mini gun. Hugh fought with a knife in one hand and a 9mm in the other. A Chinese soldier rushed Hugh; Hugh killed him with his pistol, and then shot another enemy soldier. A third enemy soldier leapt from a bolder, knocking Hugh to the ground, but the Colonel had caught the man on his knife, and he rolled the dead body from atop him. With a pause in the action, Smith called Webster's number. Just as the General was answering, a Chinese soldier came through the opening in the rocks. Hugh shot the man. The enemy soldier behind that man knocked the radio and pistol out of Hugh's hand, Hugh drove his knife up under the soldier's ribcage.

Another man tackled Smith, but he managed to get his knife in-between himself and the enemy soldier, the man's own momentum killed him. As Smith rolled the dead man off him, another enemy soldier leapt on Hugh, he positioned the knife just so again and the man's own leap impaled him on Hugh's knife. The American Colonel saw his pistol lying nearby he rolled to it and grabbed it as bullets began peppering the ground near him. While rolling, he noticed the enemy soldier was firing at him from atop a bolder. Hugh rolled to his knees and managed to fire and fell the man before the soldier could hit him. A few more shots and all the 9mm clips were empty. Hugh pulled his personal .357 from under his shirt that had been his duty when he was a cop. He probably killed as many Chinese with a knife as with a gun. He was nearing the end of his ammo for the .357 when he heard the whump whump whump of chopper blades. They were American. Two more Chinese came at Hugh and both were felled with the .357. Then he looked out to see what was next. There were no enemy in front of him. All of the Chinese he could see were retreating; the choppers were pounding them. Missile and guns dealt death from the air. He saw a missile streak from the enemy's area striking a chopper that exploded in midair and crashed in a flaming mass, but two more bore in to take its place. At least the enemy were forced back for a time.

The Colonel looked to his right to find the five closest men down. He looked to his left and three were down there. *'Though a thousand die on my left and ten thousand on my right'* Hugh thought as he looked to the right, he saw Captain Hardwick. "Captain!"
Percy came at a trot. Hugh noticed the Captain's right arm had a bullet hole in it. The superior officer bandaged the junior one.
"You want medevacked," Hugh asked.
"Wild horses couldn't drag me outta here, sir," Percy said.
"OK, Captain," Hugh smiled, "they might be back. Find out what we've got left."
Percy Hardwick trotted off to carry out his orders. Hugh looked the other way to see Tex treating a wounded soldier.
"Sergeant Saddler!"
Tex finished working on the Private and then reported to the Colonel. "Sir?"
"See what the bad guys are doing."
"Yes Sir," Tex looked around and spied one of his scouts, "Rich!'
The Private came at a trot. "Yes, Sergeant?"
"Going scouting!" The two men headed up the left rise to see what was up.

After a time, Percy came back.
"Report," Hugh asked.
"As near as I can tell, sir," the Captain was grim, "we've had over eleven hundred wounded who have been or will be medevacked, more than eight

hundred killed, and about thirteen hundred serviceable. Most of the serviceable guys are like me, sir, they're almost all wounded. Sir, we can't hold them again."

Percy looked down at Hugh's belly and pointed. There was a shallow knife slice from one side of the Colonel's belly to the other. The Colonel had known that an enemy soldier had swung a bayonet at him but thought it had missed. Hugh found a bandage and handed it to the Captain who wound it tightly around the wound.

"Captain, we held by God's grace last time," Hugh said. "If it is His will we can hold again."

It was at that precise moment that Hugh and Percy heard the rumble of armor. Tex had been gone for some time with no report. Worse yet, the armor was coming from the behind them. Hugh had been too busy to keep tabs on the other parts of the battle and had lost his radio. Smith knew they probably had nothing left that would deal with armor. Had the Chinese broken through somewhere else?

"What do you suppose that is, sir," Hardwick asked.

"Don't know," Hugh answered. "Place half the men in defensive positions facing south. Leave the others to deal with any threat from the north."

Percy did not even bother acknowledging the order verbally but was off at a run. He was little more than a hundred yards away when the lead element of the approaching unit crested the hill. He looked back and saw that it was a Hummer. The front bumper of the Hummer bore three stars. General Webster was on the way with reinforcements.

Hugh's radio buzzed on the ground a short distance away. The Colonel found it and answered. "Smith."

"Sir, its Tex."

"Tell me something good, Sarge."

"The Chinese are really retreating, sir. Their high tailing it down the valley clear to the other end," Tex said. "It's over."

Hugh's knees buckled. He fell heavily against a boulder and slid to the ground.

"Sir, you clear," Tex asked.

"I'm clear, Tex," Hugh felt the tears rolling down his cheeks. "Come home."

Hugh punched his radio off as he noticed someone was standing next to him. He looked up and saw Hardwick. The Captain had seen that the new arrivals were friendly. As the General's Hummer pulled up to them, Percy stepped in front of the Colonel.

"What happened here, Captain," Webster asked.

"Sir," Percy reported, "the Colonel placed a regiment on the left rise, a regiment on the right rise, and two regiments on the end of the valley in the rocks. The Chinese came down the valley and pushed us until the fighting became hand-to-hand. We held, sir."

Webster got out of his vehicle. "Where's Smith?"

Hardwick stepped from in front of the Colonel.

Webster squatted in front of Hugh.

"How many Chinese," the General asked.

"We were outnumbered thirty to one." Smith did not look at the General but blankly stared straight ahead.

"Hand to hand, huh?"

"For half an hour or so, yes sir."

"You won."

Hugh looked up at the General. "Don't know if we won. I lost well over half my men. I'll say we didn't lose. The choppers helped. They finished it."

Webster nodded and looked at the stacks of dead enemy soldiers. "Because you held here Colonel the entire Chinese Army has withdrawn to the south. We are going to pursue. Third Army is coming in from the east and should hit the enemy within the next five or six hours. As for you, Colonel, you and what's left of your men are to report to HQ. You'll be headquarters guard until further notice and until we can reconstitute the regiments and restaff them."

"Yes sir," Will saluted without rising from his seat.

"You did an unbelievable job here Colonel," Webster complimented, "I believe you saved the day against very steep odds."

"The men did, sir," Hugh said. "They did the dying. Besides, the battle belongs to the Lord."

The General nodded. "See you at headquarters. It'll be at least twenty-four hours before we move."

With that, the General was off to see to the remainder of the army.

Percy leaned against the boulder and slid down next to the Colonel. Hugh sat there for a long time just staring off into space, too tired to think. Finally, he got up.

"Captain, get the men moving. Have them load our dead on trucks. Make sure all the wounded get medevacked. Once that is done police up the area. Let's make sure we don't leave anything here for some kid to find and hurt himself with a year from now."

Percy was just slightly wobbly as he stood. "On it, sir."

Hugh punched a code into his radio. He needed engineers, trucks, choppers and so forth.

The sun was setting when the troops under Hugh's command marched into the area around the headquarters of General Webster. A Major was sent out to retrieve the Colonel.

"Lieutenant Colonel Smith reporting sir." Hugh did not know how much longer he could stand.

Webster looked up from his desk, "Stand easy, Colonel."

Hugh relaxed to parade rest, with all the adrenaline gone he was nearly out on his feet.

"Third Army has engaged the enemy south of here," Webster informed him. "They are continuing to push the Chinese. As for you, the Major is showing your men into an empty tent city east of here. You have assigned tents and are to use them. Get some rest. You and your men are standing down for the next twenty-four hours, clear?"

Hugh could barely raise his arm to salute, "Yes, sir."

A Lieutenant had slipped into the room without Smith's notice.

"Lieutenant, see this man to his tent," the General ordered.

"Yes sir," the Lieutenant acknowledged.

The Lieutenant led Hugh from the headquarters. When they exited, they found Tex next to the entrance waiting on his boss. "What's up, sir?"

"Twenty-four hours off, Tex." The Colonel was mumbling. "Everyone who is still in one piece is to rest and probably get ready for further action soon."

The Lieutenant got into a Hummer; Hugh got in the front passenger's seat with Tex and Percy in the back. A few minutes later they pulled up in front of a tent marked 'Lt. Col. Smith.' The Major acting as Quartermaster stood nearby.

Smith and Saddler exited, "Thank you Lieutenant."

The Lieutenant saluted then sped off.

"Where should I bunk, sir," Saddler asked.

"With me," Smith walked into the tent. Two sleeping bags were already rolled out on the floor. "I need my scout close by. Percy, find a tent on the other side of our men and get some shuteye."

Hugh sat down and removed his boots. Saddler stored their equipment at the side of the tent and then turned to speak with his commander. The boss was already out and as Saddler watched for a moment the Colonel started snoring. Tex lay down and was asleep in seconds.

When Webster found the time he made out the paperwork to nominate Hugh for the Congressional Medal of Honor. He was still having trouble believing Smith had held his ground against such odds.

7.

Tex awoke to a rapping on the wooden frame of the tent. He got up and opened the flap to find out who was there. The rapping had not awakened the Colonel. Opening the flap, he found the same Lieutenant that had dropped them off.

"What's up, L. T.?"

"Sergeant, need to see the Colonel."

"Still asleep."

"Probably time to get him up, the General wants him."

"I'm not inclined wake him, sir. We had a very long day yesterday. What time is it?"

"You've been in there for fifteen hours. I know you had a long day yesterday. We all did. Yesterday was two days long it's time to get on with other things," the Lieutenant said. "Now the General wants the Colonel."

"Lieutenant, I would guard the Colonel with my life. Have guarded the Colonel with my life. I have followed the Colonel into hell. If he needs to sleep longer then I'll let him sleep," Tex said. "When the man is up, I'll tell him to go see the General."

"Sergeant!" The Lieutenant was starting to get testy.

"It's OK Tex." Hugh showed up at the flap clapping Tex on the back. "Be there shortly, Lieutenant."

The Lieutenant saluted and left.

"Thanks buddy," Hugh said to Tex.

"Any time sir" Tex smiled.

Hugh was back in front of Webster sixteen hours after he left. "Lieutenant Colonel Smith reporting sir."

The General did not look up from his paperwork. "What you did at that pass was incredible Colonel. As of right now you have the field promotion to full bird. That would allow you a staff member. Who would you like?"

Hugh was surprised at this, but the decision had made itself. "Sergeant Saddler will do, sir."

"The rest of your men are going to remain here on headquarters guard for an indeterminate period, Colonel. You, on the other hand, have a different assignment."

Hugh was both saddened and surprised by that. After all they had been through together losing the Three-oh-First was hurtful. Well, losing what was left of the Three-oh-First. "What's that, sir?"

The General signed the documents he had been working on then looked up at Smith. "By count of the engineers there are more than 25,000 dead enemy soldiers up that valley you were defending. That's twelve dead for every one you lost or had wounded. The whole battle turned on your defense of that valley, Colonel. I recommended that you be decorated, and you are to report to the New White House in Lincoln, Nebraska for a ceremony four days from now with the President of the United States."

"Sir, I don't..." Hugh started.

"Don't want to hear it Colonel." Webster interrupted him with an upraised hand. He handed Hugh fresh orders. "Here are your orders. You are to report back here in thirty days. You may stop by your house and pick up your family. Shoot, take Tex' wife and kids too if he has any. Does he?"

Hugh was truly embarrassed. He had never asked, and Tex was very private about his personal life. "Don't know sir. Guess I'll find out."

"What's up sir?" Tex fell into step with Hugh as he left the CP.

"You and I have new orders."

"Leavin' the Three-oh-First, sir?"

"Temporarily anyway," Hugh confirmed. They climbed into a Hummer now assigned to Hugh, this one actually had brakes. "You got a family, Tex?"

"Yes sir," Saddler acknowledged.

"Well, you're going to go meet the President so we may want to stop by Illinois and pick them up."

Tex stopped the Hummer. "We're gonna meet Will Sevrin?"

"I've never mentioned it" Hugh said, "but I already know him."

"You know Will Sevrin?" Tex was incredulous.

"We're first cousins" Hugh said. "Known him all my life."

"I used to work in one of his plants before the war." Tex started back down the dirt road. "Always did want to meet him."

"Well, you're my staff now and I'll see to it that you do."

"Hot dog," Tex said.

"What about the family," Hugh asked.

"Wife and little boy," he confirmed. "I'd like them to see the new capitol, sir."

"Let's head for the transport center and get the arrangements made," Hugh said.

"I have good news tonight!" Will was doing one of his fireside chats. "First Army has met the Chinese on the field of battle and beaten them. No, our occupied territories are not yet liberated but we have defeated the supposedly invincible Chinese. As more armies come into the line, we will push the enemy back farther. As the banner of Almighty God goes on before us, we will go from victory unto victory. Now I ask everyone within the sound of my voice to give thanks to God and ask for His continued protection. Ask him for protection for our country, protection for our soldiers and protection for our lands."

With that Will signed off. Gordo was standing there.

"Do you really believe that" Kirk asked.

"With every fiber of my being," Will answered.

"Can this nation really withstand these times?"

"If we again become One Nation Under God, yes," Will nodded.

"I hope you are right."

"Don't hope, pray," Will advised him.

"I don't mean to be rude, Tex, but you'll have to stay at a motel tonight," Hugh said.

Tex guided the administrative car down the country road. "No problem. I understand, sir. You haven't seen the misses in a while."

They approached the end of the road that led to Hugh's rural home. "Stop here."

"You sure sir," Tex asked.

The Colonel pointed to the middle house of three that sat together in the remote area. "The middle one's mine. This is my wife's generational family farm. We built the house there in between her parents and grandparents home. The walk is only a little over a quarter mile. They might think the worst if an official car with two men in uniform pulls into the drive. I can sneak up on them on foot."

"My wife'd beat me if I did that." Tex smiled at the thought as he stopped the car.

"Just come get us about 0800," Hugh said.

The two men shook hands.

"See you then, sir."

Hugh exited the car and hoisted his duffel bag onto his shoulder. He watched the house as he approached. The girls were not in the yard. The van was in the drive and so he knew that they were more than likely home. Things looked odd without a black and white sitting in the drive. Hugh wondered why they still called patrol cars that when very few were black and white. He had decided to ring the doorbell so that they would know someone was there but did not want to wait at the door as they might again think someone had come with bad news. He knew that some people around Forrest County had already had a military chaplain on their stoop. He sat his duffel on the picnic table on the porch, then rang the bell, turned the handle, opened the door and stepped in.

As Hugh took his first steps past the door, Michelle appeared from deeper in the house. The seven-year-old paused for a second at the sight of a man in the house, and then her eyes flew wide open.

"Daddy," she screamed.

Michelle flew into his arms, and he practically squeezed her in half. Soon four-year-old Patti was squeezing his leg. He sat down Michelle so that he could squeeze Patti. When he had squeezed her with all his might, he opened his eyes to see Terri there, tears running down her cheeks. He sat down his littlest and took a step toward his wife. With a leap, she was in his arms, her legs wrapped around his waist, her lips on his. They clung desperately to one another for a long time.

    Tex relaxed on the motel bed. He barely remembered what a soft bed was like. He had picked up carryout from a drive through burger joint. The restaurant would not let him pay for his meal stating that it was on them. He reveled in the greasy decadence of the carryout burger. The television was a welcome distraction as he munched the fries. He steered clear of news shows and went for old sitcom reruns. He was away from the war and did not want to hear about it second hand.

    The four Smith's spent the evening on the couch talking and just holding on to one another. The girls held onto their dad until they were fast asleep. He picked up each girl in turn and carried her to her bed.
    When the girls were tucked in, he came back to the couch and Terri held her hand out to him. He took her hand and she led him to their room. When they had pleasured one another for a long time she knew she had to ask. She had seen the scar across his belly, but there was something deeper. She had recognized the emotional pain held just below the surface. She knew her man.
    "You're hurting, aren't you," she asked.
    He looked at the ceiling for a long moment before he spoke. He thought of trying to say that his body did not hurt anymore and see if he could bypass the subject that way, but he knew what she meant. "Bodies stacked up like cord wood. Their buddies died and they stepped over them or on them and just kept coming, mindless suicide. The Chinese use their people worse than we'd use dogs. And my men! So many killed and maimed!" He started to lose control. "So many widows, orphans, and broken bodies all because someone wanted more power."
    The first sob was deep. The second was deeper. He cried for nearly an hour as she held him as tightly as she could. Finally, he cried himself to sleep. She still did not let go. She did not know if she would ever get to hold him again.

    "Terri, girls, this is Tex." Hugh introduced them as he walked to the car carrying their bags the next morning.
    "Good to meet you Tex," Terri smiled, "I've heard a lot about you in the last few hours."
    "Don't believe everything the Colonel says, ma'am." Tex took the bags and stored them in the trunk. "He tends to exaggerate when he brags on his men."

"Lincoln," Terri said, "I've wanted to see it. I saw Washington before it was destroyed. I wonder if the new monuments are really as good as the ones that were blown up?"

"Same Indiana limestone they used the first time from what I hear, Ma'am," Tex offered.

"You don't have to call me ma'am, Tex," she laughed, "I don't outrank you."

"Guess you do ma'am."

"How do you figure that," Terri asked.

"The Colonel says you're his better half, ma'am. That means you rank him." Tex grinned. "So, if I salute him, guess I should be salutin' you."

Hugh and Terri looked at each other. Hugh shrugged. Tex saluted as he held the car door open for Terri.

Fifty-one soldiers, most on crutches or in wheelchairs, lined the stage on the new Pennsylvania Avenue. Hugh stood at one end. The President of the United States started at the other end pinning decorations on each soldier. Most got purple hearts, some bronze stars and some silver stars. Will Sevrin read a short citation before each medal was awarded. The President did not rush, taking his time with each award, speaking with each man.

The Colonel's mind began to wonder as the ceremony dragged on. His entourage had just arrived in Lincoln a few hours before the ceremony meeting Tex' wife and son at the military family transportation center, they would tour the new capitol after the ceremony. Most of the monuments were within walking distance of one another. They had almost a month before they had to get back to the war and intended to spend at least a week touring the capitol on the military's dime.

Hugh wondered why he was given a chauffeured limousine while most of the other guys were bused from one spot to another. Was it because he was the first cousin of the President?

Finally, Will Sevrin stood in front of Hugh.

"Last, but not least," the President was saying, "we now honor the highest-ranking soldier that will be decorated today. Lieutenant Colonel Hugh Wallace Smith, first, let me pin on your Purple Heart. The citation is much longer than I have time to read to all of you, but I'll read it in part. 'Though facing odds that exceeded thirty to one Lieutenant Colonel Smith rallied troops under his command and other nearby troops whose commanding officers had been killed or wounded to defend the flank of First Army. With little more than three thousand troops Lieutenant Colonel Smith held off a force of more than one hundred thousand enemy troops, thereby keeping this massive enemy force from getting behind the American lines. If Lieutenant Colonel Smith had failed at his task, the battle would probably have been lost. Because of his heroic actions the battle was won. Signed

Lieutenant General Arlen Webster Commanding First Army.

"The General wrote the citation. The Congress of the United States took the following actions. First, Lieutenant Colonel Smith is a Lieutenant Colonel only by battlefield brevet commission. His actual rank by army regulation is Captain, until now. By act of Congress Hugh Smith is promoted to full Colonel. Also, due to his heroic actions that saved first army at great peril to his own life Hugh Wallace Smith is the first soldier of World War Three to be awarded the Congressional Medal of Honor."

Hugh's eyes grew wide. No one had told him that he was being awarded the CMH. That was why he was riding in a chauffeured limo. The crowd cheered as the President draped the medal around his neck. He found Terri in the family section and saw tears running down her cheeks. The girls were too young to yet understand the import of what had just happened to their father.

"I ask that the first Medal of Honor winner from the Third World War would grace us with a few words." The President stepped aside and waived Hugh to the microphone.

With faltering steps Hugh made his way to the podium, stopped for a moment to think, then stepped to the microphone. "No one told me that I would be speaking today, but I need not have prepared any statement. My whole life has been preparation for this moment. Sunday school, Sunday sermons, and Bible study have all told me what I must say here. Whether with few or with many the battle belongs to the Lord. It was not humanly possible for my three thousand men to withstand the onslaught of a hundred thousand battle hardened enemy troops. Not only were we victorious, but the victory was also decisive. I am reminded of the Israelites taking the Promised Land and fighting the Amalekites. The Amalekites were said to be seven to nine feet tall and living in cities that had walls more than twenty feet tall and more than twenty feet thick. By human endeavor alone, victory is not possible in such situations, yet the Israelites defeated the Amalekites. By our effort alone, especially by my effort, victory was not possible that day at that mountain pass, but the battle belongs to the Lord and so, in His name, I accept this award." With that Hugh snapped a textbook about face then with military precision retook his place in line.

For a moment there was silence then the crowd leapt to its feet in thunderous applause.

When the applause had subsided, the President stepped back and snapped his hand to his head. All the men on the stage snapped their hands to their heads.

"I salute each and every one of you." Sevrin held his hand to his forehead. "As long as we have men like you, we will live free."

Will snapped down the salute. The soldiers followed suit. The President turned to Smith. "You may dismiss the troops, Colonel."

The President stood to the side.

Hugh strode out to the front of the stage then turned, military parade fashion, to face the other men. "Atten-hut!"

The men came to attention as best they could. Many of the injured were unable to do it properly. "Dismissed!"

The men broke formation.

"Colonel?" The President spoke.

Hugh turned and came to attention.

"At ease Colonel," Will said, "may I shake your hand?"

Hugh offered it. "Yes, sir. Thank you, sir."

"Your service to your country has been gallant and brave."

"Sir, I accepted this medal for my men," Hugh said. "Most of them didn't make it."

"Weighs heavily on you, doesn't it." Will did not let go of the Colonel's hand.

"Command's not fun when people die," Hugh agreed.

Hugh had forgotten that he was talking to the Commander-in-Chief. "When you give orders, men from one regiment go into harm's way. When I give orders, entire armies go into harm's way."

The two men shared a moment with a look. Hugh nodded his agreement. "Mr. President could you come say hi to the wife and kids."

"I'd love to."

The two men started toward the gallery as Secret Service swarmed them.

"You don't have to call me Mr. President all the time" Will offered. "We are cousins. We've known each other since you were born."

"As long as I wear this uniform and you hold the office, I will address you formally."

The two men strode down to the VIP box together. Tex's wife thought she was going to pass out as Will Sevrin approached her. She raised the phone taking several shots as Will shook the hands of the girls, Terri and Tex. He took the time to hold Michelle, Patti, and Roy Saddler long enough for their parents to get a picture. He posed for pictures with the Smith's and Saddler's. Then, just before he left, he turned to Tex.

"Your name is really Randolph Scott Saddler?"

"Yes, sir." Tex was embarrassed. He wondered how the President of the United States could know such a thing.

"You go by Tex, but you're from Illinois?" The President questioned further.

"Yes, sir." Tex was mystified.

The President started to stride away. "You meet such interesting people in this job."

"Shall we go," Hugh asked.

The others agreed as they were ready to see the sights of the new capitol.

Hugh did not expect the swarm of reporters that covered the ceremony to descend on him. They had soon crowded him away from his family and Tex. America was hungry for a hero.

"Colonel, as the first American hero of World War Three do you have anything to say to the American people?"

"I'm nobody special, just a man defending his home. The American people should remember that the real heroes are the ones that made the ultimate sacrifice." Hugh's lip quivered. "I accepted this award on their behalf. I accept this medal for all those whose heroics were just as deserving as mine but went unrecognized. I represented those who can no longer represent themselves."

"Are the Chinese beatable?"

"Yes, we proved that at what they are now calling the Battle of the Passes."

"Do you think the President is right? Does the country have to turn back to God to win this war?"

"Yes, I agree."

"The President also says we have to cleanse our land in blood. Do you agree with that?"

"It appears that is what's happening."

"Colonel, are you a right-wing Christian fanatic?"

Hugh looked to see that the question had come from Rock James.

"I am definitely a Christian. Conservative would be a good description of my political leanings. I wouldn't call myself a fanatic."

Rock James decided that there was nothing here worth covering, just more right-wing political hype from the administration. He walked away as the other reporters continued to question Hugh. The press conference continued for more than a half-hour.

Will was on his way back to the White House when he was handed a phone by the aid.

"This is the President."

"Mr. President, Frank."

"What's up, buddy?" Sevrin had really come to value time with old friends. A President did not get much time for that.

"Sir, the IP Shuttle fighter is ready."

Will knew that this could have a huge impact on the war if it worked right. "When and how will you test it?"

"There's only one way to test it," Frank said. "In combat is the only way we can see if it will function like it is supposed to."

"When?"

"If the Commander-in-Chief approves it, we'll do it today."

Will weighed pros and cons for a minute then said a short prayer. "Send it up."

Hugh Smith stood before the many times' life size Abe Lincoln. The rebuilding of this monument had been done first class. Hugh had never been to the old one, but from the pictures he had seen he could not tell the difference in the two. Lincoln was a man who stood in the gap when the country was at stake. Hugh felt the late President reach across more than a century and three-quarters to give him a manly squeeze on the shoulder.

Terri walked up beside her husband. "Talkin' to Abe?"

"We've discussed a thing or two."

"Guess I can't have you all to myself anymore," she said dreamily, "a Medal of Honor winner belongs to the people."

He pulled her close. "There are definitely parts of me that will always be yours and only yours."

She snuggled into his shoulder with a giggle then a contented sigh.

Lieutenant Shing rolled hard right as an American missile shot by just inches from scoring a hit on his jet. He tried to roll around and lock onto the American, but then another American was on him, and he had to loop.

Shing had been in the first wave Fighter Pilots that landed in Argentina. That had been easy, actually fun, almost like a video game. What was the American saying, 'Shooting fish in a barrel?' The South American pilots were seldom a challenge.

The Americans were a life and death struggle every time you flew against them. Tracers shot over his cockpit, and he rolled left to get away from that threat. The Chinese had less than a hundred planes left in theatre and fewer came back every day. They were outnumbered now.

Shing rolled, climbed almost vertically then rolled to get back toward the dogfight. He was shocked to see the Americans fleeing. He and some other pilots kicked in the afterburners to pursue the Americans.

"Stand down, gentlemen!" The Major who commanded the air wing called out to his charges. "We need gas. Everyone return to base."

Shing backed off the throttle and looked at his fuel gage. As usual, the Major was right. If he had chased the American, he never would have made it back. Shing settled in off the Major's wing. He liked his commander. The Major looked over at Shing and gave the junior officer the thumbs up. Shing returned the gesture.

The young Lieutenant almost did not notice it. A small portion of the Major's wing turned blue for a moment, then the wing exploded in flame and the Major was gone.

Shing did not have time to sound the alarm or even reason out what had just happened. The laser cut a hole through Shing's cockpit and then his chest and the

Lieutenant was dead. His plane plummeted to the ground as others followed. Of the twenty-three planes in Shing's flight that night, none came home.

Marlon called from the back of the IP Shuttle that had been converted to atmospheric combat. "No more threats on the board, sir."

"Roger." Andy Herdsman answered. He had been the Chief Astronaut and Test Pilot of the Magnetic Engine Corporation. Now he was doing test flights in combat. He switched frequencies. "IPF-1 to base."

"IPF1 go." Herdsman recognized Frank Thomas' voice. He wondered when the last time was that the man had been home.

"IPF1 advising forty-one targets engaged. Forty-one destroyed," Andy said. "No more threats on the board."

"Bring it in," Frank ordered. Looking at the clock he realized that the IP Fighter had only engaged two minutes before. That was one enemy plane shot down every three seconds. Imagine if they could bring more IP's online. The air war was over.

"Returning to base," Andy acknowledged. If intelligence that he had seen was correct his ship had just eliminated almost half of the enemy strength during a thirty-minute mission. Things were definitely turning.

"She worked flawlessly, Mr. President." Will could tell Frank was smiling over the phone. "Shot at forty-one, splashed forty-one."

"I'd call that air supremacy," Will offered.

"Yes, sir," Frank agreed. "We should be able to bring a couple more to bear before the month ends."

"We'll keep her up as much as possible. They can't have any more than seventy planes left in theatre. If they fly 'em we'll splash 'em."

"And they can't bring down what they can't see or track."

The IP had been flying at over 100,000 feet when it had engaged the enemy. She was too far away to see, and her stealth technology made her impossible to track.

"Forty-five planes," Chen asked. "None came back?"

"None, sir."

The Chief of Air Operations for the Americas was stunned. "And you say that most went down at roughly the same time?"

"Sir, we sent up forty-five planes. The Americans had shot four down, but then disengaged. Moments after the Americans turned for home the first of our planes went down. Eighty-three seconds later forty-one planes were down."

"But none from combat?" Chen could not make sense of it.

"No, sir." The junior officer was mystified. "There were no enemy aircraft in the area."

Chen picked up the phone and called General Chan, the Supreme Commander of the invasion.

"You have no explanation for this," Chan asked.

"None," explained Chen.

"We cannot win this war without air cover," Chan said. "Keep sending them up. Maybe this was some kind of freak weather phenomenon that the Americans know about and can detect."

"Weather," Chen was mocking, "the sky was clear."

"Your orders are to send the planes up," Chan answered, "this conversation is over."

"We've got a friendly flight up," Marlon Lacoste advised Herdsman.

"They squawkin' right?" Herdsman asked as their craft steadied at 100,000 feet. With the latest stealth technology, they appeared on no radarscopes.

"Right on freq," Marlon acknowledged.

"Whoa," Herdsman was watching his scope, "looks like the neighborhood bullies want to come out and play."

They had sent up fighters to draw out the enemy planes. It had worked.

"Got it," Marlon's radar showed fifteen Chinese jets go air born on an intercept course for the Americans, "heating up?"

There was a moment of silence on the radio as the equipment came online.

"Firing...now," Lacoste said as multiple lasers shot forth from the belly of the IP. "One, two, five, seven, nine, ten, thirteen, fifteen targets destroyed."

"Think we'll orbit for a while and see if anyone else wants to come up and play," Herdsman said.

The helmsman set the course.

"Fifteen more," Chan asked.

"Yes," Chen answered, "they had barely even left the ground. We've recovered some of the wreckage. There are strange burn holes in the fuselages."

Chan knew that this was an ominous development. Was this some new American wonder weapon? "Order all aircraft grounded until further notice."

"Yes sir." Chen was relieved. He only had thirty-five planes left in theatre. If he sent them all up at one time, he could be without a command in two minutes at the rate he was losing planes. "Does intelligence say anything about the Americans having new stealth craft?"

"We've nothing from our spies," Chan said. "If they have something new, we'll have to analyze it when they surrender."

Chan was still talking as if his armies were unbeatable. They had reached to southern Colorado but were now being pushed back into northern New Mexico. Supplies were running short and now they could not fly without losing the planes. For the first time Chen considered that they could lose North America.

An aide came to Webster and handed him the more complicated 'cell phone'. This was not the cell phone type radio, but the encrypted telephone that only the high command might use.

"The President." An aide informed him with raised eyebrows.

Webster took the phone and raised his eyebrows in return. "Yes, sir, Mr. President how's the Commander-in-Chief today?"

"Good Arlan" Will sounded cheery, "getting some good news from the front for a change."

"Yes, sir," the General agreed, "things are turning."

"What I called about, General, is Hugh Smith." The President got to business.

"One of our top officers," Webster said.

"That's the point," Will was apologetic; "he's the first real hero of this war. We have to have him around for a while. If he would go right back to the war and get killed that would be a morale disaster for the folks back home. He's been all over the news. We need him to stay alive at least until other heroes are in the news."

"What are you suggesting, Mr. President?"

"Give him an assignment that's likely to keep him alive." Will did not like doing this, but knew it needed to be done. "At least for a few months."

"I don't like pulling one of my best commanders out of the field, sir." Webster was bristling.

"I know, General, I don't either," Will paced as he talked, "but we need to do that for now."

"Is that an order, sir?"

"Yes, it is."

"I'll get it done, Mr. President."

"Thank you, General." Will hung up.

The General handed the phone back to the Captain. "They want me to win this war and then they take my best people out of the line. Ahh, well, ours is not to reason why."

"Do you suppose he's just trying to keep his cousin alive?" The aide spoke what the General was wondering.

The General gave the junior officer a nasty look. "I don't know Will Sevrin personally, but I do know that kind of man. He would not do that. He just wants America to have a hero for a while."

8.

Hugh had expected a combat command after the Battle of the Passes. He was surprised when he got his orders. He was to report to Pagosa Springs, Colorado and supervise the building of a supply depot there. The former cop had expected to be right back on the front line, possibly with greater responsibilities then when he left. This appeared to be the beginning of another pleasant time in his war experience. His cousin lived in Pagosa Springs and he had not seen her in some time. He also enjoyed the company of her husband, who had not been drafted into the service due to his age and job at home.

The new commanding officer of the Pagosa Springs base arrived with little fanfare. A small cargo plane landed at a nearby public airstrip carrying Hugh and Tex. Percy Hardwick who was also now on Hugh's personal staff met the plane. Percy had been named the Deputy Commander, Pagosa Springs, at Hugh's recommendation and was sporting a Major's oak leaves as a result of his new responsibilities. Tex had also grown a fourth stripe on his shoulder.
"Welcome to your new command sir," Percy saluted.
"Thank you Major." Hugh got into the front seat of the Hummer as Tex stowed their gear in the rear and jumped in himself. "How's the base construction coming?"
"Sir, we've leveled the top of the mountain and are beginning to build the structures but it's mostly still just big tents right now." Major Hardwick had been busy.
The fifty-minute drive through the Rocky Mountains of southern Colorado to get to the base was scenic to say the least. Hugh and Tex enjoyed it in silence. Finally, they started the climb up to the top of the small mountain that would be topped off by the new base. Hugh took in a lot of things as they approached. When they topped the mountain and came to the gate, he saw the men lined up. The survivors of the old Three-oh-First with about 4,500 others now under Smith's command lined either side of the drive. They cheered and waved; Hugh had Percy stop the Hummer.
The Colonel stood in the Hummer to address the men. "Men, it's a pleasure to be your commander. I hope I can be worthy of such a fine bunch of soldiers. I will get to know you in the days to come. Some of you I already know. We will be efficient in moving these supplies along to our men in the field. I accept no excuses for things not getting there on time. Be about the business of this base."
Smith retook his seat and told Percy to go to the east side of the base. This was a sheer drop. They then went to the north and west sides to find the same.
"So, the only approach to this base is from the south," Hugh approved.
Percy had chosen the spot.

"Or by air, sir," the Major agreed, "but we seem to have won the air battle over the States at least."

"Drive me back to the approach," Hugh ordered.

The three men studied that for some time.

"Major," Smith spoke.

"Yes sir?"

Hugh was looking at the terraced land on the south side of the base. This was a very tough way to approach, but it was a way to approach the base. They already had enough instruments of war on hand to supply an army and more would be coming and going each day.

"I want five defensive lines built up and down this side." Hugh was taking no chances. "Put the first near the bottom of the mountain but give us the advantage of being above the valley floor. There should be trails from the first to the second so that falling back is easy, same with the third, fourth and fifth. The fifth should be slightly below the top of the mountain. Understand?"

"Yes sir."

"Next, do we have any explosives guys?"

"Yes sir."

"Set mines, lots of mines leading up to the base of the mountain," Hugh continued. "Make sure the minefields are clearly marked for civilians, but I want to be able to quickly disguise those markings if the enemy should venture this way."

"Understood sir."

"Also, commandeer and set up some artillery for the top of the mountain." Hugh continued to build the defense. "We don't need the really good stuff, but the stuff that'll shoot a few miles will do."

"Yes, sir," Percy said, "I'll get on it right away."

Two days after his arrival Hugh was bored. The men were taking care of the labor and all his paperwork was done.

"Sergeant Saddler!"

Tex was quickly in front of his desk. "Sir?"

"Time to learn your way around town, Sergeant," Hugh said.

"Yes sir." Tex caught his meaning and started toward the Hummer. "Where to, sir?"

"One-thirty-four Mountain View Drive."

The Sergeant wondered what was there that interested the Colonel. Tex could think of other ways to spend a Saturday afternoon. It took him half an hour being directed by GPS to find the address. One-thirty-four Mountain View was a nice home in a nice neighborhood. Those who bought here were not filthy rich but were by no means wondering where their next meal was coming from. The house was neatly kept. Tex wheeled the vehicle into the drive.

Hugh exited and started toward the front door. "Wait here, Tex."

The Sergeant watched the Colonel ring the bell. After a moments wait the front door flew open and an attractive woman answered the door. He heard her say, "May I help...Hugh!"

The woman threw her arms around the Colonel who returned the hug. Hugh and the woman hugged each other tightly for some time. Tex decided not to watch, knowing the Colonel was married.

"Daryl! Daryl, look who's here!" The woman was shouting back into the house.

Tex looked back around. A man now came to the door and gave Hugh an enthusiastic handshake. Tex let out a sign and decided he could watch again.

"Well, don't just stand here on the porch, Colonel, come in," Daryl was saying.

"Is it OK if my Sergeant comes in," Hugh asked.

"Of course," said the woman.

"Tex!" Hugh shouted and waved him in.

When Tex got there, he found the front door open for him and stepped into the living room, closing the door behind him. Everyone was smiling.

"Tex." The Colonel waved him over to the other three. "This is my first cousin Pam Andrews and her husband Daryl."

Tex noticed that the woman was starting to gray noticeably and was probably several years older than his boss.

The woman put her arm around Hugh and squeezed him again. "Yes, Sergeant, this is my little cousin."

Tex noted that the Colonel was about twice the size of Pam. "Little?"

"He's the next to youngest first cousin" she said, and then admitted, "I'm the oldest."

"Now I get it, ma'am." Tex did not think they looked a lot alike. "You have some interesting cousins."

"Have the met the President" Daryl asked.

"Yes, sir" Tex answered. "I got to go to the Colonel's CMH ceremony."

"I guess it runs in the family" Daryl smiled.

"Can you guys stay for dinner," Pam asked.

"Don't know why not," Hugh answered. "We've got our radios if the base needs me."

"Daryl, entertain." Pam headed for the kitchen. "I'm going to make a meal fit for a winner of the Congressional Medal of Honor."

Hugh frowned at Daryl. Daryl shrugged a 'what can I do' shrug.

"Come on, I'll show you my shop," Daryl said.

Over the next hour, Daryl showed them the wood shop that he made some money off of. He was a retired anesthesiologist who was working again in the local hospital due to so many doctors being off to war. They had been frugal and had retired in their early fifties. The couple had kept busy enough before the war with travel and selling the pieces that he turned out in the basement of the house. Pam, a nurse, was also back to work because of the war.

While they were in the shop Tex was drawn to a display case. There was an impressive display of military medals in the case. At the top of the case was the name plate Lt. D. Andrews. While there was not a CMH in the case there was most everything else.

"You were in the service Mr. Andrews" Tex asked.

"Did six years in the Marine Corp" Daryl said.

"Looks like heroics run in the family" Tex mused.

"Ready, guys." Pam shouted down the stairs just then.

As they ascended the stairs, the smells were wonderful. All three men's stomachs were growling before they even made it to the kitchen.

There was Sirloin steak, mashed potatoes, salad, corn, green beans, and so forth. Everyone ate until they were stuffed.

"Did you enjoy it, Tex," Pam asked.

"Ma'am I don't know when I've eaten like that," Tex confirmed. "Sure beats MRE's any day."

Hugh rose from the table. "Thank you so much, Pam. We'd better be getting back, Tex."

"If you insist, sir," Tex smiled.

Hugh stopped at the door; Tex was already at the Hummer.

"Thanks, cuz."

She hugged him again as a tear glistened in the corner of her eye. "Take care of yourself little cousin."

"It appears they have stored me out of harm's way for now," Hugh frowned.

The men shook hands and then Hugh was gone.

"Sir, we've got to find a way to make an end run," Webster said. "For the last month it's been back and forth. We push them into old Mexico; they push us back into New Mexico. There's got to be some way to break this deadlock."

General Douglas walked over to look out the window of what had become First Armies HQ. Webster had chosen the third floor of an eight-story building,

"I wish we had a way to do that. There are just too many Chinese in Mexico for us to blow through them."

"Sir, we're trading the Chinese about three soldiers for one now." Webster walked to the Army Chief of Staff's shoulder. "We've gotta do better than ten to one to win this thing."

"Even if we did have an idea," Douglas turned to look at Webster, "have you seen the weather report?"

Webster nodded. "Low clouds for several days, heavy snow in the mountains."

"No air support," Douglas agreed. "We'll work on it."

Douglas left. Webster was getting desperate. He knew that they had won this stage of the war, but that they could still lose right here on their own soil. Something had to give.

At the same time that the Commanding General of America's First Army spoke to his superior, General Lian was speaking to General Chan.

"Our supply lines are too extended. Without air support or being able to resupply from the sea our supply lines are just too long. We cannot sustain an action in North America."

"But we are so close, Lian," Chan said. "If we can just wear the Americans out. Attrition will soon take its toll. The Canadians have not even declared war on us yet. If we can make the Americans sue for peace, we have conquered the entire world!"

"Not the whole world," Lian countered. "We have never conquered the Israelis and were unable to maintain our foothold on England. We've yet to invade Australia and it is very slow going in Russia."

"If the Americans fall, do you really think any of them can hold against our massed forces," Chan asked. "The English will soon run out of resources. Britain is an island; they cannot stand alone."

"There is one possible way to sustain our action here for another few months," Lian offered, "If we can take the American supply depot at Pagosa Springs in Colorado we can use the Americans own supplies to prosecute the war against them. But we must take it intact."

"That is an excellent idea." Chan liked the idea.

"If we fail, we must withdraw from the United States and retreat back into southern Mexico," Lian said. "We will not be able to hold Mexico for long and the battle for North America will then be lost."

"I am willing to take the gamble," Chan said.

"Sir, we've got a problem!"

Colonel Gray Penobscot, head of First Army Intelligence, spoke the words.

"What's up, Gray," General Webster asked.

"My scouts are telling me that a huge chunk of enemy forces have broken off from the main body." The Colonel started drawing the movements on a map. "They're heading north, sir."

"Where?" Webster was on his feet heading toward Penobscot.

The General saw that his Intelligence officer had drawn the battle lines of both armies. Arlan had not realized until then that the armies had shifted so much. Second Army, who was north of his position, had been pushed to the east. The way north was open. "Are they trying to flank again?"

"I don't think so, sir," Gray said. "Intelligence says they are running low on supplies. They can't sustain an action much longer unless they can free up supply routes."

"Fat chance of that any time soon, they can't fly because of the new MEC shuttle fighter and our fly boys keep pounding their supplies." The General was contemplating their desination. "Where are they going then?"

Penobscot had drawn a short line where the enemy force was leaving the line in northern New Mexico. He then drew a longer line; Webster's eyes grew wide.

"Sir, they need supplies to keep going. If you can't bring your own here, you go take them from someone else." The Colonel spoke the enemies plan.

"Can we turn the army to block them," Webster asked.

"Sir," Penobscot answered, "we're engaged in that area with a heavy force. There's no one who could get there in time."

Webster turned to an aide. "Get me Colonel Smith at Pagosa Springs, pronto!"

Tex was running, slipping and sliding through the ankle-deep snow as he tried to make corners. "Colonel, Colonel Smith, anybody seen the Colonel?"

Men were pointing the way. Soon Hugh stepped from a newly completed building at hearing the Sergeant calling his name. He could not see his aide through the huge flakes that were falling for a moment, and then Tex came into view. "What's so urgent, Sergeant?"

Tex stopped and saluted then handed Hugh the cell phone radio. "General Webster, sir, says we've got trouble commin'."

Smith took the phone. "Colonel Smith."

"Hugh, this is Webster." The General was gruff.

"Yes, sir?" Hugh did not like his tone.

"Hugh, about a quarter million Chinese have broken off from the main force. Due to the way that the battle lines have developed they are able to head north. I'm afraid they're coming right at you, son."

"Are you going to pursue?" The Colonel had suddenly turned ashen and the men around him knew it was bad.

"We can't," Webster broke the news, "we're fully engaged right now. We've no one to send after them."

"Air support?"

"Afraid not, Colonel," Webster answered, "have you checked your weather report lately?"

"I know it's snowin' pretty heavy, sir." Given his job he had no need to check the weather. He had a corporal keeping track of it and he was supposed to tell the colonel if any major storms were headed their way.

"Low clouds for the next four days, heavy snow for the next two. That eliminates the fast movers in the mountains. The snow has already started. That eliminates choppers for the next two days."

"Where are they heading, sir?"

"The theory is that they're getting low on supplies," Webster broke the news. "We think they'll try to take your supply dump because they need the supplies to maintain their war effort."

"I see, sir."

"So, here are your orders, Colonel." Webster paused to gather his thoughts. He could not believe that he had to say this to Smith again. "You have forty-eight to seventy-two hours to prepare. The Chinese are not to, under any circumstances, take that base intact. Under no circumstances are those supplies to fall into enemy hands. With the snow coming, we can't move the stuff out. Not to mention I don't think we could get enough people and trucks there before the enemy gets there. So, if you have to, blow it in place and you may not retreat unless there is nothing left for the bad guys to get."

"Yes sir."

"Do you understand me, Colonel," the General's volume rose to make a point, "the Chinese are not to take one bullet. Destroy everything if that's what it takes."

"I understand, sir."

"Colonel, if we destroy those supplies, we can replace them in short order. If we deny them to the Chinese, they will run out of supplies and have to retreat deep into Mexico to shore up their supply lines and we can pound them the whole way. If they can take your base intact, they can sustain their war efforts for months. We can't let them do that. Understood?"

"Understood General."

"Webster out."

"Why," Pam asked.

"I don't know why," Daryl answered, "he couldn't tell me. All I know is he says we need to get out and get out now."

Pam put her suitcase in the back of the SUV. "What about the neighbors, our friends?"

"If everyone bugs out then people will know something's up," Daryl said. "They'll know someone said something."

"What way?"

"He says go north to I-70 and then go wherever," Daryl answered.

"That means the danger's coming from the south." Pam had a realization. "The Chinese are to the south. They must be moving this way."

Daryl locked the front door. "We've gotta go."

Pam was about to get in their SUV when she heard Daryl shut the front door. Pam turned around and looked at the house wondering if it would be there when they returned. As her husband started down the sidewalk she turned around and got in. Tears started to well up in her eyes.

Hugh had gathered his staff and command personnel. After he had briefed them, he asked for suggestions.

"We've set out two thousand mines, but we've got twenty thousand more," Hardwick offered. "Those will make a rather large boom."

"I don't like the thought of runnin'," Tex interjected.

"I guess that is the basic choice," Hugh observed.

"What choice, sir," Angelo Lopez asked. The man that had graduated first academically in OTS with Hugh was now a Captain under Hugh's command.

"There are two ways to blow this stuff up." The Colonel smiled. "We can just blow it up and hope to take a few Chinese with it or we can blow it up shooting it at the Chinese."

Everyone smiled as they saw where the Colonel was going.

"What are you thinking, sir," Major Hardwick asked.

"What do we have on stock," Hugh knew that Percy was more current than he.

"Any type of rifle or handgun with any kind of ammo and pretty much as much as you want, stacks of grenades. Truckloads of mortars and some artillery. Just about everything you want."

"How far does the artillery shoot?" Hugh could see a plan coming together.

"The biggest stuff on hand will shoot about twenty-five miles accurately," Lopez answered. He had been through artillery school.

"What about the new GPS'," Tex asked.

Hugh did not know about the GPS model. "What about them?"

"These new GPS' sir," Tex explained. "We could program 'em right then place 'em in the path of the bad guys. When the bad guy's pass where the GPS is, you can turn it on from miles away by remote as long as you're in line of sight. So, the GPS sends a signal to a satellite, the satellite sends a signal to a control board here at the base and we fire arty around that coordinate. We can start poundin' 'em twenty miles out."

Hugh considered this for a moment.

"OK, we blow it up shooting it at them." Hugh said to the affirming cheer of everyone gathered. "Tex, get your scouts out there. Find the Chinese Army and set those GPSs in their path. We should be able to eliminate a large number of them with arty before they get here. Angelo set up the arty. Get it ready. I want it firing without cease until we get overrun. Percy, if we have twenty thousand mines, we need to set twenty thousand mines in their path. But we've also got to have a contingency. Have your explosives guys set the mines but save back enough explosives to blow the top off this mountain. I want the whole place wired to blow if one Chinese soldier gets through."

"How will it be triggered," Hardwick asked.

"Someone will have to sit in a bunker in the middle of the camp with a trigger of some sort and will have to blow it the first time he sees an enemy soldier."

Percy swallowed. "Who gets that assignment?"

Hugh called on the one person he was sure would set the blast off if it needed to be. "You do."

The Major's eyes closed in resignation.

"How many mini-guns do we have?" Hugh changed the subject.

"About thirty," Percy answered.

"Heavy machineguns?"

"A couple hundred."

"Split those evenly among all the fox holes in the defensive lines." Hugh paced. "Make sure there's plenty of ammo in every hole. I also want mortars starting in the second line. When the first line starts shooting the second, third, fourth and fifth can start shelling."

"I'll see to that," a Lieutenant volunteered.

"Everyone know their tasks," he asked.

"Yes, sir," they chorused.

"Go!" Hugh sent them on their desperate mission.

9.

Tex had taken a Hummer southwest from Pagosa Springs and then turned due south. He had sent another squad of scouts to the southeast. Every so often, he would stop and drop off one of his men. Each man made his way into the wilderness to scout the best targeting areas. Each knew that this was as desperate an hour as any of them would know. They had to do everything right. Not only did their own lives depend on it but so did their buddies. Maybe even their countries very existence.

Tex drove the Hummer as far as he would dare and then he drove it into a snowbank. He shoveled snow over it and marked a tree nearby so he could find it. The snow was falling at a brisk pace and was now knee deep in many places as Tex wound his way out among the trees and rocks. He could smell the enemy. He would make contact soon.

"Colonel?" A Sergeant approached escorting a civilian. Hugh thought he knew the man.

"Yes, Sergeant?" The Colonel had been helping with the preparations. He paused now to see what was happening.

"Sir, this is Jim Arvin" the Sergeant reported.

Hugh knew the name. "The newspaper guy that broke the NASA scandal."

"Yes sir" Arvin confirmed.

"What can I do for you," Hugh asked.

"I have a letter here from President Sevrin." Jim handed the letter to Hugh. "It gives me access to any military unit. I won't give away your secrets. I want to follow the first CMH winner of WW Three."

"I think you picked a bad time, Mr. Arvin."

"Please call me Jim." Arvin said as he looked around at the frantic activity. "What's going on here?"

"First, I don't know how you found your way in all this snow. I can't even see two buildings away. Second, there are about a quarter million Chinese heading this way," Hugh said. "If we're going to defend this place we might be trapped here on top of this mountain. There is only one way out of here. If that is closed off by Chinese, then we're trapped. We have no intention of running, Mr. Arvin."

"What would you do then," Arvin asked.

"If we're going to be overrun, we blow the place up."

Arvin turned rather pale. "Sounds like fun. Mind if I hang around?"

"It's your skin, Mr. Arvin," Hugh said.

Jim thought that if these guys won't run I won't either. If they all die, I'll die with them.

Almost sixty hours had passed since Tex and his bunch had left the comforts of Pagosa Springs. The scouts felt quite alone. The snow had been so heavy that they could not see fifty yards and was more than knee deep everywhere and hip deep in places. He could almost smell the aroma of Pam Andrews's kitchen. The Colonel had taken him there four times. The meals had been almost beyond belief, yet simple. Now he lay in the snow watching for the enemy to come up the valley. He had not been anything approaching warm in two days. Despite how he tried, the snowflakes continued to find its way down the back of his neck.

There, suddenly Chinese soldiers appeared through the snow. The snow had just then lightened enough that he could see them at the far end of the valley. Tex moved as quickly as he could in the brush and boulders. As heavy as the snow was falling, any tracks would soon be obstructed, but he dragged a branch behind him anyway. He wired the GPS to a tree in the middle of the valley then retreated to the north. The snow made for heavy, slow going. Five miles hence and near exhaustion he had set two more GPS'. Now was the time to head back to the first GPS.

Tex dropped from the tree where he was placing the GPS but caught a movement to his left. He froze. A Chinese soldier, obviously an advanced scout, slipped quietly around a large tree pointing his rifle in Tex' direction, but not right at the Sergeant, then the Chinese soldier looked the other way. A quick scan of the area showed that no other Chinese were in sight, but he was sure they were around. Tex drew out a throwing knife and planted it in the man's heart. The Chinese soldier fell to the ground quivering as he died.

Tex was quickly on the fallen enemy. He pulled his knife from the man's chest and scanned the area to the south with his silenced 9mm in front of him. As he scanned left to right, another Chinese soldier came out from behind a tree back to the left. Tex swept back and fired; the soldier crumpled.

Until this point the white camo had hidden Tex from prying eyes, but now bark splintered to his right. The Sergeant rolled through the snow as he heard the AK-47 barking and heard the bullets whine as they went over or heard them impact nearby. Finally, he was behind a boulder and the firing stopped. He could hear several men trying to run through the snow.

Tex scanned the area then quickly slid into a creek bed. He crawled quickly down the creek. Soon, he guessed he was on the opposite side of enemy troops from what he had been before. He popped up and saw the three Chinese soldiers approaching the creek where he had entered. Tex pulled a pin on an anti-personnel grenade, let the spoon go and then held it for three seconds. He threw the grenade and rolled back into the creek bed.

After the blast, Tex popped back up with his rifle at ready, the three Chinese lay dead on the ground. From the look of things, the grenade had blown just above them where it would have had maximum effect.

'I love it when a plan works out.' Tex thought. He knew that the snow would muffle any report of the grenade, making it hard to trace. Still, he did not wish to wait around to see if any more enemy scouts were about. He had to activate the GPS.

"How long has it been," Hugh asked.
"Almost seventy hours, sir," Hardwick answered.
"The snow must be slowing them down," Lopez offered.
"Let's hope it stops them." Hugh was wondering if his scouts had not been discovered and eliminated. He had ordered radio silence so that the Chinese would have no clue that something might be in the works. Tex had become his right hand and he would have a huge hole to fill without him. That, of course, presupposed that he survived.

The Illinois Cowboy was alive and well watching the enemy approach.
'Just a little farther,' Tex thought. Soon the lead elements of the Chinese would be surrounding where he had set the GPS. He wanted them well past the GPS so that the artillery would score a hit no matter what side of the GPS that the shell fell on. Now! He pointed the remote at the GPS. Nothing happened. He tried it again. Nothing happened.

"Doggonit," he said aloud. Maybe the angle was wrong. Tex climbed a short way up a tree. This might expose him, but he did not seem to have a choice. The tree was snow covered and his white outer garments would help hide him. He pressed the activation button on the remote and was awarded with a beep. The GPS activated.

"Yes!" Tex said to himself then dropped back to the ground and found his safe area among boulders where he had a good view of the valley.

"Sir, we have a signal!" Lopez shouted this to the Colonel who was about a city block away.
Hugh was running his way. "Fire, fire at will!"
When Smith arrived at the board, he found that the GPS was sounding to the south and slightly west. As he watched, another signal showed up east of the first one in a second valley. The guns started booming.

The snow just kept getting deeper. How does an army move with any speed in this, General Park thought. His soldiers were professionals and so were doing what they had to do, thousands had dropped by the way due to insufficient clothing, boots, and rations. To keep the pace and surprise he had to leave them behind. They would die without help, but the Americas would be lost without the weapons. He had started out with 249,000 men and had now lost nearly 25,000 to the weather. Ah well, at least the snow had stopped the Americans from using air power. They might not have made it to this point at all if they had been constantly attacked from the air, and the low clouds were preventing that. How was one supposed to win a war without air cover in this modern era?

Whump, whump, whump! All the troops hit the ground as artillery began to fall all around them.

Park stood in the jeep they had taken from an American civilian. "Where is that coming from?"

"Don't know, sir," a Major reported, "we can't see it. They may be miles away."

"If they are miles away, how can they be shelling us so accurately?"

The Major shrugged trying to think of something.

"Well, find them and silence them or we won't even get to the target," the General barked. Between blasts near him, he could hear blasts far away. "Where is that other artillery falling?"

"Sir, the other troops in the next valley are also being shelled." A Colonel held up a radio where he had gotten the report.

"They must have scouts nearby!" Park was trying to shout over the explosions. "Find them and kill them!"

"Yes, sir," the Colonel answered.

Park looked around. His troops were cowering in the snow. He jumped from the jeep. "Get up! All of you up!"

"Sir, you must get back in the car." The General's driver shouted as a shell landed nearby, showering the General with dirt and snow.

Park headed farther from the Jeep. "Get up! We must take those guns, or we will all die! If you lay here, you will die!"

Another shell was screaming in and made a direct hit on the Jeep. The vehicle flew fifty feet in the air, landing a hundred yards from the General. The driver had been his nephew. Now he was on foot like all his troops.

A Sergeant handed Hugh a radio. "Smith."

"It's Tex, sir."

"How are we doing, Sergeant?"

"Right on, sir!" Tex saw a vehicle fly into the air. "Keep pouring it on, sir."

"Keep us informed," Hugh ordered. "Who is the other scout that has us firing?"

"Sergeant Vickers, sir." A technician said who was looking at the board that tracked the various GPS'.

"How do you know that?" Hugh had not had time to learn all the ins and outs of the new technology.

"Each scout was assigned GPSs with unique frequencies. We can tell them by what they squawk."

Hugh punched in Vickers code.

"Vickers." The Sergeant whispered then Hugh heard a blast in the background.

"Sgt. Vickers, Colonel Smith."

"Yes sir."

"How are we doing?"

"The arty's takin' its toll, sir" the Sergeant answered. "Almost every shell is doing something."

"OK, Sergeant," Hugh said, "keep us on target."

Hugh handed the cell phone like device back to the Sergeant.

"How are we doing, sir," Angelo Lopez asked.

"Sounds like we're hitting the mark," Smith said, "keep it hot."

Due to the pounding that they were taking, General Park increased the pace. A blessing in disguise, he thought. This will wake up the troops and warm them. Some more men were sure to fall by the wayside due to complete exhaustion from the three-day march. He never did figure out how the American artillery was so accurately pounding them every step of the way.

"Sir, Pagosa Springs in sight," a Captain told him.

"How many men are left," the General asked.

"160,000," the Captain said, "give or take."

"We've lost that many men?" The General thought the Captain might have overestimated.

"Sir, unit commanders report that the weather had taken over 30,000. This artillery has dropped more than 50,000."

"Sir," a Colonel spoke now "I suggest we rest the men before we attack. They have been on the move for more than three days without cease."

"Are you kidding, Colonel," the General was incredulous; "we must go straight into the attack. If we pause before this artillery, we'll have no one left to attack with. Those that don't get hit by shells will freeze to death. Life is at the top of that mountain. Give the order!"

"Yes, sir." The Colonel went to comply. He doubted they could take the mountain. The men were so cold and tired they could hardly move at more than a slow walk.

The sight the American Colonel saw through his binoculars was awesome and intimidating. Hugh could see the Chinese pouring out of the two valleys to his south. He had seen such things before, but it never seemed to get less disheartening.

General Park looked at the objective through his binoculars. Three sides were clearly inaccessible. A frontal attack was all that was open to them, and the Americans seemed prepared for that. He had been told that only a few thousand Americans defended the base and thought it should be a doable thing to take the supplies. He knew he would lose many more men but would sustain the war effort by taking the supplies. Maybe he would be honored for doing a great deed to win the war against the great odds of American forces and the weather.

The Chinese troops streamed toward the objective. He was proud of his men as they walked through the lethal artillery fire toward the mountain base with no sleep and little food. Then he saw the first explosions. Mine fields. How could the Americans have been so prepared if they had not known they were coming? The snow was now starting to let up and his weathermen told him that it would soon be gone. The weather had been perfect in a way. The American satellites and planes could not keep tabs on them due to the heavy snow and now it was letting up so that they could attack the American base. Tens of thousands of men were falling to mines. How many more casualties could he take before he had to call off the attack?

Hugh watched the Chinese walk right into the mines. They walked like zombies. When the first line died, the second line did not even hesitate to die seconds later a few feet on. The enemy troops were pressed so close together in the narrow valley that several men died with each explosion. Several more were wounded. His explosive's guys had done a lethal job; it seemed that every mine found its mark.

Park was hopeful now that he saw the troops now approached the bottom of the mountain. They had apparently passed the minefield and now reached the bottom of the mountain base. Between the mines and the continued artillery, his statistic men estimated that they had lost another 40,000 men dead and wounded. If the statistic ghouls were right, he had lost well more than a hundred thousand men before they could even fire a shot at the enemy. Suddenly the whole bottom of the mountain exploded. Thousands more died.

"What was that?" Hugh asked his explosive's chief what had just happened.
"We had a lotta plastic stuff," the Lieutenant answered. "Just one more present for our antagonists, sir."

Arvin sat in his foxhole and typed into his satellite-connected laptop. 'The artillery was firing for a whole day before we saw the first enemy soldier emerge from the snow. Our scouts tell us that our cannon have done horrendous damage to the Chinese, yet on they come. A recent report says that the trail of bodies stretches back for more than twenty miles; still we look at well more than a *hundred thousand enemy soldiers storming our base. We may not survive this day, but the Chinese have already lost. If we lose our entire force, we lose only 4500 fighting men and one reporter. They will have surely lost well more than a hundred and fifty thousand before the battle is over*, JIM ARVIN, PAGOSA SPRINGS, COLORADO.

Jim showed the dispatch to the press officer. The Captain nodded. Jim sent what he expected to be his last dispatch to his paper.

Park watched as his men finally started the ascent. Now the Americans opened up with machine guns and mortars. They had those deadly guns, what did they call them? Ah, yes, mini guns. This was an odd name for a weapon with such a huge impact. His soldiers were dropping just as fast as they ever had. As each rank fell another crawled over them and continued the advance. There! The first line of Americans was retreating! Perhaps he could yet win!

Hugh watched as his first line fell back. He had to order them too, as they would not retreat on their own. He estimated that well less than half of the one thousand men made it to the next line.

The Chinese were apparently encouraged by the retreat as they now picked up their pace. Adrenalin was giving them strength. That only meant that they died more quickly. Still, they came on in huge numbers.

Percy sat shaking, not from the cold, but from his assignment. Even the bullies in school that had broken his glasses and taken his lunch money had never thought him a coward. How had this duty fallen to him? They all would die if he pushed the plunger that sat in front of him in the bunker. Then again, if the Chinese took the base and he did not do his duty, many more men would die.

He had always thought to go back home and pick a fight with one of the bullies that had tormented him in his youth. That might not be possible now. He imagined mopping up the floor with Harvey Jeffries, that jerk had tormented him almost every day of his freshman year. Percy had heard that Harvey had grown lazy and fat. The Army Major had finely tuned his body and carefully practiced the defensive arts the army had taught him. Harvey would pay.

Now the enemy was pressing the second line.

"Order the second line to fall back," Hugh said. When the order was passed, about three-quarters of the thousand men retreated.

The Colonel started forward and was stopped by his men. "Where you goin', sir?"

"Gotta check on the lines," he told them. "Don't worry, I'll get back when they get closer."

The Lieutenant looked at two Sergeants. "Go with him and make sure he comes back."

Now his men were halfway up the mountain. Park was ever more optimistic. If they could just make it a little farther, just a little farther.

Hugh was walking the forth line when he saw it go over his head. He recognized the Chinese RPG and dove for a hole. Both Sergeants who were acting as his bodyguards died.

Sergeant Carlin came sliding into the bunker in the middle of the base. He startled Percy so much that the Major almost hit the plunger.
"Sir, the Colonel's down," the Sergeant told him, "we need you outside. You're in charge now!"
Hardwick's eyes grew wide. "Do you know what to do here?"
"Yes, sir," the Sergeant said. By the look in his eyes and the quiet way he said it Percy knew the mission would be carried out if it needed to be.
The Major ran out of the bunker in time to see the unconscious Colonel carried into the medical tent. He saw blood but did not think it was too bad. If the Chinese got through, what would it matter? He reached the fifth line at a run. The Chinese appeared stalled between the third and fourth lines. More Chinese were coming up at the bottom. Percy ran to Captain Lopez.
"Captain, can you target those men at the bottom of the mountain?"
Lopez looked where the Major was pointing. "Yes, sir."
"Fire for effect!"
Lopez crews cranked the cannon down and loosed them. Some of the rounds were just going feet over their own troop's heads.

The third American line had broken, but the attack was faltering.
"Sir, we're getting to the breaking point." The casualty officer spoke.
"What do you mean," Park was incredulous, "we are about to win the day."
"By our calculations we have less then eighty thousand men left." The man was good at his job. He knew how many had fallen just by watching the battle. Park rued the day that the Army had trained and assigned these guys. Battles were sometimes won on emotion, by throwing logic to the winds. "Sir, we'll lose half of those finishing off the conquest. We won't have enough to hold the position if we can win it."
Park watched a while longer. The forward progress was almost completely gone. He turned and looked back to the other direction for a long moment.
"Your orders, sir?" A Colonel asked.
"Order the retreat."

Suddenly there were whistles blowing all over the enemy lines. Hardwick climbed on some sandbags to get a better look. Two privates immediately pulled him back to the ground.

"We already lost the Colonel, sir," one private told him, "we can't afford you to go down too."

Percy climbed back to his feet and peeked. The enemy was retreating. "Cease fire! Cease fire!"

The Chinese retreated into the valley to the right. Their dead and wounded were left behind, as they had no way to take them. Calculations said that only some 80,000 were retreating. Less than one in three who had started the campaign. This was surely the end of Park's career. He would be sent back to Beijing in disgrace. Perhaps he could at least get some of these men back to their lines safely.

Reality swam into being. His eyes opened but took a moment to focus. The pain helped them focus. He was obviously in a tent. The pain was so intense that this surely must be torture. They had lost the base!

"Colonel." He vaguely recognized the voice that spoke gently to him.

The Medic was in his face. "He's awake."

"Ohh, not good," another medic said, "got one more to pull out."

"Do it quick." The medic in front of him was watching his face.

He felt a hard pull, then a sharp pain up his spine. He screamed involuntarily.

"Done!" This one spoke from behind him.

"How you feelin' Colonel?"

"I hurt."

"Give him some morphine."

"No!" Hugh sat up. That was a mistake. His head swam with the pain.

"Sir, not so quick."

Hugh heard the rattle of battle nearby. "What's going on out there?"

"Don't know, sir," the medic admitted, "we've been patching people up."

"You done with me?"

"Need a few more stitches."

"Do it," the Colonel ordered, "gotta get back to the war."

The medic lay the Colonel back onto the table and began to sew.

"Can I walk?"

"Yes sir."

"Finish and get me up."

The medic finished the stitches as Hugh grimaced against the pain.

"Done," the medic announced.

The Colonel looked at a nearby Corporal. "Get me out there."

As the Corporal helped his commanding officer from the tent silence suddenly fell over the camp. Both Hugh and the NCO instinctively drew their side arms. Then the cheering began. With the help of the Corporal Hugh quickly made it to the lines.

Percy was hugging anyone of any rank that was nearby. The Chinese were leaving. He turned to his right to find Hugh Smith standing there, supported by the corporal. His hand flew to his forehead.

The Colonel did not attempt to return the salute. "Guess we won another one, Major."

Hardwick moved to hug his superior. Hugh placed a large hand in the middle of the smaller man's chest to stop him.

"Not a good idea for me right now, Major."

"Oh, sorry sir." Percy looked at the ground. "Forgot about your injuries."

"I guess that's why you're out of your bunker," Hugh asked.

"Oh my!" The Major's eyes grew wide, and he took off at a dead run. When he rounded the last building, he could see Sergeant Carlin staring over the bunker wall. He slowed to a walk to keep from startling the Sergeant. "Sergeant it's over. The Chinese are retreating."

Carlin wondered if the Chinese might be holding the Major at gunpoint and making him say that. He hesitated.

"Sergeant, you can disconnect the device."

Carlin still did not move. Then, he saw the Colonel come around the corner, walking with support.

"I'll disconnect it, sir." Carlin turned and very carefully, unscrewed the bolts that secured the wires to the detonator pulled the wires off the plunger. They had survived. Of course, he and the other explosives guys had a lot of disassembling to do around the base. The demo guys would find only four mines that had not been detonated. They had set thousands.

10.

A Sergeant came up to Hugh with a radio. "General Webster, sir."

"Hi ya, General." Hugh had now taken some pain medication and was a bit happy.

"Hugh?"

"Yes sir."

"You don't sound right." The General was taken aback.

"Got hit, sir," Hugh admitted, "I'm a little dopey."

"You need medevacked?"

"No, sir, I'm stitched and patched, I'll survive," Hugh said.

"How goes the battle?"

"The Chinese are retreating, sir."

"Their what?"

"We beat them, sir," Hugh explained, "their heading back your way."

"Thought I told you to blow the stuff in place." The General scowled as he barked into the radio.

"You told me to blow it up before the Chinese got it, sir." Hugh was becoming clearer. "I chose to blow it up shooting it at them."

"I'll be," Webster muttered. "You drove them off?"

"Apparently, sir," Hugh acknowledged. "I was unconscious for the last part."

"How many troops does Park have left?"

"My men tell me a hundred thousand or less, sir."

"Can we hit them?"

Hugh scolded himself for not thinking of that. The painkillers had dulled his mind. "We'll start shelling them immediately, sir."

"I'll send some jets too." Webster said as he looked at the rapidly clearing sky. "We might be able to destroy this bunch in detail."

Hugh hung up with Webster and punched Tex' code.

"Sergeant Saddler."

"Tex, Smith."

"Yes, sir." Tex' eyebrows knitted. "Don't sound right, sir."

"Got hit," Hugh explained. "They got me on some pain killers."

"What can I do for you, sir?"

"The Chinese are retreating your way." Hugh informed him as Tex pumped his fist in the air. "I need you to do the same job as they leave as you did when they were on their way in."

"Roger that, sir!" Tex smiled a predator's smile. "Those GPS' seem to still be in place."

A short way south of the Pagosa Springs base the valleys split. On the attack they had come out of both. The Americans clearly had the valleys bracketed with their artillery. Park had personally been in the right one on the way in. He decided they would take the left valley on the way back and hope that they did not have that one marked as well not to mention it was a slightly closer route back to Chinese lines.

Tex quickly found the retreating enemy force. It was hard to miss eighty thousand men. He called his scouts and got a response from four of the five. He wondered where the other one was. Only a hiker would answer that question eight years hence.

The scouts would wolf pack the area and each place GPS devices. For the Chinese it would be worse going out than coming in.

"Sir, the men must have a break." A Colonel stood before Park adamant about the men.

Park looked at the junior officer. "If we stop here, we'll probably die here."

"Watch them as they walk," the Colonel protested, "they stagger like drunken men."

Park watched for a moment. Three men stumbled and fell as he watched. None got up. They were not yet five miles from Pagosa Springs and so not yet out of danger. Still, the adrenaline had worn off. The men could not go on. He did not think the length of the break would matter to their survival. The clouds were clearing and soon those cursed silent American bombers would be pounding them. He began believing that all was lost. "Order the men to take four hours."

Tex could not believe his eyes. The Chinese were encamping right around his first GPS. *'Hot diggity!'* He punched in the Colonel's code.

"Major Hardwick."

Tex checked the code he entered. It was the right one. "Major, this is Tex need to speak to the Colonel."

"Sorry Sergeant," Percy answered, "he was in too much pain. We had to put him out for a while. I'm in command for now what do you need?"

"I'm activating my first GPS, sir," Tex said. "The Chinese have camped all around it. Tell the arty boys to fire for effect."

"Got it!" Hardwick ran to the artillery. The men with the big guns had not slept for two days and were now stretched out by their cannon. He had them up and firing in two minutes.

General Park could think of worse places to take a break. The mountains here were beautiful. This valley was undisturbed until their passing, the snow pristine except where they had walked. For the first time in three days his eyes closed.

Whump! Whump! Whump!

The artillery started again. Park was on his feet. "Colonel!"

Whump! Whump!

The man was quickly there. "Sir?"

Whump!

"Get the men up," Park ordered, "get them going."

Whump!

"Sir, I don't think they can."

Whump!

"If they stay here, they'll die," the General said, "get them moving!"

Some never rose from where they had settled into the snow whether by enemy fire, exhaustion, hypothermia or loss of will to live when he called an end to the break. Park looked at his watch. He had trouble remembering as lack of sleep was taking its toll on him as well. He thought their break had been less than half an hour. He watched as the Colonel ran along getting the men up. Whump! The Colonel disappeared in the direct hit of a shell.

Arvin was back in his foxhole writing. 'We survived. Do you remember Lt. Col. Hugh Smith? If you do not, he was the first man to win the Congressional Medal of Honor in World War III. He won that medal because he held off 100,000 Chinese with 3000 men. How can you top that? He just did. 250,000 Chinese attacked this time... Colonel Smith's base was manned by only 4500. The Chinese retreated in tatters. Some have asked if we can win this war. As long as we have men like Hugh Smith and a First Family that is unashamed of praying on their knees this reporter is sure that America will win this war. **Jim Arvin, Pagosa Springs, Colorado**.

General Lian learned of Park's defeat via the intercepted newspaper article that had been transmitted on an open frequency. Things were going badly in America. He wondered what setback was next.

Percy watched the helicopter come in. He stood at attention as the General stepped off.

"Where's Colonel Smith?"

"Still in the medic tent, sir." The Major pointed. "We've got him sedated because of the pain from his shrapnel wounds."

"He needs to be in a proper hospital, Major." Webster was intense. "You second in command here?"

"Yes sir."

"OK, so now you're in command." Webster started toward the medic tent. "You load the Colonel on to my chopper and you'll get him back when he's well. Understood?"

Percy saluted. "Understood."

Hardwick had just come back from issuing the orders at the medical tent when Captain Lopez found him. "Sir, the Air Force, for you."

"This is Major Hardwick."

"Major, this is Colonel Renner of the Fifteenth Fighter Group. We've got those Chinese in our sights that are retreating from the bloody nose you gave them. If you'll have your arty cease, we'll finish the job. We are heavy with ordinance and it's all hot."

"Cease fire, Captain," Percy ordered.

"Cease fire! Cease fire." Lopez yelled the order as he ran down the line of guns.

When the guns had ceased, Hardwick was back on the radio. "Colonel Renner, the guns are silent. Fire for effect."

"We're clear, Major, rolling in as we speak."

Hardwick handed the radio back to the Captain, a bloody nose? He thought it was more like a broken nose, broken teeth, raccoon eyes, cauliflower ears, broken ribs and a broken jaw, just what he had imagined doing to good 'ole Harvey back home.

"Burner to flight," Colonel Renner called, "lay 'em in patterns. Let's take out as many bad guys as we can, bomb on me."

The silence was deafening. The artillery fire had been unceasing after two hours and now all was silent. Perhaps they had finally run out of ammo.

Kawhooomp! Park was thrown from his feet, head over heels and landed on his back. He could see the planes passing overhead, dropping bombs. The General knew it was over.

The first round of American planes was deadly. He was sure more would come after them, "How many men have we left, Colonel?"

"Maybe sixty thousand, sir." The Colonel said shaking his head.

"Radio."

The radio was handed to Park by another new radioman. This was his fourth radioman since the start of the campaign. The first radioman had frozen to death. The second radioman was in the Jeep with his nephew. The third one had succumbed to the shelling not an hour ago. Park hoped this one would live, would survive the war. He doubted that would happen. If he didn't get on the radio none of them would survive.

He had little more than contacted headquarters to inform them of the situation before General Lian was yelling at him. "How could 5000 Americans defeat 250,000 of our best soldiers? Did you forget all your tactics? Why should you not be sent back to Beijing and executed?"

"Sir, I am calling to inform you of our surrender."

"Surrender?" Lian's volume increased. "You will not surrender! You will fight to the end! That's an order!"

"General, my men have not slept in nearly four days. They simply can't go on. If we attempt to fight it will be rifles against planes and artillery."

"I order you to fight!"

"I did not call to ask your permission," Park said, "I just called to inform you."

Lian opened his mouth to argue but realized the connection had been broken.

Park watched as yet another of those terrible, silent American planes dove on his men. He was sure that another five thousand of his men had died since he started the efforts at contacting the Americans. Suddenly the plane he was watching peeled off without dropping anything.

"Sir, we've contacted the Americans," General Ying told him, "they want to talk to you."

Park took the radio. He spoke in perfect English. "This is General Park."

"Park, this is Arlan Webster. Do you remember me from Oregon State." They had known each other in college.

"I do, General Webster!" Park thought back on much more innocent days. "How are you, my friend?"

"Better than you, I guess." Webster had never really cared for the arrogant Chinese Officer. Still, if he could work the angle. "It has to be unconditional."

"Understood," Park said. "Then you accept our surrender?"

"Yes," Webster agreed, "let's talk details."

"I will leave the details to General Ying." Park handed the radio to Ying and walked a short distance away. The Commanding General of the Ninth Expeditionary Force of the Nineteenth Army of the People's Republic of China looked at the mountains, then at the clear blue sky. He watched a bird fly for a moment, then listened to another sing. With that, the General drew his sidearm, put the muzzle to his temple and pulled the trigger.

Hugh came to half awareness. He had the sensation of flight. These were good drugs, and he could see how people became hooked on them. Surely this helicopter flight was a dream. The pain was coming again. The Colonel felt a prick on his arm and consciousness faded.

Lian looked back to the north as his troops streamed south. They could no longer sustain an action in the United States. The American Navy pushed farther and farther south, as did American air power. Resupply this far north was impossible. They had finally learned of the new threat from the MEC space shuttle. How would they deal with that? They could not detect the thing in the air, so how do you shoot it down? Not to mention none of their aircraft could fly nearly as high or as fast. Apparently, the new craft could detect and target multiple targets in seconds and the lasers it fired were deadly. They simply had nothing that could combat or evade America's new weapon.

They would not merely retreat into Mexico. They would have to fall back into southern Mexico to shore up their supply lines. This was the first time his armies had retreated from anything. He would work hard to make sure it was the last. He knew it had to be the last if he wished to keep his command. If he had many other failures it would cost his life.

Will had never thought he would enjoy press conferences. His interaction with the press had become one of the highlights of his time in office, except for The Rock, of course. That was one of the pains in his backside.

As he walked from the Oval Office to the Pressroom, he encountered General Douglas Chair of the Joint Chiefs.

"Sir, General Webster just radioed this." He handed the President a note.

"Thank you General," Will stopped to read it then smiled. "Thank you!"

"Yes sir, Mr. President."

Will walked to the Pressroom podium. "I know that I said I was only going to take questions today, but I do have a statement."

Sevrin's statements tended to be long and so the some in the press corps groaned. The President held up his hand to silence them as he laid his papers before him. He placed the dispatch from Webster on top. "I told you about the complete destruction of a quarter million-man force of Chinese at Pagosa Springs, Colorado a few days ago. Well, there is more good news. This was just handed to me as I walked this way from the Oval Office. Excuse me if I stumble a bit as I've only read it once.

From: Webster, Commanding First Army
To: Douglas, Chair Joint Chiefs

Today, at approximately 1100 hours the Chinese Army retreated into Mexico. There are, at present, no Chinese soldiers on the soil of the United States. What is ours is ours again.

The room exploded in celebration. The press conference was broadcast over every press outlet that night and was in every paper the next day. Headlines screamed 'America Free Again' in different ways all over the land. Even The Rock could not come up with a reason not to broadcast it.

Hugh Smith was getting restless to get out of the hospital. He was mostly healed and believed that he could resume his duties. Due to his rank, they had tried to put him in a private room, but he would have none of it. He would be with the men. What was good for a Private was good for this Colonel. He had already devoured four books on Military Tactics and was now starting a novel.

"Daddy!" He heard the scream from across the ward, immediately recognizing the voice. Michelle and Patti were running for him, Terri walking and smiling through tears. The girls jumped on their dad, causing a jolt of pain that was overcome by the joy of seeing his family.

"My girls, my girls," he almost shouted. He held them perhaps a little too tight. Then Terri was there. She sat on the edge of the bed, and he encompassed her in the hugging circle. For five minutes the family group shut out the world.

"I almost lost you," Terri said.

"I'm OK." Hugh said.

"I love you," she said.

"I love all of you," he answered.

Then Hugh noticed some men standing at the foot of his bed. He looked up to see General Webster and Vice President McCoy quietly waiting.

Hugh saluted. "Forgive me for not getting up, Gentlemen."

"I don't have a problem with it," McCoy smiled. Hugh noticed Jim Arvin and other press standing a few feet away.

"What's the pleasure of this visit, sir?"

"If you'll give us the Colonel." Webster was speaking to Terri and the girls. "I promise you'll get more time when we're done."

Hugh's family moved off to each side, but still did not leave the bed.

"Colonel Smith," McCoy was being official now. "Once again you have shown great heroism in the face of the enemy." The Vice President pulled a medal from his pocket. "You have been awarded a Silver Star to go with your Congressional Medal." Hugh leaned forward so that McCoy could pin the medal on his clothing. "Oh, yes. Almost forgot." The Vice President produced another medal. "And you also get your second Purple Heart."

That was pinned on the Colonel as well. The media cameras caught every move.

"Any comment, Colonel," Jim Arvin asked.

"It's easy to be a hero when you command the fine soldiers that I have had the privilege to command." That was all Hugh could say. He thought of the ones who died and was choking up a bit.

The brass and press were then escorted out. Terri and the girls spent the day in the ward. Many fathers and brothers lay there near Hugh. That day they all were a part of the Smith family.

Just a few days later Hugh came to attention before the General's desk. "Colonel Smith reporting, sir."

"Glad to see you up and about, Colonel." Webster stood in front of a map of the battle lines on the other side of the desk. "How do you feel?"

"The Doctors gave me a full release, ready for active duty," Hugh told him. "Anxious to get back to my command, sir."

The General turned to face Hugh. "Well, you don't have a command anymore."

Hugh was shocked.

"You get in too much trouble when I let you go off by yourself." Webster grinned at Hugh. "I'm placing you on my staff."

"Your staff, sir?" Hugh was puzzled.

"Colonel Suarez just got his first star and has been placed in command of the Free Mexican Army. You're taking his place here."

"I see, sir."

"You'll be in charge of press relations and imbedded reporter assignments plus some other things. Your new office is just down the hall to the left, your names already on the door." The General continued. "You'll have a staff of your own choosing. You're allotted two men. The secretary pool will provide you with a secretary."

"I'd like Sergeant Saddler and Major Hardwick for my staff, sir."

"Good choices," Webster nodded, "they'll be here in the next day or two."

"I'd like to see them get some perks too, sir."

"Such as?"

"Promotions."

"You like to push, don't you, Colonel?"

"What good is a CMH if I can't use it for leverage to do nice things for my men, sir?"

"Well, I'm afraid Hardwick's out of luck. A Lieutenant Colonel can't serve on a Bird's staff," the General lightened, "but I will get Saddler his fifth stripe."

"Thank you, sir."

"Both men have also been put in for Bronze Stars," Webster informed him, "they'll get them too."

"Thank you again, sir."

"Dismissed."

"Sir?"

The General sat at his desk, and then looked up. "Yes, Colonel?"

"I've never been a press officer," Hugh stated plainly, "I don't really know the job."

"You didn't know how to be a soldier a matter of months ago," Webster observed, "I think you've done all right with that. You'll do fine. Besides, with all that hardware on your chest, you're the darling of the press. I suggest you wear those medals every time you do an official briefing."

The General got to his paperwork and the Colonel went to find his new office.

For fifteen minutes the Praise and Worship band had wound the crowd to a fever pitch, then, to thunderous cheers and applause, the featured speaker stepped onto the stage.

Sandy Sevrin was dressed in an ankle length, conservative dress. There were nearly fifty thousand people gathered to hear her speak in Atlanta. The prayer movement had only gotten stronger as the war continued.

"Do you think the praying people of America have had an impact?"

"Yes," the crowd screamed.

"You're right! The Chinese rolled over army after army on their way to the United States. When they got here your prayers stopped them cold!"

A huge cheer rose from the crowd.

"Do you know that for all the parts of the world that they have conquered to date the Chinese Army was unable to completely occupy any single state in the Union?"

"Praise God!" The crowd shouted nearly in unison.

"The battle belongs to the Lord," Sandy shouted.

"Praise Jesus!"

"If God stands with us who can stand against us?"

"Praise Him!"

"But there is much yet to do."

The crowd had been on its feet. They quieted and sat back down in their chairs.

"There are many peoples yet under the tyranny of Chinese rule. My husband has promised that we will not stop until the yoke of tyranny is thrown off all peoples on this planet."

The prayer movement had printed a book that listed all the things that needed to be prayed for every day, it was called the Freedom Prayer Journal; there were also numerous blank pages in the back for other prayer concerns.

"Get out your Journals."

Everyone complied pulling the books out of backpacks purses and pockets.

"It says in the Word that where two or more of you are gathered in His name there He is also. I'd say there's a little more than two here today."

Attendees shouted the affirmative.

"The prayer of so many gathered in one place will have great power," the First Lady started. "We must send our armies on the trek to free the world with all the power that we can call down from Heaven."

Hands rose in worship all over the stadium.

"Pray with me."

For more than an hour Sandy knelt on the stage as she and those gathered prayed from the journal. They prayed for each thing listed, for weapons, for soldiers, for wisdom, for victory. Prayer requests were then taken from the audience and lasted for two more hours.

When, at last the prayer was over, Sandy was exhausted. As the crowd settled in for yet more speakers, the First Lady was escorted to her motor coach and immediately fell exhausted into bed. The experience of these conferences was both intense and draining.

11.

Webster stood at the front of the conference room filled with Army brass laying out the truth. "The simple fact is that we can't keep slugging it out yard by yard. At one point in the US, we were killing almost twenty enemy soldiers for every American lost. Now the rate has dropped to three to one. In the Rockies, we had the high ground and they had to attack us while we were dug in. Now we have to attack them while their dug in on good ground.

"Gentlemen, we can still lose this war. We've got to find a way to break out. We need to do some open field running. I want plans from each of you on my desk tomorrow morning that will change the situation in Mexico, dismissed."

Hugh looked at his aides sitting behind him. What would they come up with? He rose to attention as the General left and then turned to Percy and Tex. "C'mon guys, we have some work to do."

They strode down the hallway in silence.

As the three men approached the office, Percy spoke. "I really don't even know where to start in this."

"Do you have the statistics that the General handed out," Hugh asked.

"Yes, sir." Hardwick held up a booklet.

"Where is the most lightly guarded spot in Central America," the Colonel asked.

The three stood in Hugh's office as the Major studied the figures "Central America. Lotta troops in Mexico, over ten million in South America. Quite a few in Honduras, Nicaragua has less than a hundred thousand. Panama has a bunch because of the canal..."

"Stop there." Hugh was pacing. "I was in Nicaragua three times in the five years before the war. I know people and know my way around the country. That's a narrow strip of land. What about Costa Rica?"

"Hundred and twenty-five to one fifty, sir." Percy was studying the statistics.

"I've got an idea." The Colonel smiled.

Webster ordered that each staff member present their ideas. Hugh, being junior, went last.

The first staffer thought they should mass forces in the middle and punch through the enemy lines. Webster appeared bored.

The second staffer proposed that they do an amphibious landing just behind the enemy lines. Webster yawned repeatedly during the presentation.

The third staffer said the same thing as the second. The staffers smiled at one another. Webster appeared depressed.

The fourth staffer, the last before Hugh, stated that he did not think they could do anything with their current force levels. They needed to wait for more men. Webster cut off this presentation prematurely and told Hugh to go. The General was now slumping in his chair.

Hugh, Percy, and Tex strode to the front of the room. Percy set up a large computer screen, called up maps and charts on it and then Hugh started to speak.

"In studying the problem, gentlemen. We have come up with the following suggestion. The force levels for the Chinese occupation force are the smallest in Nicaragua and Costa Rica."

Webster sat up.

"I have been to Nicaragua and know the country quite well. Nicaragua is a very narrow strip of land. As long as you control the water on either side, the narrowness of the area provides an advantage. There's little room for the enemy forces to get around you. The Navy has pushed their lines down to Brazil on the east and Columbia on the west. Sea action is therefore possible anywhere in Central America."

The General was now leaning forward elbows on knees.

"As we push south in Mexico the land mass gets narrower. Four armies are stumbling all over each other now trying to fight. Can you imagine what it will be like even farther south? I suggest we withdraw Forth from the line and send them to California for R and R. We then send the Fourth back into the line and the Third to R and R. We keep doing this for deception purposes until First Army rotates to California. The Marine force is back to strength and has been practicing for amphibious landings. Amphibious is a Marine specialty. I suggest the First Marines land on the East Coast of Costa Rica and sweep across the country, taking up a position to block the Chinese from sending reinforcements north from South America. This will also cut the supply lines to their army in Mexico. With our navy where it is and our air power with complete supremacy the Chinese can only resupply by land. The Second Marines would land on the east coast of Nicaragua, sweep enemy troops from there and take Managua. Once Nicaragua is secure, the Second Marines would then go south to reinforce the First Marines. Intelligence says there are only about ten thousand Chinese in Managua

"What I propose for us here at First Army is that we land on the beaches on the Nicaraguan West Coast."

"We've not practiced amphibious stuff." The Colonel who said they needed more men pointed out.

"I know," Hugh agreed, "we might not be able to get a lot of practice in either, but we can practice in California. The beaches on the northwest Coast are fairly tame in Nicaragua. There appear to be no fortifications on the coast there. We should be able to use hovercraft and choppers to make landfall. We ought to be able to pull it off with little practice. So, for deception purposes the Marines leave right from Camp Lejeune and hit the east coast of Nicaragua, going south to block the land route for the Chinese to reinforce or resupply their northern forces. First Army hits the western beach and sweeps north. We clean out Central America and then come up behind the major force that is now in Mexico. If Second, Third, and Fourth armies keep pushing the Chinese now in Mexico making them use up their supplies and since both of these actions should completely cut off all supplies to the bunch in Mexico, they should fall apart by the time we get to Mexico."

There was a very big smile on Webster's face.

"It has a few rough edges, but I like it." General Winston Sabota, Marine Commandant, agreed with Websters analysis of the plan.

Hugh had just finished the second presentation of his plan. This time he was before the Joint Chiefs.

"I believe that this is the best way to start making forward progress again," General Webster said.

"I'm behind this plan," General Douglas agreed. "Just remember that we met disaster in Central America once. We'll really catch it if that happens again."

"I'm on board," Admiral Tingle agreed.

"Let's do it," Air Force General Tom Bennett said.

Hugh came into Webster's office where he had been summoned. The General had his back to the door and was staring out the window.

"Colonel Smith reporting sir."

The General turned to face him with almost a parade snap about face. "Hugh, I'm going to have to take you off the planning of the invasion."

Hugh was taken aback. "But, sir, that's my plan."

"I know, Hugh," Webster said, "but it's mostly done now, just detail work. Besides, I need you to plan something else."

Smith's curiosity was piqued. "Sir?'

The General picked up a remote and pointed it at a big screen. A map came up. Hugh instantly recognized the area.

"Have you ever been to the Chinandega area?"

"Yes, sir, northwestern part of the country I have some friends there."

That was music to Arlan's ears. He moved to a new map. "Recognize this?"

Hugh had to look for a moment, but he soon recognized the mission of his friend the Padre. "That's a Catholic Mission. It's in the southern part of Chinandega. Looks like the Chinese have made some changes."

"Yes, it's a prison camp now," Webster confirmed. "We estimate that there are five to seven thousand men from the old First Army being held there."

"Sir, that's awfully close to where we will be landing."

"I know," Webster nodded, "do you think you can free that camp about the time we hit the beach?"

"I've got the contacts." Hugh was thinking. "How many Chinese are in the city?"

"No more than five hundred."

"How's the resistance in Nicaragua?"

"Almost everyone in the country is undermining the Chinese."

"Give me a hundred men of my choosing and put me in four days before you hit the beaches and I'll do it, sir."

"Mr. President, the shortages are unbearable." A congressman spoke of necessities being diverted to the troops. "What's America if you can't go for a fine steak? We're just simply diverting too much material to the Army. Most restaurants can't offer them during the week because so much is being shipped to the army."

"I'm sure the Army could find ways to conserve." Another Congressman smiled at the President while agreeing with the first. "The Military wastes so much! They'll have to do more with less."

Gordo could see that the President was red in the face. He was barely holding his temper. This small group of Congressmen just wanted to send as much pork home as they could. If men died in the field to get them re-elected, they did not care.

"Lady and Gentlemen," the President started low, "I have a son that is nearing draft age. He will undoubtedly want to join the service and fight for his country. I will not send my son to war without the very best in food, weaponry and whatever else I can provide them, not my son or anyone else's son. I will not withhold even one pork chop, one bullet, or even an ounce of sugar if our troops say they need it. Your constituents will have to sacrifice if they want to live in a free country."

"Mr. President." The tone of Congresswoman Abigail Fafford was condescending. She was sure she had a much clearer view of things. After all, she was born upper class. She did not come from working stock like he did. "This will be a long war. We can't ask our constituents to give up the staples of life for a decade. Like it or not these things have become a staple of American life. What do combat troops need with chocolate? We can withhold that and make children happy."

"Congresswoman Fafford," Will's tone was biting, "you live in your nice mansion and make your huge salary because men died to give you that right. If we withhold needed supplies from the troops that means the war will last longer. If the war lasts longer, we will lose more men than we need to lose. I will not spend one more life then is absolutely necessary to win this war. That means that we must give our troops the best so that they can do the job the quickest."

"Be real, Mr. President." The Congresswoman smiled in her way that said she was lowering herself to speak to the unwashed masses. "You are upper class, new money mind you, but upper class like me. Our family has maintained its status for more than a century because the cream always rises. Armies are made up of the chaff of society. If the war lasts longer, we will only have less bums lying in the gutter after the war."

Gordo had known Will almost his entire life. He had seen him lose his temper maybe a half dozen times. He had never seen an explosion like the one he witnessed that day.

Will was immediately on his feet. "You are little more than a self-righteous bitty! You don't care about anyone but yourself and your power, all of you! If I could turn you over to the Chinese, I would! I'd pay them to take people like you! You think you're so much better than other people because you've got a little money! If you ever set foot in my office again, I'll have you arrested!"

The Congresswoman and her troop were already heading for the door.

"Dixon," Will shouted.

"Mr. President?" The Secret Service agent stuck his head in the door.

"If Fafford ever sets foot on the White House grounds again throw her rather wide butt in jail! Do you hear me? Throw her in jail and throw away the key!"

Dixon smiled. She treated civil servants like dirt. "Yes, sir. I'll escort the Congresswoman and her friends out."

"You can't do that Mr. President" another congressman said, "we're in Congress!" Through fright he kept heading for the door.

"War powers act" Gordo said with a grin "yes he can."

Will let the steam bleed off for a long moment before he spoke. "I guess that one might say that was a little less than Presidential."

"On the contrary, Mr. President," Gordo could think of no person in Washington that more people loved to hate than Fafford, "I believe that most of the people in the United States, including her constituents, would be on your side. I must say that your language was much better than what most people would have used."

"Make sure she is at the top of our list to beat for Congress in the next elections," Will ordered.

"I'll start grooming a candidate tomorrow." Kirk wrote that on a list of things to do.

"I suppose she'll twist this meeting to make me look like the villain." The President knew how she could twist things to her advantage.

A grin spread across Gordo's face. "Turnbloom!"

A mousy technician opened a hidden door from a tech room and stuck his head in. "Yes, Mr. Kirk?"

"Did you get all that?"

"Every word," the Tech said.

"You had the recorders going," Will ask.

"The whole time, sir," Turnbloom answered.

"I know you don't like to do such things, but that tape is going to somehow get out before the elections," Kirk said.

"I don't work like that. Don't release it no matter how she makes it look," Will ordered.

Turnbloom disappeared back behind his wall. He knew Gordon Kirk would do what the President said. He slipped one DVD after another into the machine and made several copies. Gordon Kirk would never release it, but he would. He would download it from an anonymous internet café, bounce it all over the place and have it delivered to every major news outlet except ATCN, Rock would not show it anyway.

"They think they have it so bad because they can't go for a steak whenever they want one." Gordo shook his head. "At least we don't have to ration gas this time. Almost every vehicle in the service has an MEC engine in it now. That saves lots of gas."

"Have you seen the latest reports from England?" The President fell heavily into his chair and became reflective.

"No, Mr. President."

"You've studied the blitz in World War Two?"

"Pretty much leveled London," Gordo said.

"That was child's play." A tear showed in the corner of Will's eye. "The Chinese can't seem to get even a toe hold on the island but blast them from the sky day and night. I've approved an IP fighter to be deployed there. It'll be a week before it can get there. The ship will have to fly from here every time so it will have to be modified to carry extra pilots and techs. It's getting medieval over there. They're living under ground."

"Maybe Arthur and Lancelot will rise again to rescue them." Gordo was staring into space at nothing as if he was seeing the horrors across the Atlantic. "Maybe even Robin Hood."

"I'll tell you one thing," Will looked his Chief of Staff in the eye, "when this is all over Prime Minister Prescott's leadership will make the miracles that Churchill did look insignificant."

"I wouldn't think he could even stay in touch with his people, or us, with the pounding he's taking."

"Fiber optics," Will offered the explanation, "he addresses the people via Internet."

"Technology can be grand," Gordo offered.

Staff Sergeant Segundo Vasquez wondered what he was getting himself into. His orders told him to be at gate C7 at 1800 hours. This was the right place at the right time. Gathered in front of the gate were more than a hundred men, all Latino. A Caucasian Major and Sergeant were watching the gathering troops.

They were not allowed inside the gate. Segundo wondered what was on the other side. He knew that there had been a lot of activity there in the last month or so. Rumor had it that a whole town was being built somewhere inside the fence. When the appointed hour struck the door to the building just inside the gate opened.

"Attenhut." The Sergeant addressing them growled in a southern accent.

A full bird Colonel walked from the long building just inside the gate to where the Latino's were gathered. Segundo thought the man looked familiar.

"Form ranks!" The Sergeant barked the order as the men complied. "Listen up!"

The Colonel stood looking at them for a moment. "Men, I know you don't know why you're here, but you can't know yet. Unless you volunteer for this mission you won't know. This is a voluntary mission. You have all been selected for this mission because of skills you possess and because of your ancestry. The mission that we will undertake, if you agree to come along, is an honorable one.

"If you don't know me, I am Colonel Hugh Smith. I have won the CMH and Silver Star. I have two purple hearts. I was in command at the Battle of the Passes and the Battle of Pagosa Springs. The two other men standing up here with me are Sergeant Saddler and Major Hardwick; they were with me at The Passes and Pagosa Springs.

"If you will follow me on this mission, I will do everything in my power to see that all of you come back alive, but make no mistake, this is a dangerous mission. We will be behind enemy lines for several days. I cannot guarantee that any of us will come back.

"You have fifteen minutes to decide if you will take part in this mission. If you volunteer come through the gate behind me and take a seat in the building that I just came out of. Once you enter those gates, you will not be able to leave for any reason until the mission is finished. Your mail will be censored; you will not be allowed phone calls. Even if you wash out for the mission you will stay within the fences until the mission is complete. If you are disqualified due to a training injury you will not leave the compound. If you are caught outside the compound, you will be sent to the stockade without even the benefit of a court martial until after the mission is complete.

"Men, your country needs you. You would not be here if we did not need you." Hugh looked at his watch. "In fifteen minutes, the gates will close. If you're inside you've volunteered. If you're still outside, report back to your unit."

Hugh turned and went into the building just inside the gates. Percy and Tex followed.

The men gathered in small groups. The short stocky sergeant known as Segundo spoke to the man next to him. "Sounds like double oh seven secret spy stuff."

"Yeah, what do you suppose it is," Another soldier was mystified.

"Don't know," Segundo admitted, "but my curiosity is gonna make me go in that gate."

"Curiosity killed the cat," the other soldier said.

"But I ain't no cat," Segundo smiled, "and I ain't a coward. If Hugh Smith says that the country needs me, then I'm going."

"Can't argue with that." The two men followed others into the building where the Colonel waited.

Hugh, Tex and Percy had set out one hundred chairs in the building. When fifteen minutes had passed the seats were all full and several men stood at the back.

"Tex, check and see if there are any men left outside. If they're outside the gate, close it and send them on their way. Lock the gate. If you find any inside the gate, but not in the building tell them to come in or leave."

"Yes, sir." Tex saluted and went outside. No one was between the gate and building. One man fidgeted near the gate, unsure of what to do. Tex started to push the rolling gate closed. The soldier near the gate fidgeted even worse. The gate got closer and closer to closing, and then suddenly the Private pacing just beyond it sprinted through the opening and into the building.

Saddler came into the back of the room and nodded at Hugh. The Colonel walked to the front of the room. "OK, men, let's get started. Next to this building are four barracks. You will each be assigned to one of them. Major Hardwick will make those assignments when we finish here. You will eat, sleep, and train as A, B, C, or D squad. Each squad has its assignments. In the case of this mission, you will all know the overall mission and know your squad's mission inside out, sideways, upside down and backwards. Your training officers for this mission will be the Major, Sgt. Saddler, and I. I know that some of you outrank the Sergeant, but for training purposes, he outranks you and you will do what he tells you to."

Hugh walked to the screen in front and clicked it on to reveal a map of Central America. "As you men know firsthand, we have been slugging it out with the Chinese here in Mexico and making little headway. We are part of the plan to change that." He pointed to Nicaragua. "The problem is that there are five thousand or more American POW's being held in Nicaragua."

The brought a murmur from the men. Many of the men knew someone in the old First Army.

The Colonel changed the map to a more detailed one of northwestern Nicaragua. "The POW camp is here in Chinandega. Before the war I spent a half dozen weeks in the area and have contacts there. We are also receiving detailed intelligence from the area.

"The overall plan is this. A little over a month from now the First and Second

Marines will hit the east coast of Nicaragua and Costa Rica and become a blocking force to keep the Chinese from sending any troops north from South America to reinforce the troops in Central America or Mexico. The First Army will hit the beaches west of Chinandega and go north, sweeping Central America clean of Chinese and then coming up behind the Chinese Army now in Mexico.

"We have less than a month to train because four days before the invasion we are going to be choppered from ships offshore to this area." The map changed again. "This is the village of Monte De Los Olivas, northwest of Chinandega. We will meet with contacts there and with some of my personal friends who will act as guides. They are also part of the Nicaraguan resistance. I understand that the Nicaraguan resistance has been quite active and that over a hundred thousand of them have given their lives in the fight. These are good people. Most of them don't have much, but they'll give it to you if you need it.

"So, once ashore we will move to a point here," he pointed, "southeast of Chinandega. Each squad will go by a different route but wind up at the same place. The Nicaraguan resistance has built a village there to hide supplies and fighters. They have tunnels and other things that will be useful in hiding us. You may have seen a lot of construction traffic around the base lately. We have built an accurate mockup of the POW camp. Gentlemen, we will blow the thing up several times before we actually go to Nicaragua. Now you understand why we're being so secretive. If the Chinese get word of this operation before we go, we'll all die."

A Lieutenant had raised his hand.

Hugh pointed, "Yes, Lieutenant?"

"When do we hit the POW camp?"

"We don't know the date yet," Hugh admitted. "We will be in position the morning of the invasion. When the ships start blasting the shore, we should be able to hear it. That will be our sign to go."

Hugh pointed at a Sergeant who had raised his hand. "What kind of shape are our guys in?"

Smith frowned. "If you mean the POW's, not good. We will liberate them and then move them toward the coast to meet First Army. We know from spy film that most can walk; we question how far they can walk. We have made plans for some of them to ride if they have to."

More hands went up.

"Guys we'll get more into this in the morning," Hugh said, "right now report to Major Hardwick and get your squad assignments. We start training bright and early. We are going to hit that mockup camp at dawn, so we'll be up well before that. Get some sleep."

"All right all you heroes!" Tex was walking down the aisle in A Barracks. "You want a vacation in the tropics of Central America? Then you're gonna have to work for it, on the line in five."

Tex was out the door.

Segundo rolled over and picked up his watch. It was three-thirty a.m. He mumbled to himself. "Oh man I volunteered for this?"

Hugh stood in a guard tower. He saw the explosives guy approach the south fence and fired his fully automatic paint ball gun at him. Several of the rounds struck their target. "I see you!"

The man stood. There was the whap of a small charge taking out the north fence.

"That's the way to do it," Hardwick encouraged.

Hugh pointed to the man on the south fence. "You do it again."

"How are you today, General Green?" The Commandant of the POW camp was all smiles.

"I'm in your stupid camp, how do you think." General Green tried his best to stand at proper attention before the other man, but his body was just not strong enough to hold it now.

"You are never nice to me, General. Or can I call you Paul?"

"Only my friends call me Paul. You don't qualify."

The Chinese Major jumped to his feet and slammed his fist on the desk. "We will rule your people for the foreseeable future! Soon, America will fall."

"You've been tellin' me that for months." Green smiled since he was aggravating the commandant. This stuff gave him hope. The man would not waste his time with Green if America had been conquered. He guessed it would probably be months at least, maybe years before he would be liberated, but he believed he would be liberated.

"You had better learn to get along with me, General."

"That'll never happen," Green snarled.

The Major came around the desk, getting close enough to Green that when he spoke the spittle hit Green's left cheek. "You will learn respect for me!"

Green turned to his left and looked down into the man's eyes. "I doubt it."

The Major decked Paul with a single blow to the face, something he had been unable to when Green had first come to the camp. "Get out of my office!'

"Gladly," Paul said. He started to get up but was felled by a kick to the ribs.

"Crawl," the Major screamed. "From now on you will always crawl in my office. Whenever you come before me you will come on your hands and knees."

Green had made it out the door. "I'll die first."

They were two weeks into the training and just did not get it. They had been training to shoot Chinese while riding on a school bus down a dirt road.

"What do you make of all this?"

"I admit I don't get it either." A tall, thin Corporal named Suarez spoke.

"Why are we riding in school buses in civilian clothes to go shoot the enemy." The other Sergeant asked more obvious questions. "Why not use tanks?"

"I'm sure we'll understand in Nicaragua." Segundo said as he leaned back against a tree. It was nice to be out of the sun as they took a break in the shade during a pause in training. Someone had gotten hurt, and the Colonel had taken the injured officer away in a Hummer.

"And we attack a fortified church." A private spoke now, shaking his head. "This thing is getting weird."

Tex had been just the other side of a brush pile and heard the conversation. He would mention it to the Colonel when he came back.

Hugh came roaring back up to the mockup of the mission minutes later. Tex approached him as he stepped out of the Hummer and relayed the conversation that he had overheard. Hugh nodded.

"Men, gather round."

All the men made a circle around their commander.

"I understand there are some questions about the training we've been doing. Most of the time we would not be explaining ourselves, but in this case we will. You are all volunteers you deserve to know. I said we have to get from Monte De Los Olivas to Chinandega. In Nicaragua they use old US school buses as their public transportation. That's how we will get from one place to the other. You are to avoid contact with the enemy, if at all possible, but you had better know how to fight from that bus if you are discovered. Not to mention that everything you will need for the mission will be on that bus, your weapons, explosives, everything.

"By the rules of war this does make it more dangerous. If you are caught behind enemy lines in uniform, you are taken prisoner. If you are caught behind enemy lines in civvies you're shot as a spy."

Hugh looked at the ground for a moment to gather his thoughts. "Guys, there are several thousand fellow soldiers down there in that prison camp. We are their only chance of getting out of there alive. Believe me all this training will make sense when you get there. Get back to it."

The men got up to attack their training with more vigor than before. They would ask no more questions.

"Sgt. Saddler," Smith waived Tex over.

"Yes, sir," the Sergeant asked.

"You know about the injury."

"Yeah, how is the Lieutenant?"

"Torn ACL."

"How we gonna replace the guy this late?"

"That was my problem, Tex." Hugh suppressed a grin. "We can't replace him with a new guy he'd never learn the job in time."

"Quite a problem, sir;" Tex nodded, "I don't have a solution right now, but I'll think on it."

"I have a solution and General Webster thinks it's a good one."

"What's that, sir?"

"Replace the Lieutenant with someone that already knows the job," Hugh smiled. "He's already issued the order that gives you these."

Hugh handed Tex a pair of golden bars. Tex took the bars and looked at Hugh with mouth agape.

"It's just a brevet rank," Hugh took the bars from Tex' hand and pinned them on his collar, then stepped back and saluted. "General says that you can go to OTS when we get back from Nicaragua. Congratulations, Lieutenant."

12.

The two Generals were up on the mountain to see the battlefield. Up here, they could see things they could not see from ground level. This reminded Chan of a game of chess. He often stood when playing Chess to get a better look at the board. He looked over at Lian, only to find him facing the other way. Chan looked there but saw nothing of interest.

"What are you looking at, General," Chan asked.

"The scenery," Lian answered.

"Scenery?" Chan could not believe his ears. "Look at the battle, man. We came up here to size up the situation, not sight-see!"

Lian was only mildly irritated by his superior's tirade. This was Chan's personality; his idea of relaxing was playing war games. "I know the situation, sir. Being up here and seeing it only confirms what I suspected."

"What, then, are your plans, General?"

"Sir, we cannot maintain this fight so far from our supply base. If the Americans can get a force between South America and us, they can destroy this army to a man. If we consolidate our gains, we will return to the United States some day and win."

Chan was shaking with rage. "Give back what we've won, never!"

"The mistake that Hitler made in World War Two was that after he conquered Europe, he turned immediately to conquer other territories. If he had consolidated his hold on Europe, all of Europe would still be speaking German and paying homage to the Fuhrer. If he had moved more slowly, then he would have kept what he conquered."

"We have won!" Chan was almost screaming. "No army can conquer us. This has been a short setback. In the end we are the superior race!"

"General," Lian was focused, "intelligence says that the Americans are practicing amphibious landings. We must pull back to a place where we can hold what we've gained."

"I forbid it, General!" There was death in Chan's eyes. "You will not retreat!"

Chan walked away without another word. Lian could see disaster coming but could do nothing to prevent it.

'Never thought I'd be sleeping with the President of the United States,' Sandy thought as she watched her husband sleep. With everything going on it seemed to be the only time that he was not troubled. The gray hair was overtaking more of his hair, and some had fallen out. She wondered if the stress would kill him. She seemed to notice new wrinkles weekly.

When she had married him, she knew that she had gotten a special one, but never guessed the ride that they would have. She married a poor farmer and got the world's first trillionaire. She married into the simple life and watched it get more complicated every day. She married a man who cared nothing about politics and watched him become a great president at a difficult time. If she could do it over, she would change nothing. The ride had been wild, but she would have missed none of it.

"You ready to do this, Lieutenant," Percy asked.
Tex had just finished smearing camo on his face. "As I'll ever be, sir."
"We'll have quite a lot of stories to tell our grandchildren, won't we." The Major checked his camo in a mirror.
"Yes, sir." The new Lieutenant nodded. "They'll probably be readin' about 'em in a history book. Were you really there gramps? Why yes, I was. I was with General Smith when he did all that."
"Yeah," Percy nodded, "we've had the adventures. We're about to have another. Think of the book we can write if we just live through it."
Tex snorted a short laugh and nodded. There was the crux of the problem, living through it. Somehow Hugh Smith always brought them through. Off we go with Hugh on just another trip into the very mouth of hell. Just then the Colonel signaled for them to get on the choppers.

Hugh sat in the back of the chopper; earphones hooked up so that he could talk to the pilots. He switched off all interior lighting as the bird lifted almost silently from the deck of the carrier. The Colonel wondered, with the new technology, if the headphones were still necessary. Oh, well, the MEC powered bird was quiet, but still made enough noise to cause a miscommunication. The old choppers had been so noisy as to prohibit talking without the phones. The new one just had the whirr of the blades. No engine noise.
The men seemed nervous. Nervous was good, that kept them on edge, ready. He just had to keep them from getting too on edge. They had chosen to use smaller birds so that one malfunction or one being shot down would not have so great an impact on the overall mission.
The hand-chosen group left the friendly confines of the USN Carrier nearly a hundred miles offshore and flew through the dark. Two of the men were returning home. They had been legal immigrants to the United States and then joined the Army to defend their new homeland only to end up defending their old one as well. There was no light from the choppers or the sky. The moonless night made it difficult to see and then Hugh heard a private say he could see land after they had been in the air for better than half an hour. Hugh donned night vision and saw the profiles of approaching shore.
"Five minutes, Colonel." The pilot signaled then to get ready.

Hugh held up his hand and spread his fingers. "Five minutes."

The men started making sure of their equipment, tightening ties, etc.

"Remember, touch and go," Hugh said, "choppers won't be on the ground long."

Soldiers nodded around him.

The aircraft sat down without a sound a little inland from the Nicaraguan coast. Hurricanes etc. had stripped the land of large trees and good cover so the men were off and instantly out and running to the brush that was available for cover. In two minutes, they were reasonably sure that no enemy soldiers were around. Three minutes after that more choppers were landing.

When the next bird sat down Lt. Saddler was the first one on the ground. "Move, move, move."

The chopper was back in the air less then fifteen seconds after the first skid touched. Tex and his crew headed for the brush. While Hugh's bunch held the LZ, Tex took his group to scout further inland.

As he headed into the darkened landscape Tex spoke only loud enough for him to hear. "You ain't in Illinois anymore Toto."

Hardwick's group was the third to touch down. As with everything, Percy was a fanatic about doing it right. His bird was down no more than ten seconds when it climbed back into the air. He pushed his men into the bush. The passage was safe as he went through the Colonel's group and Saddler's. When they started past Tex they slowed down. Now they were in potentially hostile territory and on point.

The fourth group pushed out of the LZ, through Saddler's and Hardwick's men until they were almost two miles further inland. Hugh went through the friendly lines and to the front again, pushing the American force farther inland. Tex' group then pushed on farther. The new Lieutenant, himself was on point with his group passing an occupied shanty when the home's door swung open with such force that it slammed against the wall. Tex and several of his men dove for the ground and then swung their weapons in the direction of the house and started to squeeze their triggers. There was no hostile fire.

As the men's fingers were relaxing somewhat on the triggers a loud harumpff was heard and almost drew a hail of bullets, but they managed to refrain. With that a man, staggered from his home. Unsteady with sleep and probably drink, he staggered to the outhouse. Tex and his charges slumped with relief. Tex waived the men forward.

At 0200 hours the American force reached the outskirts of Monte De Los Olivas. Hugh called Sgt. Vasquez. "This is the part where you and Enrique infiltrate the village. Side arms only, conceal those. We should have you in sniper sights most of the time."

The two men nodded at each other then moved off toward the village.

"My friend's name is Herman just like you practiced it." Hugh pointed, "Go down the village street between the two rows of houses. Herman's house is the third on the left. Knock on the door; Herman will be grumpy when he answers. Ask him if he knows a man named Hugh Smith. He'll ask how I know him. Tell him that he was the construction foreman. Then bring him here."

Sgt. Vasquez and his partner sauntered out of the bush as if they did it every day and walked toward the sleeping town. All was quiet. There were not even guards posted. A couple of dogs barked, but quickly lost interest. He would have to remember to speak in Nicaraguan Spanish, American Spanish or even Mexican Spanish could get him killed. Their senses on hyper alert they walked to the third house without seeing a single person. They were also hoping no one had seen them. If an observer was going unnoticed, they were at a distinct disadvantage. Vasquez knocked on the door. The lack of an answer made him quite nervous. Both men wanted to swivel their heads, but that would be a dead giveaway. Instead, they stood back-to-back and moved their eyes. Segundo did not want to knock too loudly because of the type of mission but knocked louder.

"What? Who is there?" An angry male voice came from inside the house.

Segundo relaxed some. "I need to speak to Herman."

"Why, what do you want." The angry voice was closer to the door.

"I must see, Herman."

Now the voice came from just the other side of the door. "What is so important at this hour?"

The Sergeant lost his accent and switched from Spanish to English as he spoke quietly. "I am a friend of Hugh Smith."

The door flew open as a man in a nightshirt hustled them inside while checking from side to side. He looked around to see if anyone had heard but saw only pigs and chickens.

"How do you know Hugh?" Herman spoke Spanish from the dark. The room was too dark for the US soldiers to see the man or if anyone else was in the room. A Chinese squad could have been standing within five feet and they could not have seen them.

"He's our commanding officer." Both were now speaking Nicaraguan Spanish.

"Where is he," Herman asked.

"Just outside of town."

"Can you answer the question?" Herman knew the code that had been set up through the underground. It only dawned to him now why they had chosen these words. No one had told him the American coming would be his friend Hugh.

"Yes."

"How does the American know me?"

"You were the construction foreman." Herman thought back to the mission trips in which Hugh had helped them build homes for those wiped out by the hurricane.

There was suddenly another presence there in the dark. Segundo reached for his gun.

"Welcome to Nicaragua, men." The new man spoke American.

"I know that voice," the Private said.

"I'd shake your hand if I could find it," the voice said, "I am Gary Patton with WNN."

"Who is here, Herman?" A woman's voice spoke from the next room.

"Shhh, mama," the Foreman said. "The middle room."

Herman led them into a middle room and closed the doors. No more was heard from the woman. They guessed correctly that she knew not to ask the goings on in the middle room. There were no windows to the room, no outside walls, just a small doorway. Once they were inside with the door closed, he turned on a light. They found Herman to be in his fifties, but strong from hard work.

"I do know you," Segundo said, "I've seen you on the news."

Patton was not easily recognized because he looked like a wild man. His beard and hair had not been cut in months; it did not look like a comb had been near them in some time also.

"Seems like a lifetime ago," Patton admitted.

"Where is my friend Hugh," Herman asked again.

"We have come to take you to him," Vasquez said.

"I will get dressed." The Nicaraguan went off to get his clothes on. He was careful to turn the light off before he opened the door.

"I'm coming to," Patton said.

"I don't know, Mr. Patton," the Sergeant said.

"Look," Patton was firm, "you wouldn't be on this mission without me. I've been behind the Chinese lines for months. I know where everything is and how to get there. I found the POW camp, doubtful that the US would even know about the POWs without me. I'm coming."

Segundo just nodded. This was something for the Colonel to deal with.

At 4 a.m. Segundo Vasquez and the others were stumbling through the bush. The moon did not rise tonight and so they had no light to maneuver by. They had no night vision, as they could not afford to carry anything that would identify them as Americans. They even carried Russian 9mm side arms instead of ones of American manufacture that were now the standard issue of First Army, because they were the norm in South America.

"Don't breathe, my man." The voice spoke in Spanish.

"I'm Sgt. Vasquez." Segundo said it in English, they had finally stumbled into the American lines.

"Herman, my friend." The Colonel used the night vision to recognize the group.

"Hugh!" Herman squinted to find his friend, and then put his arms around him.

Herman's night vision was beginning to get adjusted enough to see the men around him. "What is this mission for which you have brought so many men?"

"You have not been told," Hugh asked.

"He was only told that he was to get us to the resistance village," Gary Patton spoke. "This thing's compartmentalized, it's best to keep it that way."

"And who might you be," Hugh asked.

"Gary Patton, WNN." Gary said in his best announcer's voice.

Hugh wondered if the stress of being behind the lines for so long had begun to get to Patton. "OK, men, what's the drill?"

"We will move you to better cover for the next day," Herman said. "I will have to send messengers to bring the buses. It will take more than a day to get them here."

"O.K." Hugh nodded "let's get going."

"Follow me," said Herman.

A little more than a day after Hugh and company got to the little Nicaraguan village a school bus still painted and lettered, as it had been when it was a US school bus, pulled off the road and into the bushes. There were maybe ten Nicaraguans on the bus already. Percy and his troop of twenty-four boarded the bus with all their equipment. The native Nicaraguan's lifted the seats on the bus to expose smuggling compartments in the floor. The US Army men threw most of their things in the compartments but kept their rifles. The M1A1's were hidden under jackets and laid on the seat next to them. The bus backed onto the road and was gone. The whole thing took less than two minutes.

The wait of a half-hour was made harder since the sun was starting to come up. The second bus pulled into the brush, the natives lifted the seats, the US soldiers boarded and put their stash in the compartments, the seats were replaced, everyone sat, and the bus backed out.

"So far this thing's goin' slicker than snot on a doorknob," Tex observed.

"I like a positive attitude." Hugh then he got a mental picture of what his Lieutenant had just said and frowned. "We're one percent complete, but it's a successful one percent."

"Kinda like the optimist that fell off the hundred story building," Tex said.

Hugh waited for a moment to see if Saddler would go ahead with the punch line and then asked. "What about the optimist who fell off the hundred story building?"

"When he went past the fiftieth floor a guy working there had the window open and heard him say, 'So far so good.'"

The Colonel laughed. "The moral?"

"It' always is good until that sudden stop at the end," Tex smiled, "sir."
The men shared a laugh. A bus was heard straining up the hill.
"Sorry, sir, gotta go, got a bus to catch."
A few minutes later Hugh and his squad were the only ones left.

Gary Patton squatted near Hugh.
"Thought you would have left with one of the other groups," Hugh said.
"You're the CMH winner," Patton observed, "thought I'd stick with you. Action always happens around you from what I hear. It seems to find you."
The Colonel laughed. "That's too true."
They heard a bus grinding up the hill and soon it pulled into the bushes. In few minutes they were aboard and rolling down the gravel road. None of the roads were well enough maintained to allow the bus to carry much speed and since they had to take a circuitous route, the trip that normally would take little more than an hour in the U.S. would take two days. Herman was a passenger on this bus.
"Won't the Chinese miss you if you're not home?" Hugh asked the question, knowing his friend was a prominent man in the village.
"No," the Nicaraguan shook his head "our village has not been important to them. They do not know me. I picked the people on these buses because the Chinese do not know them, but they have been active in the resistance."
Except for Hugh and Patton, everyone on the bus appeared to be just ordinary citizens of the Central American country. Herman had not told him that each was armed in some way. If the Chinese stopped them, the Colonel and reporter would have to hide. One thing did worry him. There were no children on the bus. This was, of course, an operational necessity. This would also make obvious to an observant Chinese soldier that this was not a normal bus.
"We have to avoid the main roads where the Chinese occasionally put up check points without apparent rhyme or reason." Herman was speaking again. "We will have to ride this bus for two days to get to the safe village."
"Where will we spend the night," Smith asked.
"We have another village that will hide us for the night." The Foreman looked down the road. "You need not worry."

Not far away Percy had the first worry of the trip. As the bus wound slowly down another gravel road near the coast, a truck with Chinese soldiers rounded a corner a half-mile away.
"Chinese! Chinese!" The people aboard the bus said in a desperate whisper.
Percy hit the floor in the aisle way, the Latino soldiers lifted the seats and he rolled into the box like opening.
The bus slowed to a halt as the truck pulled across the roadway to block their progress. Five soldiers exited the back of the truck as an officer shouted orders at

them. There were at least twice that many soldiers left in the truck. The Chinese, brandishing AK-47's approached the bus. Every soldier on the bus slid his hand under his jacket or bundle that lay on the seat next to him or in his lap to grip his rifle. As four of the Chinese stood in a half-circle around the front of the bus another approached the door. The driver opened the door and spoke in Spanish. The soldier spoke passable Spanish.

"Where are you going," the Solider asked.

"The next village," the driver answered, "and then the one after that and so on."

The Soldier stepped up on the top step and looked toward the back of the bus everyone avoided the soldier's eyes. After a moment he stepped back down without speaking. He walked back toward the truck; the other soldiers followed.

The American's finally relaxed their grips on their weapons as the truck backed up to unblock the road and roared past and on down the road.

When the truck rounded a bend to disappear out of sight, Percy was let out of the compartment.

"What happened," he asked.

"We fooled them, sir," a Sergeant said.

Saddler saw the roadblock coming. This one would not be easy to get by. He knelt in the isle rather than hiding. He had dark skin from spending summers in the sun and wore a floppy hat that helped disguise him. There were four vehicles in line waiting at the checkpoint, the bus being the last. The ten soldiers that manned the roadblock were thoroughly searching everything that passed. Suddenly a soldier shouted, the Nicaraguan driver of a heavily loaded pickup truck ran for the bush but was riddled with bullets twenty feet from his truck as a half dozen assault rifles barked. A plan quickly developed in Tex' mind, he called his men to the back of the bus as the Chinese pushed the truck to the side of the road and told them what to do.

When Tex was finished all the men went to their tasks.

A Hispanic-American soldier walked up to the another truck in front of the bus and spoke with the driver. "Do you want to see some bad guys die?"

"That would be a good thing," the Nicaraguan said.

"As the line creeps forward let your truck drift to the right." The soldier instructed him of the plan.

The driver nodded.

"When the shooting starts you should get on the floor."

The driver's eyes grew hard, but he smiled and nodded.

The American kept moving up the line and telling people to get down if shooting started. No one cried out or objected. They were all anxious to see those who occupied their country die. The Chinese paid him no attention.

When the truck was far enough to the right some of the Americans slipped from the back door of the bus and into the bush. Their movements shielded by the truck. As the line crept forward some of the Americans worked their way through the brush as the others prepared to fight from the bus per their training. Every soldier still on the bus had their firearms out and their windows down.

Saddler led his men through the thick brush right up to within twenty meters of the checkpoint before he showed them his balled fist, indicating that he wanted them to stop. The underbrush here was thick enough to conceal them and it was starting to get dark. The men took aim. The vehicle being checked moved on and the next one stalled as the driver tried to bring it up to the checkpoint. The car would not start. This left an open shot at the enemy soldiers without civilians in the way. Tex had planned to wait until their bus was next in line to open fire, but this presented a better opportunity.

"Fire," Tex said.

The firefight was short. There were only ten Chinese, and they were quickly felled. Only a few bullets came the American's way before eight Chinese lay on the ground, unmoving. Tex counted. Eight? Wait a minute there were ten.

Suddenly the engine of the Chinese truck fired, and it began to move toward the bus as fast as the old engine would grind. The Americans ran out into the road and opened fire, but the truck made it past the bus. Tex heard the thump; thump of two RPG's being fired. Both RPG's impacted in the open back of the truck and it exploded in flames. Half-dozen American soldiers approached the truck to find the driver dead.

Then the Soldiers heard a shout. The tenth enemy soldier was running. The Army men raised their rifles, but a shot rang out and the soldier dropped before they could fire. No one could see the shooter and so they approached with caution.

The woman looked to be eighty and held an old US Colt .45. She looked at the US soldiers and smiled a toothless smile, then put the pistol back into her bag and walked back to the car she had been riding in.

"Sir!" A Sergeant spoke to Tex as his voice cracked.

"Sergeant?"

"Sir, Rodriquez got hit." Tex was quickly back to where his man had fallen. The Private had taken a round in the shoulder. The medics were working feverishly on him.

"How is he, Doc," The Lieutenant asked stood over the medic as he worked on the wounded man.

"He'll live," the Medic answered, "needs a real Doctor, though. A hospital wouldn't hurt anything."

Tex had not noticed the natives gathering around him.

"Where do we find a hospital," Tex asked the air.

"Sir," a Nicaraguan man spoke.

"Yes?" Tex asked as a soldier translated.

"Are you here to kill Chinese?"

"Yes."

"The Chinese truck has to be moved. Your man needs a hospital. This will slow you, no?"

"Yes."

The speaker waived at the twenty or so natives gathered around, "We will move and hide the Chinese truck and bodies. We can also get your man to a doctor. Will this help you?"

Tex closed his eyes in agony at the thought of abandoning one of his men, yet he knew it was right. "You will do this for us?"

"We can do this for you if you will run the Chinese out of our country for us." The man was quite enthusiastic. "Your soldier will be safe and will be properly treated for his wound. I'm guessing that if you take him with you, he will be neither."

Tex knelt over the fallen soldier. "Did you hear the deal?"

"Yes, sir," Rodriquez nodded, "breaks of the game."

"Is there someone who you want to go with you?"

"Vasquez," Rodriquez said.

Tex turned to the other soldier. "Vasquez?'

"I'll take care of him, sir. Sure, do hate to miss all the fun, though." The other private shrugged.

"Side arms only," Tex ordered.

Vasquez nodded and then put their other equipment back on the bus. He retrieved a pistol for him and one for Rodriquez. A vehicle left in one direction with the wounded soldier on board. The other Nicaraguans started moving the truck and the bodies as they bus moved on down the road two passenger's lighter.

Smith's entourage pulled into a village as the sun was setting. Everyone in the village stopped what they were doing and started toward the bus, which made the Americans nervous for a moment. The bus pulled into an open spot in a sugar cane field as the villagers built a wall of cut cane stocks behind it. No one would see the bus from the road. Then the villagers went to work stacking cane over the bus, turning it into one giant shock. Their transportation was now camouflaged from land and air.

Herman had been speaking to a local man since they had arrived. He motioned Smith over.

"This is Cortez," Herman explained, "he is the elder of the village. He says that each house will host one of your men, claiming them as a son if need be. You will be in a house that has a cellar that is hidden since you don't quite look native." Herman smiled at the tease. "Do you want to post your own lookouts, or will their guards be good enough."

Hugh trusted Herman, but "I'll assign two men per shift. Other than that, let them do it. They know the territory and what is normal for the Chinese."

Herman spoke to Cortez who nodded. Soon Hugh's men were bedded down. He let a Sergeant assign the watches. If he were to lead this mission, he would need some sleep.

"Colonel Smith!" The voice spoke American in a loud, urgent whisper.

After a moment the Colonel shook himself out of a deep sleep. "Yes?"

"Chinese sir."

The Colonel was wide-awake. "What are they doing?"

The soldier held down a hand to help Hugh from the cellar. "This way, sir."

Hugh and the private crept into the brush at the edge of the village. Herman was there in the brush as the village elder was speaking with the soldiers. The Chinese were angrily demanding something in Spanish, but Hugh did not know what.

"The Chinese officer is saying that they have come here for the women" Herman explained. "He says that tonight is the lucky night for the women of this village. The Chinese will grace the women of the village by raping them."

Hugh turned to Herman and told him of a plan. As Herman worked his way around to the hut that the Village Elder was going to, Hugh started moving his men.

"The women of our village say that they will be thrilled to spend the evening pleasuring men such as you and your friends." The village elder told the Chinese interpreter pretending to be subservient to them. "They do request a short while to freshen up and put on a nice dress."

"We have no problem with that." The Interpreter, as with all the others, was quite drunk. "I don't know why they need dresses though. They won't be wearing them long."

The Elder led them to a long brick building at the edge of the village. "This is our community center. Await your pleasures in here."

The Chinese staggered into the building. The enemy soldiers flipped on the light in the building, lighting it against the night. Like many buildings near the equator, there were no windows. The American's slithered up to the walls around the building and, as the Chinese celebrated loudly, they rose to the window openings. Just as the Chinese started to notice someone in the window the Americans opened fire from two sides of the building. All the Chinese soldiers died in seconds.

Hugh turned to a nearby Sergeant. "Hide the bodies and the truck."

Hugh would later learn that this group of Chinese had systematically raped women in several villages.

The bus carrying Smith and the rest of his troupe rolled into the safe village two days before the scheduled strike. Their old school bus was unloaded and back on its way in minutes.

"Follow me," A young man with a rifle acted as their escort.

The Colonel started to take the lead but was brushed aside by three of his men. Hugh had noticed this being a more frequent occurrence. The boys were not about to let their Colonel get hurt if they could stop it. The privates had 'ordered' the colonel to stay off point. They followed the villager to a stack of sugar cane stalks. Another nearby man cranked a handle, causing the cane to rise and expose an opening. The soldiers followed their guide down into the mouth of a tunnel. The tunnel was high enough to walk upright in and wide enough for the Americans to walk two abreast.

"This is your office, Colonel." Herman had stayed to interpret. "There is enough room here in these tunnels for all your men."

"Other exits," Hugh asked. Herman put it to the guide. The man guiding them pointed to four of the twenty or so branching tunnels and spoke.

"Each of the four wide tunnels is an exit. They each go out in different directions." Herman stopped speaking as the ground started to move.

Hugh looked with trepidation at the walls and ceiling of the tunnels.

"What was that?" Hugh asked as he looked at the walls when the shaking stopped.

The guide was speaking in Spanish.

"A small temblor," Herman grinned. "They know how to build tunnels here. The walls and ceiling will hold. He says that a nearby volcano is growing restless."

A picture of General Webster heading an investigation looking into what had happened to the lost commandos under Colonel Smith flashed through his mind. He could just see some investigator saying that they could never be sure, but he thought that the heroic Colonel and his men were buried under a couple of hundred feet of lava. All he said was, "Wonderful."

"As I was saying, Hugh," Herman continued, "the larger tunnels are exits. The smaller one's lead to rooms that will house your men." He pointed to room that opened off the hall. "This will be your office."

The 'office' had dirt walls and ceiling, but otherwise was pretty nice for what it was. The floor had a rug; the furnishings consisted of a desk, cot, and nice chair. There was no wall and so no door to the hallway. Privacy was in short supply in the tunnels.

Hugh could hear men coming down the tunnel, a different tunnel then he had come down. He gathered his men in strategic positions and awaited the approaching noises. Donning night vision Hugh shut off the lights and waited as the men closed on their position. Soon the new arrivals rounded the last corner. Hugh immediately recognized Tex. The Colonel stood, "Welcome, Lieutenant."

"Good to be here sir," Saddler said, "I'm two men short though."

"What happened" Hugh asked.

Tex explained about the roadblock.

"You did the right thing Lieutenant" Hugh said. "We'll get them when this is over."

The Chinese hit the village the wounded man and his friend were in a day after they got there. The entire village was massacred as it was thought to be a hotbed of resistance. Neither man's remains was ever recovered.

"When do we do the scouting" Tex asked.

"Tonight," Hugh said. "The other two bunches are not here yet. Besides, your men need some rest."

Smith assigned a Corporal to show Saddler's men to their rooms.

13.

"Sir, an odd report from the Nicaragua area." An aide addressed the General.

"What would that be," asked General Chan.

"More than twenty soldiers have gone missing in the last day."

"A single group?" The General was puzzled how so many of his men could be taken.

"No sir, two separate groups."

"Deserters?"

"Doubtful, sir." The aide continued. "One group all ranked Lieutenant or higher."

"It doesn't make sense that the US would have commandos so far behind the lines." Chan thought aloud. "Are any of these disappearances anywhere near the POW camp?"

The aide looked at a map. "Not all that close, sir."

"Is Major Mau available to begin an investigation?"

"The Major has to finish up his current one, sir." The subordinate told him. "He should be available in a couple of days."

"Probably just local resistance." The General thought aloud. "Place it next on the Major's agenda."

"Yes sir."

When dark had fallen, Hugh went to the village Elder. "Who will show us the way?"

The Elder pointed to a man in the corner of the room. "He will."

Hugh had not noticed the man before. The man was obviously American who was of average height and weight.

Hugh stuck out his hand. "Hugh Smith."

The man shook his hand. "Call me Wilson."

The Colonel thought that the man did not look like much. Then again, if an American could get so far behind enemy lines undetected he should listen to him.

Wilson, Hugh, Saddler, Patton, and five other soldiers took brush trails for nearly two and a-half-hours before the moon rose. With the help of the night vision equipment no one stumbled or made a sound. Finally, they were on the hill overlooking the camp a half-mile away.

"What is your count," Hugh asked Patton.

"About five thousand," the Reporter answered.

"Five thousand one hundred and eighty-three according to their official records four days ago," Wilson said.

The others looked questioningly at Wilson.

"Don't ask," he said.

"From what I can see," Hugh said, "Tex, you can take third and fourth squad in through the neighborhood to the north and come up near the fence. Hardwick can bring first and second squad through the brush to the east and hit from that direction. What time do they bed down the prisoners?"

"About sundown depending on when they get to it," Wilson answered. "They bring them out a half hour to hour after sunrise."

"Guard towers," Tex asked.

"At least two men per tower at all times."

"Total staffing?"

"Two hundred give or take."

"Lieutenant," Hugh spoke, "We move to here tomorrow night and then move to our assignments. We've got to be in place before sunrise."

Everyone nodded.

"Let's get back to the village and get some rest."

On the way back to the village Hugh turned to Wilson. "Your obviously American. How did you come to be here?"

"Do you know who Frank Thomas is" Wilson asked.

"He works for my cousin" Hugh answered.

Wilson gave Hugh an odd look. "Your cousins with the President?"

"First cousin" Hugh nodded.

Wilson was surprised he missed that. He seldom missed anything.

"My mom and his dad are brother and sister." Hugh informed him.

Wilson nodded wondering at the gap in his intelligence. "Frank asked me to come down at the request of the President. He provided me with the means to get here."

Hugh would have to ask his cousin about the strange little man when he saw him again. "Do you know the President?"

"For a number of years" Wilson said.

When Will entered the Oval Office that morning he found Scott Douglas already there. Will was not surprised, as he got his military briefing first thing every morning and General Douglas, Chair of the Joint Chiefs, usually did it. What was unusual was that Scott stared pensively out of the glass doors near the back of the office. The General came to attention and saluted when the President came in.

"At ease, General," Will said. "What's up?"

"I'll start the briefing, Mr. President," Douglas said.

"No," the President said, "there's something more on your mind. Let's have it."

Will and the General had taken chairs opposite each other in front of the President's desk.

"On six June in 1944 America did the largest amphibious landing in history.

Thousands of men died. There were a lot of amphibious landings in the Second World War. Now we start them in the Third World War."

Sevrin smiled. "I don't think this is quite the scale of Normandy."

The General nodded agreement. "I can't argue that sir. But I do know that at some point we will probably do such a landing. However, the amphibious landing was just called off for today. Hurricane Betty is in the area."

"I should have prayed for clear weather," Will frowned.

"You can't take responsibility for everything." The General raised his eyebrows.

"I am the President," Will stood and started pacing. "As Harry Truman said, 'The buck stops here.'"

"My favorite saying is give your troubles to God He's going to be up all night anyway." The General was now standing since his commander and chief was also standing.

Will nodded and smiled. "Good point. I think I'll do that. I'm sure He's waiting for His perfect timing and the invasion won't happen until then."

Hugh's heart was thumping. From his place on the hill, he could see Saddler's men moving down the streets of Chinandega. The people of the town were starting to bed down for the night, but those yet awake were quickly disappearing behind the walls of their homes as the soldiers moved past them. The Colonel looked at Patton and Wilson. "Gonna move down with my men and the Major. You guys stay here."

Hugh rose from the hill and took the trail that would lead to the east side of the POW complex that had once been a Catholic Mission. He knew that Tex would be approaching the fence to talk with the POWs, though he could not see him. He had barely made five meters when his radio vibrated. They had been on radio silence since their landing, so it startled him. Hugh squatted behind a bush. "Colonel Smith."

"Hugh, its Webster."

"Yes General?"

"How are things going?"

"Just waiting for the Navy to start pounding the beaches, then we go," Smith said. "We're almost in place, sir."

"I thought they were waiting too long to call this one," Webster said. "You need to stand down."

"Stand down, sir?"

"Got a hurricane in the gulf so the Marines won't be able to land for at least a couple of days," the General explained.

"Great timing," Hugh observed.

"Yes, Colonel, Mother Nature doesn't consult us about such things."

Smith did not believe in Mother Nature, but he did believe in God. Somehow the timing of this operation needed to be set back to fit in His plan. He knew that Percy's troops were already in place. "I'll withdraw my men. I'll be waiting for your call on when to reschedule, sir."

"See ya when it's over, Colonel." Webster broke the connection.

Hugh punched in Percy's number and put it on standby and then dialed Saddler's number. When the connection was made the men answered at one time, "Hardwick, Saddler."

"Guys, stand down, return to base," Hugh said.

"What's up, sir?"

"Guess there's a hurricane in the gulf," he answered, "postponed at least two days."

They each cleared him and were at the rally point in half an hour. They were back in the village well before the sun was up, the people in the village were surprised to see them.

The rain was falling as hard as it had ever fallen in the last two days, effects of the hurricane. At least it had now started to pass to the north. As the rain had now been falling for nearly forty-eight straight hours everyone was wondering when the mission would come off. Putting it off only made the men more on edge. Despite water standing everywhere and running as quickly as it ever had they were ready to go, rain or no rain. The tunnels they called home had gotten damp and so offered no comfort. In many parts of the tunnels, there was standing, sometimes flowing water.

Patton sat just within the entrance to the tunnel where he had been watching the Colonel for twenty minutes. Smith had been standing in the rain about twenty feet from the tunnel entrance for some time, appearing to be deep in thought. Patton strode out to Hugh. "What are you doing out here, Colonel?"

"Could ask you the same question." Hugh shot back his retort as the reporter approached. The Bible said to pray where no one could see you. He had been praying where everyone could see and so did not want to admit that he was doing that. He did not kneel due to the water.

"I just came out," the Reporter retorted "you've been out here for a good while."

"Claustrophobia," Smith said, not lying at all. "Had all of those tunnels I can stand for a while."

The reporter was about to ask another question when the Colonel's radio buzzed. Patton did not hear the radio; he only saw Smith's reaction.

"Colonel Smith."

Patton watched as Hugh listened.

"Good news, sir."

Hugh listened some more.

"We'll be ready sir." The Colonel snapped the radio shut.

"So," Gary asked.

"The Hurricane's cleared the Gulf, made landfall in Mexico," Hugh acknowledged. "The Marines are seasick, but ready to go. We are to be in place before sunup."

The Colonel went looking for his officers. Patton went to make sure his camera was fully charged as he intended to film the whole thing. He knew it would not make the news for some time, but this would be an historical record. A reporter did not get such an opportunity often.

The sun came out for the first time in three days, but it would be just another day in captivity as far as Tim Blair was concerned. The Captain was one of the highest-ranking officers in the POW camp and was in charge of moral. Moral was in free fall, and he was running out of ideas how to keep the men from plunging into the depths of despair. There had been two suicides in the last week. He leaned against the fence and thought for a moment.

"Pssst," a voice said, "hey, Captain."

Blair looked around; no one was near him.

"Outside the fence Captain."

Tim started to look for the voice.

"Don't look this way," Tex said. Tim would not have been able to see the Lieutenant anyway. He was camouflaged head to toe and beyond.

The Captain tried to relax into the posture he had taken before. "American?"

"Lieutenant Tex Saddler, sir."

"What's up?"

"Need your help."

The Captain laughed. "I'm the one on the inside how can I help you?"

"You can help me get you outta there."

"I'm all ears, Lieutenant."

"How long do the Chinese let you stay out after dark?"

"We might be able to push it to an hour."

"They don't mind you leaning on the fence?"

"Don't seem to," the Captain grimaced, "guess they reckon we got no place to run."

"Get your men leaning on the fence about sundown? They need to line the north and east fences," Saddler explained his plan. "We're gonna place charges on the fences to take them down. Once the charges are placed you need to get your men inside and they need to stay there and might see if you can barricade yourselves some so a stray bullet doesn't get you. When you hear the arty start on the beach, we'll be commin'. Get down and stay down until we come get you.

Got it?"

"I get the guys to lean against the fence about sundown until you get the charges placed. We get barricaded in our barracks and hunker down until the shootings over and you come get us."

"You got it."

"Lieutenant, can you stay there for a moment?"

"Not too much longer," Tex said, "this stuff is hot."

"Be right back." The Captain was gone two minutes before Saddler saw him returning. A black man who wore three stars on his one shoulder though the other shoulder in his shirt was missing accompanied the Captain.

"Sir, lean against the fence," Blair said.

The General did as he asked. "What's up, Tim?"

"You still there, Lieutenant," the Captain asked.

"Yes, sir," Tex said.

The General did not look around. He looked straight at Blair and spoke to Saddler. "Who are you?"

"Lieutenant Tex Saddler, First Army." Tex silently scolded himself. "Sorry, sir. The new First Army."

"Who commands First Army now," Green asked.

"General Webster," Saddler answered.

"Good man," Green said, "what's up?"

"He already explained everything to me," Blair said, "I just brought you here to show you I wasn't hearing things."

"If you are, we both are," Green observed, and then joked. "Knew this place would drive us batty sooner or later."

"I'll leave you to brief the General." Saddler slithered off into the bush.

"So, Captain," Green said, "what's First Army up to?"

"Major Mau reporting." The Major came to attention before Chan's desk.

"Your latest investigation is done," the General asked.

"I've yet to quite finish my report," Mau admitted. "It will be finished yet today, sir."

"I know the investigation was long and arduous," Chan said. "You did a good job on it. You deserve some time off. Unfortunately, we have had nearly thirty men disappear in the Chinandega area in the last week. I need you to find out why and stop it."

Mau was outraged by what he heard. "I will be there in the morning. This will stop and the rebel natives who did it will pay with their lives."

Saddler and his scout's belly-crawled up to the fence of the POW camp, which was lined with prisoners, the guards did not seem to notice. Saddler approached the fence where he had talked to the Captain earlier. As he started to press the shaped charges against the fence, he noticed Captain Blair.

"That you, Lieutenant?" Blair looked toward the center of the camp.

"The same, Captain."

"This what you wanted?"

"Just what the Doc ordered, sir." Tex was puzzled. "Don't the guards see anything unusual in the way you guys are acting?"

"Some kind of big holiday in China," Tim said. "Even the guards in the towers are drunk and that should make your job easier."

Tex had thrown a tantrum when the mission had been postponed because of the hurricane. Hugh had told him that God had a better plan and that was why it would be better done later. Tex said that he thought that God needed to get his act together and get it done. From where Tex sat now, the Big Guy had the better plan. In fifteen minutes, the four camouflaged commandos had their charges placed. Sunrise was hours away. The drunk Chinese did not notice the time, so the prisoners put themselves to bed.

No American slept that night. The Chinese, except those pulling duty, slept the fitful, though deep sleep of the highly intoxicated. The Americans outside the fence were on edge all night, waiting to be found out by enemy soldiers that were passed out.

Armed American soldiers were crouched in the bushes. American POW's were lying on the floor with their bunks turned over to protect them. The Chinese soldiers were mostly still passed out.

Hugh heard a distant thump and then another. The third thump was the confirmation. The Colonel punched a code into his radiophone and punched a preset button that called Tex and Percy. "Go, go, go!"

From his vantage point, Hugh watched two of the RPG equipped soldiers rise up and saw all four fire. Three of the RPG's found their mark and two of the towers tumbled while the third stood and burned. The explosions blasted the fourth tower's guards out of their stupor, and they lit the night up with their machine gun. They were firing into the hills beyond, doing no damage to the attacking troops. As the fourth tower opened up, the fences blew, but with the tower shooting the men did not move.

The front door of the barracks opened as the next round of RPGs fired. One RPG hit the fourth tower, silencing the machine gun. A second hit the motor pool, disabling vehicles. The third one fired literally hit a Chinese soldier as he tried to exit the barracks. The fourth RPG struck the barracks.

The American troops moved up to the holes in the fence and fired the third round of RPG's. Two of the RPG's hit the barracks and one hit the motor pool while the fourth hit another building. With that the men broke into a run, heading for their assigned areas to sweep clean of enemy. Percy's group was heading for the barracks to get the POW's out.

Hugh heard the burp of an AK on full auto just before someone hit him with what felt like a sledgehammer. The blow came in the Colonel's left thigh, spinning him to the left; he landed on his back. Looking up he saw that there was a man on the porch of the command hut. The man quickly died from massed American fire.

"Colonel's down," someone yelled.

Hugh could hear the moaning of at least two other men.

"Colonel?" A medic was over him.

"Left thigh," Hugh said.

The man started working on his Commanding Officer. "Not too bad, sir."

With that assessment the Colonel turned to look at the wounded soldier that had been next to him. There was a blank look in the man's eyes. "Just patch me and then work on him."

"Sir, he doesn't need my help," the Medic said.

"He's hit, isn't he?" Hugh was not getting it.

"He's dead sir." The Medic knew how the Colonel took such things. "Sorry, sir."

Now the POWs were pouring out of the barracks. Per the plan, the prisoners were going directly to the armory where about one in four would get weapons.

Percy was at Hugh's side. "How's the leg?"

"Hurts," Hugh said. "Get me a couple of men to help me around. Take charge until I tell you otherwise."

"Yes, sir." Hardwick suddenly turned at the sound of large, military trucks approaching from town. "Excuse me, sir, business."

Percy was up and running for the fence. "RPG's, first and second squads!"

The medics drug Hugh to the side of the buildings. From their vantagepoint they could see five trucks pull up with some of the garrison from town. Hugh saw Percy rise up from cover as the four men with RPG's shadowed him. Four RPGs fired as one, each hitting a truck before they stopped. Two men on fire jumped from the trucks, but quickly fell. Ten men managed to get out of the fifth truck before two RPG's struck it. The Chinese ran back toward town, most fell before they could get but a few feet.

Hardwick pointed after the hand full that was getting away. "Saddler, third Squad!"

Saddler and the men trotted off in pursuit.

Percy was back in Hugh's face. "Sir, some of the prisoners are pretty shaky on their feet. I don't think they can walk to the coast."

Hugh looked over at the other man who was hit when he was. The corporal was hit in the chest and would need transport. There was also the matter of the dead private that lay next to him.

"I'm going to need a ride," Hugh said. He looked at the fallen soldier next to him. "And we ain't leavin' him behind. Have Herman bring the buses up."

The pop of small arms fire was heard from town. Saddler had found the runners.

Hugh heard more heavy vehicles coming. They were coming from the opposite direction that the first one had.

"Don't worry, sir," Percy said, "Herman was nearby."

Two soldiers helped the Colonel up and they headed for the buses. Two more gathered their fallen comrade's body. The third man was placed on a stretcher and carefully loaded on the back door of a bus.

Gunfire popped again in the town. This time it lasted longer. As the Colonel eased his way down into a seat, his radio buzzed.

"Smith."

"Saddler, sir."

"How goes it, Lieutenant?"

"We got the one's that got away."

"Good work," Hugh let out a slight cry as he adjusted his seated position.

"You OK, sir?"

"Got hit, Tex."

"How bad?"

"Not bad," Hugh grimaced. He would not take pain medication until the mission was over. "Round went through my thigh, but it was clean, didn't hit anything vital."

"One of my guys caught it in the shoulder and another one didn't make it," Saddler informed his commanding officer. "Anyone else get hit?"

"One KIA, one chest wound," Hugh informed him.

"That makes two that didn't make it," Tex was upset.

"Yeah, he was running right next to me when that guy opened up from the porch of the CP."

"My KIA was just a few feet from me. That guy that shot you was the Commandant," Saddler said. "Sir, did they tell you what Major Hardwick found in there?"

"No," Hugh said.

"Better ask him that one yourself," Tex was reluctant to say more. "I'll be back in the camp in a few minutes. I'll get the men moving toward the coast."

The window was down on the bus. "Major Hardwick!"

The Major was there in seconds. "Yes, sir?"

They both paused. Something was different. Both looked around for a moment.

"The shelling stopped," Percy finally said. "Guess the boys are about to hit the beach."

Hugh nodded. "What did you find in the CP?"

Percy fell heavily into a seat and took a moment to compose himself before he could speak. "There were four women, native women. They were bound by handcuffs and leg irons to beds. The room appeared to be the Commandants bedroom."

"Did you document this?"

Hardwick looked at the floor. "I could not take pictures of the women. They were bound nude. After I removed the women, we took pictures."

"Have we accounted for this animal?"

Percy looked up to look Hugh in the eye. "He's the one that shot you, sir. He caught about fifty bullets a half second later."

Hugh nodded. Just deserts.

Hardwick went away without saying another word.

Percy had barely left the bus when Tex came aboard.

"I thought you were organizing our march to the sea." Hugh teased.

Tex sat down hard, reminding him of how Percy had fallen into the seat across the aisle.

"Something wrong?"

"On our way back from town we had several people stop us," Tex was clearly upset. "I don't habla, so I had to wait for someone to interpret. I could tell they were upset."

"And?"

"Seems that about a month ago the Chinese went around and gathered up the locals they thought were with the resistance. There's a mass grave of about fifty on the edge of town."

Hugh thought for a moment. "Let's go find First Army. When we've swept the area clean of bad guys, we'll find that grave and document it."

14.

The ragtag group of Americans moved west from Chinandega. The men from the new First Army led the way; they had been in their clothes for a week and smelled bad but felt fortunate when they compared themselves to the men from the old First Army. The firefights and walking through the brush had also ripped and torn their cloths and skin. Next came the men of the old First Army that could walk. Their uniforms barely held together, were thread bare, and had been worn for over a year. They had ceased to notice the smell. Paul Green was determined to walk but was getting shakier all the time. The General was bent like a man twice his age. Finally, the buses brought up the rear. The natives helped to man the buses and care for the wounded and weak. There were eight buses in all, nearly four hundred men that could not make it on their own.

Tex saddler was out in front of the five-thousand-man American force when he saw something he did not like. An American chopper swooped down over the road firing, then back up. A rocket shot up from the ground and barely missed the chopper. The enemy troops that had made it to the coast were retreating in the direction of Smith's Raiders, as they had taken to calling themselves.

Tex started shouting orders. He had the men take cover on a ridgeline that commanded the road. He did not have time to see to all the men. "General Green!"

"Yes Lieutenant?"

"Unfriendlies coming back this way," Tex said, "get some cover."

"You mean we can shoot some Chinese," Green smiled.

"Yes sir."

Green was suddenly erect. His posture fit his age. "You heard him men! Let's get ready to kill us some Chinese!"

A cheer went up from the former prisoners as they found positions of advantage.

Tex looked back as the helicopter dove in again. The chopper stopped firing halfway through its run, and then sped off toward the coast.

'Must be outta ammo,' Saddler thought.

The Illinois native climbed aboard the first bus to find the Colonel in the first seat. "Sir, we got company."

"Chinese," Hugh asked.

"Yep," Tex said, "looks like their runnin' from our guys on the coast. I got the troops dug in, but we need to ditch these buses."

"Where's that Wilson guy?"

"Don't know, sir." Tex had not thought about the man. "Haven't seen him since we hit the POW camp."

"Herman!"

The man was there in a second. Hugh explained the situation.

Herman barked out orders and the buses headed for some brush. The brush did not exactly hide the buses, but it somewhat concealed them.

Tex nodded at the Colonel and headed back toward the front.

The Chinese, perhaps two thousand were pouring over the hill heading for Chinandega.

Green grinned. "Gimme that RPG."

He was handed the weapon.

"No one fires until I shoot this thing." Green was back in command. He was the General again. "When I fire this RPG, we all fire for effect. Pass the word."

Percy knew the former POWs needed this. He passed his rifle to one of them. The others in Smith's raiders followed suit. After months of torture and abuse these men would be getting some payback.

Green let the enemy force walk/run right up on their position. The Chinese were not retreating in good military fashion, but rather in full panic. With panic making them blind, they walked right past the Americans on the ridgeline without seeing them.

Green stood to his full height, making some of the enemy troop's halt with eyes wide.

"Time for a little payback!" The General shouted as he fired the RPG into a cluster of Chinese soldiers nearby. "Eat this!"

The whole valley exploded in a wall of fire, most of the fire coming from the Americans and toward the Chinese. Very little fire returned. Many of the Chinese had lost their weapons in their flight.

When the firefight was over several hundred Chinese lay dead or dying while several hundred more were captured and a couple of hundred wounded. Hundreds more had again headed for the coast while others went in yet another direction. The wounded were loaded on trucks and buses that were scrounged from nearby villages.

A half dozen former POWs died in the fight and nearly twenty were wounded. Not a man believed that it was anything but the right thing to do. No one would have missed the fight.

Hardwick had the Chinese prisoners sit down on the roadway with their hands on top of their heads. He would only use Smith's raiders to guard them. Percy had seen the glee in some of the ex-P.O.W.'s eyes as they had killed their old tormentors and worried what might have happened if he let the ex-prisoners watch the new ones.

An aide handed the phone/radio to General Webster. "Colonel Smith, sir."

"Hugh, where are you at?" The General asked the question as he looked over maps of the developing battle.

"We're hunkered down about twenty miles inland, sir."

"Hunkered down?" The General was puzzled; they had met little resistance at all. "Why?"

"Just ran into a couple of thousand bad guys, sir."

The General laughed. "If I know you their all dead."

"Wasn't in command, sir," Hugh admitted, "I got hit again."

"Bad?" He did not want to lose his best commander.

"Thigh wound." Hugh felt it twinge and noticed that the wound was seeping blood again. "Not bad. Just gotta stay off my feet."

"Who commanded?"

"General Green."

Webster closed his eyes. His friend and academy mate Paul was alive. "He in good shape?"

"Only met the guy a time or two," Hugh admitted. "If I remember him right, he needs some hospital time. I'm guessing he's lost at least fifty pounds."

"The other POW's?"

"Similar shape."

The General barely held his fury. "Did you get the Commandant of the camp?"

"Swiss cheese, sir," Hugh said. "None of the guards at that camp survived."

"Good riddance," Webster said. "You take any casualties?"

"I lost two men," Hugh choked a bit. "We lost about a dozen POWs at the camp or in the firefight we just had."

"How many POWs made it?"

"Five thousand give or take a few." Hugh could not help but grin.

Webster was smiling too. "Good work, Colonel. We should be to you in an hour or so."

Gordo handed the radiophone to Will. "General Webster."

"General!" Will sat at the desk in the Oval Office. "How's it going?"

"Can't say how the Marines are doing." Webster seemed in a good mood. "I just wanted to tell you that we've got five thousand POWs to send home."

Will closed his eyes as a tear left the corner of his left eye and rolled down his cheek. "I guess Colonel Smith did it again."

"Yes, and he got hit again," Webster admitted.

Will's heart jumped at the mention of his cousin being wounded again. "How bad?"

"Not bad, Mr. President," Webster said. "I ordered him to get on the first chopper and get to the hospital ship, but the man refused a direct order. He would not be moved until every POW, wounded man, and KIA went ahead of him."

"I don't guess a court martial is in the making about that." This was more of an order than a question.

"No, sir," Webster said, "I would have done the same thing."

"I guess I'll have to decorate him again." The President smiled. "Great first cousin."

"Yes, sir, Mr. President," Webster was glad the President brought it up. "I'm recommending a Bronze Star, Purple Heart, and his first star for his shoulder."

"I notice you call it his first star," Sevrin said.

"Yes, sir," Webster said, "this war is far from over. I'd bet there are more stars in his future."

"I wouldn't bet against it," the President admitted. "I'll have the bill for his promotion and decorations before Congress tomorrow if you can get me the specifics for the citation."

"Sir, I'll have one of my aide's type it up and send it to you within the hour. Thank you, Mr. President," the General said, "Webster out."

"We have someone both old and new with us tonight," Galena Gomez said. "We have known where he was for the last year or so but have been unable to say. Now we can say."

Gary Patton came onto the screen with a fresh haircut and shave. "Hi, Galena."

"Good to have you back, Gary," she smiled. She had come to admire the reporter as she watched him struggle to keep the government informed from behind enemy lines.

"It's good to be back." Gary thought she looked particularly ravishing tonight, but he thought any American woman looked good right now.

"What have you been doing for the past year?" She asked a question from a script.

"Well, I got trapped behind enemy lines for the better part of a year," he started. "The entire time I had a camera with me and was sending footage back to WNN, which was forwarded on to the Army for intelligence purposes. I'm now going to spend quite a bit of time on our side of the lines while I edit that film together to make a series of stories that tell the story of the war in Nicaragua especially, but also Central America."

"I understand you have some of it for us tonight."

"Yes, I do, Galena," Patton nodded. "I went on a raid with some commandos the other night. Here's what I shot."

The film started to roll. It showed the guard towers blow and then followed the raid of the POW camp from there.

"What are we seeing here, Gary?"

"A few days ago, I accompanied the already famous Colonel Hugh Smith on a raid of a POW camp where officers and men from the old First Army were being held in rather deplorable conditions."

"Oh, some men got hit there."

"Yes," Gary acknowledged, "that was the famous Colonel himself and two other soldiers."

"Is Colonel Smith alright?" Gomez asked the question she knew all Americans wanted to know.

"The Colonel was wounded, but he'll recover. I wish I could say the same for the other two men," Gary answered. "The most important thing is that we freed over five thousand Americans from that awful camp."

"Do you have an interview with America's, I guess three times now, hero," she asked.

"He wasn't in the talking mood." Gary shook his head. "They lost about a dozen men in this operation."

"And this was all part of the invasion of Nicaragua?"

"Yes, I met up with Colonel Smith and his men almost a week before the invasion." Patton revealed as much as the Army sensors would approve. "They had to get in country and in place to pull off this rescue before the invasion started or the Chinese probably would have simply executed our men."

"Gary, looking forward to those other reports." Galena turned to another camera. "In other news today the First Marines landed on the east-coast of Costa Rica while the Second Marines landed on the east coast of Nicaragua and are now engaged in heavy combat with the Chinese. The Chinese are attempting to send forces north from South America to reinforce their troops in Central America. The Marines are holding their ground. First Army on the other hand has invaded the west coast of Nicaragua and, after taking care of the liberated prisoners that you just heard about, are beginning to move north against the enemy troops there. In the meantime, Second, Third, and Forth armies continue to push the Chinese Army in Mexico to the south."

Twelve-year-old Pam Green had been asleep for some time when she heard her mother scream. The scream was gut-wrenching. Pam flew from her bed and hit the ground running as fast as the tight hallways of their suburban home allowed. As Pam rounded the last corner, she could see her mother kneeling on the floor pounding her fist.

Pam slid to a stop on her knees next to her mother just as her brother Nathan landed next to the both of them. Teenage Nathan scooped up his mother in his arms. "What is it, mom?"

Andre Green started the cry and laugh at the same time, frightening her children.

"What is it mommy!" Pam was almost at a scream herself.

"Praise Jesus," Andre shouted, "I saw him, he's alive!"

"Mom," Nathan held his mother at arm's length "we know Jesus is alive."

Andre shook her head. "Not Jesus, your father! I just saw your father on the news and he's alive!"

The screams of joy brought the neighbors over to see what the commotion was and soon the entire neighborhood was celebrating.

Terri Smith had been watching the late news and screamed when she saw her husband fall from enemy fire. She was glad that the children were asleep and had not seen it nor heard her scream. He had already been wounded twice, but she had not seen film of that. They said that Hugh would be OK, but she did not know that for sure. She worried about the wives, mothers, and children of the other men. The reporter said that the other two men who had fallen with her husband were dead.

When Hugh had been deployed to the front Terri had decided to move out of base housing and gone back home to be near the support of family and friends. She enjoyed the comfort of life on the farm where five generations of her family had lived. Still, she was not there to help those ladies who had just lost their husbands. She did not have service wives to comfort her when she saw her man go down.

The phone rang, "Hello?" There was a crack in her voice.

"Terri, its Pastor Bentley," the voice said. "I saw the film on the news are you alright?"

Maybe it was good to be home. Here she had her church family. Her family had helped found the non-denominational church just a few years ago and the church family was very close, even if it now bordered on a thousand members. Both Hugh and Terri's dad had served as Elders in the church, so the staff felt especially close to the family. "They say he's going to be OK, Mark."

"So, they called you?"

"Haven't heard a thing," she said. "I saw it on the news just like you did."

"I'm sure Hugh would call if he knew you'd seen it. Are you sure you're OK," he asked.

"I'm OK," she confirmed.

"Call if you need anything."

"I will, Pastor." She smiled. "Thanks for calling."

"See ya Sunday."

The swim was quite lengthy even for someone in as good as physical condition as he. That was one secret to his success, his stamina. He had thought of buying a surfboard to help his swim out, but that could have caused a panic and a useless search when it washed ashore unattended. Finally, the GPS said that he was over the site.

Wilson dove to his sub. His aquatic home was bottomed out in one hundred and thirty feet of water. With the top of the tower and, therefore the airlock being at the top of the sub, that would leave him an eighty-foot dive.

The former spy dove into the depths, but the sun shone down to show the way. In a few moments he was opening the air lock. Once inside the craft he closed the seal on the air lock. With the flip of a button the water drained from the lock as it filled with air.

Soon Wilson was in the fifty-by-forty living space. He walked to the kitchen area where he made a couple of sandwiches and then carried them to the control area. Once in the seat at the controls, he sat his plate of sandwiches aside and worked on the navigation program.

When the Navigation computer was set, the sub rose from its spot on the ocean floor, moving out to sea. Coming up to antennae depth, Wilson sat back to watch the TV news while his craft carried him to the good 'ole USA.

Terri's phone rang at three in the morning. This caused panic to well up in her, even though she was not completely awake yet. What if something had gone wrong with Hugh's recovery? "Hello?"

"Hi, babe," Hugh said.

Terri started to cry.

"What's wrong," he asked.

She controlled her tears and then spoke. "They showed that awful film on WNN last night."

"What film?"

"The film Gary Patton got of you being shot."

This was the first Hugh had heard of it. "I'm sorry, Honey, I didn't know. If I'd known you'd see that I would have called sooner."

"Could you have called sooner," She asked.

He thought about it for a moment. "No. I guess this was my first chance."

"Where are you?"

"Can't say." He sighed like a love-struck teenager. "I miss you."

"I miss you to." She sighed the same sigh. "It's going to be too long until I see you again."

"A weeks too long?"

"A week?"

"I'll be home in about a week."

"Why...how." She was ecstatic.

"I'm going to be decorated by cuz again," he said. "You and the girls are going with me."

"You keep this up and Sandy and I'll be best friends."

They both laughed.

"I would be quite happy if you did not do this again" she said.

"I'll try to stay out of the way of bullets and bombs" he said.

He laughed, she did not. There was a long pause in their conversation.

"See ya soon babe" he said.

"Can't wait." She tried to sound cheerful but did not quite make it. She wondered if he would survive the war and wondered what she would do if he did not.

In the first week since the invasion, the American troops were starting to roll. The Chinese had slammed themselves against the Marine blockade in Costa Rica time and again, only to be repelled. The Second Marines had finished sweeping through Nicaragua and reinforced the First Marines.

The Chinese had tried to swing around the coast through the water to flank the Marines several times. They had paid for it each time. Five tries, five disasters. The Chinese had retreated into the mountains of South America.

The Red Forces next tried to reinforce and resupply their Mexican forces via supersub. The Supersub was sunk by American subs less than halfway across the ocean. The Chinese had built four and three now had found Davey Jones' locker.

Webster had quickly turned north and was on the double-time march driving the enemy before him. In only a week, First Army had driven most of the way through Guatemala. With such speed they had left a few Chinese soldiers in their rear, but no distinctive fighting force. The Chinese between First Army and the First Marines were dying on the vine without supplies. Locals were also hunting them. In southern Mexico it seemed that every able-bodied male owned a firearm. The Chinese were losing thousands to snipers and could not seem to do anything about it. A gentler fate might have been to fight the American's head on. At least it would have been quicker.

Hugh remembered what it had been like to slip his arm around Terri when they were first falling in love, the thrill that shot through his body. Years of marriage had dimmed it somewhat, but all of it was back now. He loved the feeling. He loved the woman.

Hugh remembered what it had been like the first time he made love to his wife. Even with his wounded thigh, it had felt like that again. Wow! He was married to that babe in the front row!

"Colonel Hugh Smith," Will Sevrin announced.

Hugh snapped out of his reverie and stepped forward. He turned as smartly as one could turn on crutches, making his way to the President.

"Colonel Smith was wounded while leading a rescue of about 5000 of our POW's." The President continued, "Colonel Smith and his men spent about a week behind enemy lines to pull this off, way behind enemy lines. Since Colonel Smith is already the recipient of the Congressional Medal of Honor, the Silver Star and two purple hearts I award him, by Act of Congress, his third Purple Heart."

The President pinned the medal on Hugh chest.

"Colonel Smith is also awarded the Bronze Star."

The President pinned that medal on also.

"And finally," Will continued, "we will now address him as General Smith."

The President pulled out a single star for each side of Hugh's collar, removing the Eagles. As he was away from his microphone and leaning in toward the new general, he spoke to his cousin rather his cousin. "Hugh would you and your family have dinner with me and mine tonight?"

Hugh had been looking straight ahead like a good soldier, not believing he was being promoted again. He looked his Commander-in-Chief in the eye. "We would be honored, Mr. President."

"I'll send a car about six," the President said.

"How should we dress," Hugh asked. "Terri will also want to know who else will be there."

"Just the Smith's and Sevrin's, I mean all the Smith's and Sevrin's kids too. We have kids about the same age they need to get to know their cousins better," Will said. "I suggest a T-shirt and blue jeans. I don't know about you, but I like to get outta this monkey suit when I can."

"Should be a good evening, sir." Hugh was tempted to say that with all the kids the President had he was bound to have some about the age of Hugh's kids but thought better of it. The proliferation of the Sevrin clan was great fodder for the late-night comedians but was probably out of line for the General even if he was the President's cousin. He was also trying to remember the last time that he had worn cloths other than a military uniform.

After the ceremony Hugh made his way toward his family. It was slow going. There was great demand for pictures of America's Hero, so the press was always buzzing around him now. All the military types wanted to salute and shake the hand of a CMH winner. All the politicos wanted their picture taken with America's hero. Finally, Hugh leaned over the railing and kissed his wife.

"We've been invited to the White House for supper tonight." Hugh mentioned it casually.

Terri had a deer in the headlight look. "What can I wear? I didn't bring anything formal. I don't have anything formal. We have to go shopping. After all, a general can afford an evening gown for his wife."

They had been walking along the rail until he could pass through. "You don't need an evening gown. The President suggested blue jeans."

"I don't have any of those with me either," she said. "Neither do you."

Hugh let the girls pass into the limousine first, then Terri. When he was in and the door was closed, he looked at the driver. "Wal-Mart."

Lian stood on a hill facing north watching as his troops retreated yet again in the face of the onslaught of three American armies.

"How are our supplies," Lian asked.

Colonel Dong hesitated before answering. "We can sustain one more month's good fight, maybe two. We might last three months if we can avoid fighting every day."

"And then?"

"We run out of supplies and either surrender or die."

Lian nodded, and then turned to face south, placing his hands behind his back in a parade rest stance. "Resupply?"

"The Americans have made that impossible," Dong answered. "They have complete sea and air superiority."

"These Americans are sure hard to conquer," Lian observed. "They should lay down their arms and surrender. If only more people were like the French."

"If there were more people like the French, we wouldn't need an army. All we'd have to do is say boo and they'd surrender," Dong smiled. Lian laughed for the first time in some time.

"So here is our quandary, Colonel." Lian started to pace. "To the north we have three American armies. To the south we have only one, but there are also two Marine divisions. Which way should we go?"

"The choice seems obvious enough." Dong had worked for the General long enough that he knew when the man was trying to teach him something. "Go south against the smaller force, especially when that gets you closer to needed supplies."

"Yes, it would seem so on the surface." Dong stopped pacing and shook his head. "To our north are three American armies. To the south is just one army, but under their best commander."

"You think Webster is the best they have," Dong queried.

"Yes," Lain answered without hesitation.

"What about that Hugh Smith?"

"He is not yet of command rank," Lian said. "The Party help us if he ever even gets his own division."

The Colonel was clearly troubled. "What are we going to do, sir? We cannot just stand here until our supplies run out."

The General shook his head. "No Colonel that is what I have been contemplating. We must turn south and take the American First Army head on. It is the only chance we have of breaking through to resupply in the south."

Dong bowed slightly. "I will relay the order."

15.

Hugh held up a new pair of jeans and wished for his old, worn ones at home. Worn jeans were so much more comfortable than new ones. The newly minted General tried to ignore the crowd that was gathering around him. Several Wal-Mart employees had left their posts and were watching the Smith family shop as the ever-present photographers snapped pictures. Hugh was getting used to being in a fishbowl but doubted he would ever like it.

"I believe we have proper attire for the evening." Between Terri and the girls, she had filled the shopping cart. Oh well, after all, he was pulling General's pay now.

Hugh threw his new clothes on top of the stack. Moses would have been proud to see the way the human sea parted as they made their way to the checkout. A polite applause broke out among the onlookers as the Smith's made their way forward.

Terri and the girls sat the items on the counter as the clerk rang them through.

Hugh turned to face the crowd. "Thank you. Thank you very much. Thank you."

"Honey," Terri pointed to the clerk.

Hugh handed the clerk a credit card.

The clerk put up her hands. "Sorry, already been paid for."

"Oh, come on." Hugh pushed the card at her again.

The Clerk pushed the card back. "Your money's no good here, General."

Hugh turned back to the crowd. "Thank you. Thank you so much."

The gathered customers and employees cheered as they walked out the door and climbed in the back of the waiting limousine.

"Motel," Terri asked?

"You still want that evening gown," he asked.

"I don't need it," she said.

"Do you want it?"

"Yes," she confessed.

"Let's go get it." He smiled; glad he could do this for her.

Terri turned to the driver. "The Fashion Shoppe."

The next day most news shows in the States had pictures of Terri in one gown or another as she tried them on. She modeled several for the paparazzi so that they would leave her alone while she was trying them on. Some magazines carried several pictures of her in different gowns. One magazine even dubbed her the America's new Cinderella. A newspaper called America's Second lady, something of a snub to the Vice President's wife. This gave Sandy an idea.

Hugh recognized the car that pulled up in front of their motel at precisely 1800 hours. This was one of the armored SUVs like the President rode in. The General, now sporting blue jeans, a navy T-shirt, white socks, tennis shoes, and a baseball cap escorted his family, who were dressed in like manner, toward the SUV. Even though they were getting into an armored limousine, the press, who were camped out in numbers outside the motel, did not swarm them. Such cars were a dime a dozen in Lincoln. They were all waiting for General Smith to come out and did not recognize citizen Smith even though he was still on crutches.

Hugh had expected to be stopped at the gates of the New White House and that to be an ordeal. He was sure all of them would be examined with a magnifying glass.

The driver stopped at the gate and rolled down his window. "General Smith."

To Hugh's surprise, the guard waived them on through. Soon, they were at the door of the residential section of Lincoln's new executive mansion. Sandy Sevrin stood at the door. Her jeans were properly faded, and she looked as natural in the Christian T-shirt as she did in an evening gown.

"Oh, it's so nice to have you." The First Lady came out and gave Terri a hug. "I've seen so much and read so much about 'America's Hero'. I'm just glad to see you guys again."

"Yes, ma'am," Terri nodded. "I've been to your prayer rallies too. I just loved it."

"How are your girls?"

"They miss their dad so much," Terri said, "but they understand why he's gone."

"Well Mary and Mark have missed them." The First Lady started ushering them into the residence. "One thing that we must get straight, Mrs. Smith."

"Yes ma'am?" Terri thought that she had surely managed a major mistake in her first minutes at the White House.

"We are not in public. In public ma'am would be the correct way to address me. We are in private. I can't stand any more formality than what's required of me by virtue of my position. Here we are family. I call you Terri and you call me Sandy."

Terri nodded, amazed that the wife of the most powerful man in the world held no pretense. Even living in the New White House, she was still just a good old country gal. "OK, Sandy."

Hugh and Terri looked at one another and burst out laughing. They were remembering how nervous she was. In truth they had not spent a lot of time with the President and family before the war.

"What's so funny," Sandy asked.

"Private joke," Hugh informed her.

"OK." Sandy smiled. "Let's get you settled into the residence while we wait, Will should be home from the office shortly."

When the Smith kids were settled with the Sevrin kids Sandy headed for the kitchen. Terri started to sit down next to Hugh but changed her mind and joined Sandy in the kitchen. She could not believe that the First Lady of the United States was cooking the meal.

Later that evening Will and Hugh were alone in the living room when the President dropped one on the General, he did not see coming.

"Have you ever thought of politics for a career after the war," the President asked.

Even here, Will Sevrin was still Mr. President and the Commander-in-Chief. "Not a politician, sir."

"Neither was I," Will said. "Sometimes you have to stand for what's right. God often calls us to places we never would have ventured on our own. I can only serve one more term and then we need someone else to run."

"Sir...I..." Hugh stumbled over his words as he shook his head. He was still having trouble dealing with joining the army as a Private and already having a star.

"What's the quote," Will ask. "The only thing evil needs to triumph is for good men to do nothing."

At that point the ladies came in. Sandy spoke. "Just been checking on the kids. What are you two talking about?"

"I'm trying to get Hugh here to run for President after my next term," Will answered.

Both ladies looked like they just had been slapped.

Sandy plopped down beside her husband on the couch as Terri took a seat next to Hugh.

"You haven't won a second term yet, love." Sandy's face showed that something had just dawned on her. "In fact, you haven't won a first term. Kenton won the election."

"President," Terri raised her eyebrows at her man. "What happened to that simple cop that I married?"

Hugh squeezed her hand. "He's still here. I politely declined."

"Simple cop," Sandy's eyes twinkled. "I married a simple farmer."

They all laughed at that. Then one of the servants was there.

"Ladies and Gentlemen, dinner is served."

"Servants everywhere." Terri said as they started toward the dining room. "I thought you made supper.?

"The servants take some getting used to." Sandy took her by the arm. "I made the meal, but they insisted on serving it."

"I think I could get used to that." Terri smiled as she admitted it and both women giggled. "I'd even let them cook."

The General stood and waited for the President to pass. The President, ever the host, waived his still hobbling guest in front of him.

"I'm serious, Hugh," the President said. "What we need here in the nation's new capitol are people who are not politicians. We need to change the way things are done in the government. We have a new capitol, we do not need, nor do we want the same old politics."

"I thought you were doing that, sir," Hugh dodged.

"I am," Will nodded, "but we don't have a majority in either house yet. We've passed some reforms, but we've a long way to go. We need people who aren't here for powers sake, but the good they can do with that power."

"The American Party needs the next generation of leaders," Sandy agreed. "What do you think, Terri?"

Terri smiled at her husband. "I think it would be a great idea. He'd be a great President."

Hugh gave her a dirty look.

The families sat down and Will said a prayer.

"Work on him." Will struck a fork full of potatoes in his mouth. "We need him."

"I'd show you how to be a First Lady" Sandy joked.

"At this point, Ho, we have serious doubts that we can advance further at this time." Chin a member of the Politburo was meeting with the Premier and other high party officials. "Our supply lines are stretched much too thin. We have problems with the Americans, Israeli's, and English."

"It would be my suggestion that we consolidate our gains," Ho said. "We dominate much of the world now. If we tighten our grip on what we have gained, we will someday be able to launch our forces in victory against the remaining nations."

"I told you the plan was too ambitious when you proposed it," Chang spoke sharply. "We could have had all of Asia with hardly a fight. Trying to conquer the whole world stretches even our massive army to thin."

Ho was angry. "If I had listened to you, we would have Asia and only Asia! Now we control Asia, Africa, Europe and South America. The only places not under our influence are North America, Australia, the Middle East, and the British Islands. Now is the time to tighten our controls. Now is the time to consolidate our victories."

"What do you propose?" Chin spoke again.

"We stop where we are," Ho said. "In our generation we may go no farther, but we will develop a master plan to complete our world domination. We make sure that we give back no more territory to the Americans or Israeli's. With the domination of areas already conquered our standing army can go from two hundred million to a billion once we have indoctrinated the populations. My original timetable may not work out, but the results will be the same in the end."

"Chang?" Chin looked to him for approval.

"Very well," Chang nodded.

The 50,000-seat stadium was sold out. The crowd murmured to one another as they patiently waited in their seats. The stage was empty except for several microphones and musical instruments that were set up.

A lone, slight figure emerged from the curtain at the back of the stage and strolled to the front microphone. The crowd was instantly on its feet and roaring. Sandy stood in front of the microphone as she waited for the roar to die down. When the crowd noise started to diminish, she held up her hand to silence them. Those present quickly complied, retaking their seats.

"I think we are forgetting something," Sandy chided. "A number of years ago there was a very good praise band at a church. The church service became all about the praise band. The praise leader then wrote the song, 'We're getting back to the heart of Worship.' That's what we need to do today. That's what we are here to do. Never forget that it's all about Jesus and His Father, our God."

Hands started to rise in worship all over the stadium.

"This movement has started to become more about me then about God," Sandy continued. "Some of the people who have regularly appeared on this stage have started to be listed above our God in the playbill. Remember that Satan very seldom will try to totally derail the train, he just tries to throw a switch and send it onto a sidetrack where it will become ineffective."

Several Amens were heard.

"Our battle is not against the Communist Chinese so much as it is against the Prince of Lies, the deceiver, Satan. The battle is not against flesh and blood, but against principalities!"

The Amens grew louder.

"The Lord must do such battle for us. The battle belongs to the Lord," she shouted.

"Praise God," the crowd responded.

"For fighting our battles for us is He not worthy of praise?"

"Yes," the crowd screamed.

"Come on out then." Sandy turned back toward the curtain.

An all-female praise group strode out onto the stage and took up their instruments.

"Remember," Sandy held up her index finger, "first is praise." Sandy held up her middle finger beside the index, "Second comes prayer."

The band started to softly play.

"We will pray as we have in past gatherings," the First Lady said, "but first, for the next hour, join the band in praising the name of the Lord our God!"

The band hit it hard, and the crowd praised God for ninety solid minutes.

General Green was finally sufficiently recovered from his time as a POW to return to active duty. After being discharged from the hospital in California, he hopped a transport south to Chinandega, Nicaragua where the US First Army HQ had been set up. He was walking up to HQ when he saw the graveyards. He detoured to them. The bodies had been exhumed, identified, and then reinterred. The first graveyard he came to was that of native resistance fighters. Four hundred and eighty-three graves had been marked. He had seen them marched by the camp where he was held. He had heard that they were executed and buried in a common grave. Webster had seen that they were honored.

After a moment of silence at the graves of the Nicaraguans, Green moved on to the slightly bigger cemetery. The larger plot of ground held five hundred and thirteen of his men. Some had died of disease, their captors had murdered some, and some had killed themselves when they could take no more. The tears started to flow from the General's eyes, then his knees wobbled, and he sank to all fours. The sobs were unashamed, he had been responsible for these men, and he had failed them.

Green jumped when the hand touched his shoulder. He looked around to find General Webster squatting next to him, he had no idea that anyone was there or how long he had been crawling among the graves, reading each name, crying. Webster's staff stood at a respectful distance.

"Are you OK, Paul," Webster asked.

"I'll make it, Arlan." After a moment he leaned against a headstone. "Should we get on with it?"

Webster thought he noticed something in the other General's manner. "What do you think you're here for?"

"My court-martial, sir," Green said.

"Why would you be court-martialed," Arlan asked.

"I got my men into an untenable situation." Green looked at Webster. "My command, an entire army, was destroyed in detail due to my errors."

The two men were silent for a moment, and then Webster spoke. "No war was ever won unless commanders take chances. You took a chance and it bit you. There will be no court martial, Paul. I've summoned you here to offer you a command. We need good officers."

Green was surprised at being offered another command. He looked at Webster. "I need to go talk to my men," he waived toward the cemetery, "see what they think."

Arlan nodded his understanding. "Take your time."

General Green walked among the tombstones. There were many thousand more buried where he had lost them in Honduras, other bodies had found their way home. His knees were still wobbly, but he remained upright until he saw the name, Private Larry Campbell. Green's knees again betrayed him. In a controlled descent he knelt in front of the grave of the Private.

"Sign it or he will suffer." The scene replayed in the General's mind. The Commandant swung the baseball bat with force and, yes, with glee shattering the Private's kneecap. Campbell had screamed in pain. "Sign it!"

The Commandant brought the bat down on the Private's lower leg; Green heard the bone break. The Private screamed.

"OK, OK, I'll sign it," Green had finally broken. He would sign, confessing to war crimes he had not committed.

"Noooo!" Campbell came up halfway off the table until the restraints caught him. "Don't you sign that!"

The Commandant used the bat to strike the Private in the chest, knocking the wind out of him. The Chinese officer walked over and handed Green a pen.

"No sir!" Campbell had regained his wind. "I'll die before I'll let you sign that on my account."

The Commandant took a full swing to Campbell's face with the bat. Blood flew everywhere and the Private was silent.

"Sign!" The Commandant screamed it.

"No" Green said quietly. He would not dishonor his soldier's wishes.

The Commandant swung full at Green, breaking multiple ribs, then turned on the Private and literally beat his head until it came apart. Covered with blood the Commandant came back over to Green. Pointing at the corpse of Private Campbell he said, "That is your fault."

Green was back in the present. "What should I do, Private?"

Green came to attention in front of Webster's desk.

"Made a decision, Paul," Webster asked.

"Yes, sir!" Green snapped to attention.

"And?"

"Sir, the men wouldn't let me give up when they were still alive, how can I give up when they've given their lives so that we might carry on and win this thing?"

"Good decision General." Webster walked around the desk and offered a hand. "Welcome back, General Green."

Green shook the offered hand. "Good to be back, sir."

"They tell me that it is wrong for me as President to speak of my faith." Will was giving one of his fireside chats. "They are wrong. The greatest military force ever assembled on Earth has assaulted us. They have invaded our territory with the intent of subjugating our people. If things were left to men alone, we would now be going through the throws of occupation. The saying is that God plus one is a majority. The truth is that God alone is a majority. If the Creator of the Universe stands with us, who can stand against us? The proof is in the results; no one can stand against Him and since he is with us no one can stand against us.

"In the past when God has rescued a people, they have made one of two fundamental mistakes. They would either take credit for their victories themselves or they would enjoy the prosperity that comes after the victory and forget the God that delivered them. First, we have not yet won this war. We must continue to petition the Maker of All Things to bring us final victory, and then we must remember from where victory came and honor that.

"Remember the Lord your God each day and we shall be His people and He shall give us victory over our enemies."

Air Force One landed on MEC's private strip. Few men had the power to summon the President of the United States anywhere, but Frank Thomas was one of them. He stood next to the hanger as the First Jet rolled into a hanger. The hanger doors shut, and stairs rolled up to the door.

When the door opened the first four people out the door were all Secret Service. Dixon was the next one out the door and the President did not appear until Dixon had surveyed the scene and nodded his approval. Will made his way down the stairs at a trot, which, of course, made Dixon nervous.

"What's so urgent that we had to stop here," Will asked.

Frank motioned Will to a room in the hanger. "I think you'll like this."

Once they were inside the room Will noticed several of MEC's best engineers around a table. A multi-media presentation was set up on the table that was in the middle of the room.

"The President's in a hurry," Frank barked the order, "roll it!"

The animation started with what sounded like a professional narrator. When Frank did a project, it was always first rate. "This is the proposed new MEC-1 missile." The missile on the screen looked like any other missile. "With magnetic technology our new generation missile can stay aloft indefinitely. With this simple squawk device," a small nodule showed on the screen, "all our vehicles will be safe, our planes will be safe, our shipping will be safe but the missile, detecting anything moving without the squawked signal, will destroy it."

The animated missile dove on an animated Chinese truck and destroyed it.

There was much more to the presentation.

"Stop the video," Frank ordered.

"How good is this thing," Will asked.

"You can launch it over a battlefield with the guidance program set to detect any movement," Jack Hewitt explained. "It will ignore any vehicle that is squawking and destroy any vehicle that is not or squawking the wrong frequency. There are even settings that will let it detect enemy camps or troop movements."

"How soon can this be deployed?" The President could see an early end to the war.

"A few months," Hewitt said, "maybe a year."

"Can we expedite," Will asked.

"We will," Frank said.

"Sir, one more thing," Hewitt spoke again. "Let me tell you about the complete potential of this missile."

"Go on," the Commander-in-Chief said.

"With the MEC engines we could fire missiles from here to China. The missile could orbit for as long as it needs to until it finds a target. With the targeting programs it would be just as effective night or day. The only thing that we might worry about is weather."

Will looked Frank in the eye. "Get this done."

With that the President left.

Frank turned to his crew. "You heard the President. We have to get this done. I don't care if it takes sixteen hours a day. Move!"

There were no smiles in the group. Everyone knew that Frank could be a slave driver but they also knew that if they did not get the job done there was still a chance that they would be slaves.

Frank Thomas returned home to his lonely apartment. He wondered how many people had an apartment in the office building where they worked. He had been thinking about renting a place off the grounds but ditched the idea. He would seldom be there if he did rent someplace. He had spent months sleeping at MEC while developing the IP Fighter, now he would stay until the missile was done. So much for a social life.

There were many single women at MEC that wanted to date Frank. Due to his position, he would not consider a woman that worked for him. The lawyer in him thought sexual harassment suit.

The CEO of MEC no longer lived out of suitcases. He had managed to get some nice furniture for his place at MEC. MEC was his life. He wished he had what Will Sevrin had but was unwilling to give control of his life to anyone, even God. At 10:30 p.m. he lay down. He would start the crash program on the missile the next morning. He had told everyone to be at work by six a.m.

16.

Hugh Smith's first desire was to be with his family. He had been told he could have two months off because of his wound. He was gone less than a month. Second, he desired to be with his men. The newly minted General did not trust anyone else to lead them. The desire to be with his men got him back in the field quickly.

Hugh crawled the final yards on his belly where peered over the top of the ridge and could see the huge group of men moving toward them designating the location of the Chinese army.

Tex was on the General's left and raised his binoculars to his eyes. "Yep, them are Chinese alright."

Hugh sized up the situation through his binoculars. The enemy had turned. The Air Force was pounding them as they moved south, he could see the planes bobbing and weaving, diving, and climbing. Still the Chinese were putting distance between themselves and the other US armies. They were running in desperation and coming directly at First Army.

Hugh rolled over onto his back and punched a code into his radio. "Let me talk to General Webster."

"Webster, what ya got, Hugh?"

"Sir, have the boys dig in on the ridge you're on." Hugh looked back at the advancing enemy. "We don't have time to make it to the next ridge."

"How close are they?"

"Sir, we should be engaged late tonight or in the morning," Hugh said as Tex indicated his agreement.

"We'll be ready." Webster would enjoy getting into the fight again. Oh, sure there had been some fighting coming up from Nicaragua, but nothing major. "Now get back here before they slip up on you and capture our most decorated officer."

"Smith out." Hugh looked back through his binoculars for a moment, and then turned to Tex. They were almost two miles beyond their lines. "Let's get back to friendly lines."

With the night vision and infrared technologies, the time of day did not matter for the fight. Night offered little cover; yet the old school commanders still considered moving under darkness an advantage.

All along the American lines the squad leaders were seeing movement with their night vision. They had been ordered to maintain silence and hold their fire until the Chinese were nearly ready to step on them. When the first shot was fired, they would open fire up and down the line. First Army was holding its discipline.

Percy saw the first Chinese step from the brush on the other side of the valley and cross the road. The lead elements started up the US side of the ravine unaware that the Americans stared down on them from the heights. The Chinese disappeared into the brush again but were obviously coming on toward the American lines.

Hardwick did not see another enemy soldier for some time, though Hugh, who was using infrared, kept him apprised of how close they were getting. The brush broke only fifteen feet from where the Americans lay. Still, no one had fired. Ten feet then five the men began to raise their rifles when someone to their far-right opened fire. The entire ridge, miles long, erupted in fire. The Chinese had been taken completely by surprise. Thousands of Chinese fell before they could even defend themselves. The remainder of them retreated in a panic. The American troops jumped up celebrating and shouting taunts at the retreating enemy.

"Should I call 'em down, sir," Tex asked.

"No, let 'em celebrate a bit," Hugh answered. "Then we need to move to the next ridge."

"Sir, we've engaged First Army," Dong told his commanding officer.

"Where?"

Dong rolled out the map and pointed. "Here, sir."

"The results," Lian asked.

"We were driven back to the north side of the valley."

"Can we reorganize the troops before sunrise?"

"I believe so, sir," Dong nodded.

"I want the entire army on the south side of the valley below the top before sunrise," Lian was about to take a desperate gamble. "At dawn I will blow a whistle and all our troops will be committed. We hold nothing back."

"Yes sir!" Dong moved back off to give the orders.

Lian saw the first pink of sunrise in the east. For a moment he wondered if it might not be his last sunrise. He knew it would be the last sunrise of many a good soldier. The General raised the whistle to his lips and blew.

Hundreds of thousands of Chinese troops roared with a battle cry and charged out of the brush, up the hill to the top of the ridge and into abandoned foxholes. Confusion reigned. They were told that the Americans would be here. Where were the Americans?

Whump, whump, whump, whump, whump, whump the entire valley exploded into a wall of flame. Artillery was sited in from the next ridge and was killing with extreme efficiency. As the surviving Chinese tried to run back to the north side of the valley the planes swooped in. The carnage was terrible. In less than a half-hour more than half of Lian's army died.

Hugh sat on the ridge examining the carnage. He was still limping from his injury but just could not stay out of the fight.

"When you plan a battle a lot of people die, you know that sir," Tex observed.

"God gives everyone a talent," Hugh observed, "mine just happens to be killing people."

Tex laughed a short humorless laugh. "Yeah, killing lotsa people in short order. I'm sure glad you're on our side, sir."

"Sir, the other American armies will be on us in less than a day," Dong informed his commander. "We lost two hundred thousand men today with more than twice that number wounded. Another day like that and our army will cease to exist. We must sue for peace."

"Surrender," Lian thundered, "never!"

"What good does it do to lose all these men," a Colonel asked. "If we are taken prisoner, we might someday be liberated and be able to fight for The Party again. Not to mention all the resources the Americans will have to spend keeping us in POW camps."

Lian paced, deep in thought for some moments. "I will not entertain surrender. We will attack the American First Army again in the morning."

"Sir, that proved to be little better than suicide today," the Colonel offered. "What makes you think it will be better tomorrow?"

"We attack at dawn." Lian walked out of the command tent.

The attack never came. As the Chinese troops settled in for the night just after dark, the American planes swooped in. The only light on the cloudy night was the flash of high explosives. The Americans pounded the enemy troops until well after midnight without letup, then, suddenly there was silence.

After a few moments the Chinese soldiers started to rise from their holes, thinking the night's battle was over. There had not been much of a battle. The Americans had pounded the Chinese position and the Chinese had lay there and taken it.

There was a burst of small arms fire from out of the dark. Many men fell before they could make it back to their holes. Using their night vision, the Americans had advanced on the Chinese positions. The Chinese could not fight back effectively as their supplies were running out. Some simply had nothing left to fight with. General Lian died in the first burst of fire, and then Dong radioed a surrender order. Those who did make it back to the holes quickly ran up white flags.

Will was awakened by the knock on the bedroom door. He looked over at his wife, who slept soundly, then back at the clock that showed 0213. This always made him marvel as such a knock on the door awoke him immediately. Sandy, on the other hand, would be wide-awake if one of the children let out a whimper down the hall in the middle of the night. The child would have to be screaming bloody murder before he woke.

Sandy had explained it by their responsibilities. She was a woman, born to nurture. She heard kids. He was the President of the United States; getting awakened in the middle of the night was part of the job. Will put on his robe and shuffled his slippered feet to the door.

"Yes?"

Jeter, the head of the night watch on the Secret Service was there, he held up a radio, "General Webster, sir."

Will knew it was important for the General to awaken him at this hour. "This is the President."

"Mr. President, I thought you'd like to know that the Chinese Army of Central America is no more."

"Surrendered," Will asked, "annihilated?"

"Mr. President, the Central American group gave up in small units at first, then larger and larger," Webster sounded tired. "There was no organized surrender. There are still some Chinese units that haven't surrendered, but they are negligible. It's over in Mexico and Central America."

"Not quite over in Central America," Will said.

"What do you mean, sir?"

"The Marines are holding on by the skin of their teeth in Costa Rica," the President informed him. "The Chinese have thrown at least ten million infantry at them."

There was silence on the General's end for a moment. "In a day I'll be done here. I'll get First Army turned tomorrow. I'll start a division or two south yet today."

"Second Army is on the way to boats." The President yawned. "They should be there in less than seventy-two hours."

"Thought you'd like the news, Mr. President." The General was ready to get back to the war.

"Thank you, General." The President smiled. "It's good news."

Webster turned in his chair to the staff members assembled before him. He scanned the group, but his eyes settled on Smith. "Hugh, I need you to hop a transport and get down south. I need a complete report on how the Marines are doing, how quick we need to get there and where we're needed the most. If I have to, I'll pull out and leave the cleanup to the locals, they'd relish that."

"Yes sir," Hugh nodded. "How soon do you want me to leave?"

"How soon can you get your duffel packed," the General asked.

"Soon," Hugh answered.

"I'll have a plane warming up," Webster said. "You taking Percy and Tex?"

"Yes sir."

"Three passengers it is." The Commander said as he picked up a phone radio. "Yes, this is General Webster…"

There were explosions all around as the picture stabilized on WNN. "This is Gary Patton reporting from Costa Rica!"

An explosion that was very close caused Gary to duck in his foxhole, dirt rained down on the camera as it fell over. The change in Patton was remarkable. He had obviously been eating better since he had gotten back on the American side of the lines and his hair was cut GI style. He set the camera back up. "My, that was close."

"Things a little hot there, Gary," Galena Gomez asked.

"Yes, they are Galena." The reporter was almost drowned out by the nearby rattle of small arms fire. "The Chinese are trying to do whatever they can to break through the Marine bottleneck here in Costa Rica. They are determined to regain some of the territory that they once held. I also doubt that they have been told of the surrender of their Mexican contingent. They probably are still trying to break through to their Comrades up north, not knowing that they are not there anymore."

"How are the Marines holding out," Gomez asked.

"They're doing well, Galena," Patton answered, "but the simple fact is the Marines are wearing down and in need of relief as the Chinese have thrown human wave after human wave at the US lines and we've beaten back every attack. The problem is that the attacks have kept up night and day for days on end with no relief in sight. The Chinese have the manpower to throw different units into the fight at different times, but the Marines must fight twenty-four, seven. The Marines are simply wearing out."

Hugh lay on his belly at the top of the hill with Percy on one side and Tex on the other.

"How many does this make," Hugh asked.

"That's eight major attacks on our lines in six hours, sir," Hardwick answered.

"Don't they ever run out of men," Hugh shook his head.

"From what intelligence says they've gotta be gettin' thin," Saddler said. "At least thin for the Chinese."

"I don't know how much more the Marines can take," Percy noted. "They're getting exhausted from the sheer volume of the fighting."

Hugh's phone/radio buzzed. "General Smith."

"Hugh, it's Webster." The familiar raspy voice growled on the other end. "I'm here with the main body. Where do we go?"

"Sir, I'd move 'em straight into the front lines." Hugh slid below the crest and sat up. "The Marines need some sleep and a hot meal. I'd especially relieve them on the East Coast. That's where the enemy is attacking heaviest now, sir."

"OK, I'll get it done," Webster commented. "Second Army should be landing in the morning. We should be pushing south within a week."

"Yes, sir," Hugh answered, "Smith out."

The General punched a button on the phone, breaking the connection. Just then a Marine Colonel from the General Staff rolled up in his Hummer.

"When can we expect support, General?" The Marine asked as he exited his Hummer and headed for Hugh. "Some of my men are so tired they're falling asleep in combat!"

"Should be today," Hugh answered.

"I hope so." The Colonel did not seem too sure of Hugh's promise.

"Look there," Hugh pointed to the road coming across the valley floor from the north. First Army was coming over the horizon.

"Hallelujah!" The Colonel sat back down in his Hummer. "Let's go show the Army where to go. This is one time where we can tell Army guys where to go without getting punched."

The Hummer roared off while Hugh returned to the top of the hill to watch the battle.

The sign on the door was in Chinese, but it translated:

Commander
South American Forces

"Come in," General Hu answered the knock on his door.

The Major from intelligence came for his morning briefing.

"How is your report this morning," Hu asked.

"Disturbing sir."

Hu had been catching up on paperwork, a task he abhorred. He put down his pen and asked, "How so?"

"Sir, I believe we have the complete picture here now."

"Go on."

"The best we can tell General Lian is dead, his army defeated." The Major knew his report was grim, but he needed Hu to see the big picture. "Our entire Mexican army has surrendered or been eliminated, sir. This we have from radio messages from troops and reports in the American media."

Hu motioned for the Major to continue.

"We have badly depleted our forces in attempting to break through to our

Mexican army and are now well below four million in strength with little hope of reinforcement. Our supply dumps are stocked well enough to carry us for some time, but while the American Marines could not last much longer against our numbers, they do not have to. The US First Army is moving into the lines along the East Coast now, while it is reported that the American Second Army is docking in troop transports on the West Coast even as we speak. With these reinforcements it will be suicide to try to break through to the north and with our Mexican army gone we have no reason to waste any more troops."

"Your recommendation," the General asked.

"That we fall back to the mountains and jungles of Columbia and await the Americans there," the Major was candid. "We get the high ground and make them attack."

Hu considered the desktop for a moment. "Very well, write up the order and I will sign it, dismissed."

The Major turned about smartly as if to leave, and then turned back to the General. "Sir, I forgot to congratulate you."

"Congratulate me for what?" The General was dubious.

"With General Lian gone you are now in command of all Chinese Forces in the Americas."

"I am not sure that is such an honor, Major," Hu said. "I may preside of the biggest military debacle in history. I always thought we were underestimating the Americans. Now I see I was right."

"Sir, the Prime Minister on your line," Will's private secretary said.

The President picked up the phone. "Hiram how goes it?"

"I have lived through another day, Mr. President," Hiram Prescott observed. "Over here, that's an accomplishment."

Hugh knew that the pounding never ended in England. "Well, Mr. Prime Minister, we've pushed the Chinese into South America, it shouldn't be too many months until we can come across the pond."

"To tell you the truth I don't know if we've got months," Prescott sounded depressed.

"What do you mean, Hiram," Will was worried.

"Will, you are a good friend, but you can't understand what we're going through without being here."

"Churchill stood the blitz," Will said, thinking it hollow.

"When you compare the two, Churchill looks like a wimp compared to what we've had to put up with," Prescott said. "If we can't stop the air raids we'll have to quit."

"I know I said I would stop the raids. The problem was we needed those assets here to win the Americas back."

"I just can't let my people take any more of this."

"I'll stop the raids. Then can you hold on?" Will asked his question knowing the IP fighters had been delayed in striking across the Atlantic.

"Hold on," Prescott asked, "we'll attack. But how can you stop them from America?"

"Sorry, old chum, still secret. Need to know. While I won't tell you over the phone, I will tell you in person when I see you. Has a lot to do with why we're making such good progress," Will said. "Call me tomorrow and tell me if the raids weren't at least lighter. Just make sure you keep all your fly boys on the ground tonight."

"What are you going to do," Hiram asked.

"Just trust me, Mr. Prime Minister" Will encouraged him "just trust me."

"Whatever you say, Mr. President," Hiram said. "I look forward to a quiet and restful night."

When they had hung up, Will dialed General Bennett, Chief of Staff of the Air Force.

"Bennett."

"Tom, this is the President."

"How are you today, sir?"

"Feeling like an idiot," Will said.

"Why is that sir?"

"How many IP Fighters do we have in service?"

"Four, sir."

"How many could we divert to England?"

"Well, sir." The General thought for a moment. "The Chinese have no air power in the Western Hemisphere. We'd need to keep one here just for safety, but we could send three."

"Do it," Will ordered. He had meant to do this some time ago, but it had simply not been possible until now. "I want at least one of them to orbit over the British Isles twenty-four, seven until further notice."

"Sir, I…" the General started to object.

"Tom, if we don't stop the Chinese from pounding the English the Prime Minister says they'll have to surrender," Will informed him. "They need some relief."

"I'm on it, sir."

"And now, Investigative Reports with Rock James." The announcer said this with great gravity, though he doubted anything of great gravity could come out of that empty suit of an anchorman. The announcer knew that Rock did none of the actual investigating since he had proven inept at it. All Rock James could do was read Teleprompters.

James went to investigator after investigator, asked them leading questions, then let them tell whatever they had made up that appeared to be a story. None of the reporters had even ventured out of New York while 'investigating' the story.

"So, what you're saying is that there never was a Chinese threat," The Rock asked.

"Yes," the reporter nodded, "no Chinese soldier has even left the borders of China except to go to a few countries where they were invited and where China maintains a garrison. I've actually spoken with the Chinese Premier and he has assured me that this is true."

"So where are all the body bags coming from?" Rock continued the line of questioning.

"There are no bodies in them if that's what you mean."

"Where does all the money we spend on the war go?"

"Rock, the money goes in the body bags, which are actually shipped to a numbered account in the name of the President, Secretary of War, or other high officials. There is no war. There are no casualties."

Both Will and Sandy had paused with their forks halfway between the plate and their mouths. Neither could believe what they had just seen but were watching it because of leaks about the stories content.

"How can anyone believe that stuff and delude themselves to that degree," Sandy asked.

"They tell me that the reporters filing the story haven't even been out of New York State," Will answered.

"All they have to do is go to South America if they wanna find the war," Sandy was shaking her head.

"A few months ago, they could have found it in Colorado." Will changed the channel.

"Do you think a scandal of this magnitude can do anything but bring the President down," The Rock asked.

"I don't know, Rock," the reporter said. "President Sevrin controls all the other media and most of the money in the world. He could probably pull this off if people won't go out and find out for themselves."

Rock turned back to the camera with a stern look. "Rock James, ATCN."

Will strode into the Oval Office at his usual time of morning. There were few emergency calls to work when the enemy was in retreat. His secretary opened the door that led to her office.

"Hiram Prescott is on your line for you, Mr. President."

Will picked up the phone. "Mr. Prime Minister, did you sleep well."

"Couldn't catch a wink!" Hiram sounded almost disgusted. "I'm so used to loud noises and my bed shaking all night that I couldn't sleep without the disturbance."

"The disturbance should be over," Will assured him. "You'll get used to it."

"My radar chaps tell me you felled one hundred and eighty-three Chinese planes, not to mention the missiles." The Prime Minister yawned. "I need to know how you did this."

"Next time we're face to face," Will assured him, "not over the phone. Not even when the line is secure as this one."

"We shall have to call a summit," Prescott said. "I shall see you soon, Mr. President, but until then be assured that England is standing firm. Our upper lips just got quite stiff. Your unsinkable aircraft carrier is again available."

"Very good, Mr. Prime Minister we will probably make use of it." Will ended the call. "See you soon."

"As I sit here in the new White House today, I can't help but think of how much a year has changed the fortunes of so many people." Will spoke in the week's fireside chat. "A little over a year ago the unstoppable juggernaut of the Chinese Army was moving north from the southern tip of South America. They would move north with little more than a hiccup until they drove their way into southern Colorado.

"Then the American Army stood up. Now, as the American Army liberates each country, the Allied Army grows. The two hundred-million-man army of the Chinese was insurmountable to one country, but as countries work together, we come to a point where we have as many men in our army as they in theirs. At some point our army will be even bigger than theirs. Have no doubt that we have only begun our march to worldwide freedom, but we have begun that march. Have no doubt that we will continue the march, no matter the time it takes or the miles we must cover to walk this walk, until our mission is accomplished.

"We must not forget how we got here. God has fought our battles. Tonight, before you take your rest, thank the God of the Universe for his providence. Continue to thank him until the job is done. Continue to thank him even after the job is done. Good night."

Will had no more finished his chat then Kirk walked in. "What's up Gordo?"

"Mr. President" Gordo said, "I believe the mission you gave me to win the peace is under way?"

"What are you doing?"

"We started with Mexico and are working south" Gordo started. "We are trying to put democratic institutions in place where none existed before. We will soon start Guatemala."

"Perhaps we can win the peace this time." Will smiled.

17.

The staff of First Army was gathered in the large tent field headquarters. At this point headquarters was just outside Medellin, Columbia. "OK, gentlemen, how do we speed up this march? We are marching quickly toward Cape Horn, but we can do it more quickly?"

A two-star raised his hand. "Sir, should we mess with a good thing?"

Webster frowned. "That's what both Hauser and Glenn said. Well, Second and Third Armies can sit on their cans if they want, but that's not how I play the game. I say when you have an advantage you press it while you're looking for a greater advantage."

Percy spoke up. "Sir, how many troops do the Chinese have in South America now?"

"three to three and a half million," the General answered.

"Is the navy interdicting their supplies, sir," another officer asked.

"Some," Webster nodded, "they are still getting some of their supplies. They also have quite a stockpile."

"What's the possibility of stopping their supplies via sea, sir," Tex asked.

"Can't do it any time soon and maintain security for the homeland."

Now Hugh spoke up. "Can they resupply by air, sir?"

"We have complete air superiority. I don't think they even have effective anti-aircraft capability left."

"Then there is only one way to shut them down more quickly." Hugh continued, "We have to cut their supply line."

"How do we do that," Arlan asked.

"We land a force south of them, sir," Hugh said.

"No one has ever attempted a landing at Cape Horn," Webster shook his head. "The seas are just too rough to do that."

"Who said anything about an amphibious landing? We can invade from the air."

The commanding General of First Army walked over to the map wall and clicked through the maps until he found the right one. Hugh and several others joined him there. "What's your suggestion, Hugh?"

"I don't have a specific place in mind just yet, but let's loosely say southern Argentina or Chile or both. We chopper in and take any given area big enough to bring in an MEC lifter. We can bring an entire army and all their equipment via MEC lifters in a few hours. Like the Chinese used their super subs, we can put a hundred thousand men in lifters and place them in there. Before they know it, we can have a whole army behind their lines and their supply lines are cut."

"Sounds doable," Webster nodded, "I suppose you want to be on the first chopper."

"Can't lead from the rear, sir," Hugh offered. "I would plan for one contingency."

"Go on."

"Keep the Naval task force that launches the choppers off the cape to do evac if needed," Hugh said. "When we kill their supplies, they will probably attack south. With that many enemy forces fighting for their existence we could get pushed into the sea unless we have a way off. If we evac when they push south, we can trap them between our forces and the cape. As you said there has never been a landing on the cape. I'm betting they cannot evac via the cape. With the Navy then off the coast they also won't be able to resupply."

Webster nodded. "I'll run it past the Joint Chiefs."

Ora Pittman had never had much of a life. Both of his parents were drug addicts. His mom overdosed when he was three. The boy was raised by his drug dealing father until a drug deal went bad and the seven-year-old watched his dad bleed out from the stab wounds that a customer gave him.

Ora just lived with his aunt one more year as she hooked to support him and her ever-increasing drug habit. As the habit grew the money free to spend on him dwindled. He often went without food and sometimes the other necessities of life.

Ora's aunt was turning her latest trick one night when things became violent, and the john strangled her. For four days, no one thought much about the boy staring out of the car window despite the near freezing temperatures. Since he and his aunt had been living in the car for nearly two weeks before her untimely demise, it was not unusual for the boy to be left in the car alone for long periods of time. In the drug infested neighborhood kids were often left alone or in cars at very young ages for long periods. Finally, an anonymous call was placed to police and Ora went into state custody.

Ora could find no one to love him and seldom spent more than a few months in any given foster home. Most of the foster parents in the area were more interested in the money they could get for the boy than in doing anything good for him. Feeling more and more hopeless and less and less in control of events the boy's behavior became more and more disruptive.

At age fourteen he ran away from his last foster home. The foster parents did not bother to report him as missing. They still got the money for him if he showed on their books and his disruptive behavior was no longer a problem.

To survive the young man, who was now growing into a handsome blonde, blue-eyed hunk, sold himself to the predators that cruised the back streets looking to pay for sex. His first arrest not only landed him in juvenile but landed his foster parents in jail for fraud.

Ora was introduced to Satanism while sharing a cell with an avowed Satanist in the secure Juvenile facility where he was placed after his fourth arrest. His cellmate promised him power over the world if he would only bow to the Lord of Darkness. Ora jumped into the satanic world with both feet.

By the age of twenty-two Ora Pittman was not only the head of the biggest coven on the east coast of the United States he was also one of the best known and most feared people in the Satanist community. He no longer needed to turn to crime for his income as his followers supported him. When meeting with the higher ups from his group he often called to Satan for an appearance and was often obliged by the manifestation of demons. You might say that Ora Pittman was Satan's right-hand man in the United States.

Ora petitioned for a legal name change. His lawyer found a liberal judge who granted it without question. He was no longer Ora Pittman but rather Satan Demon Devil.

The real Satan was unhappy with the way events were turning in his plan for world domination. He had thought the forces of the godless Communist nation would conquer the world. The Prince of Darkness had empowered their military while he blinded the leaders of the West to the goings on as China built an army many times the size of any ever known. Those who claimed Jesus were beginning to win again and he needed to do something to change that. Satan had a plan for Ora Pittman AKA Satan Demon Devil.

She had expected pain to be more evident than pride. Yes, she could see the pain in the eyes, the pain of a mother forced to bury a child. Yet, there was more pride in those eyes than pain. There she saw the pride of a mother whose child had laid down their life in the defense of freedom.

A large woman, tall with broad shoulders, was the first to approach Sandy and shake her hand. "Madam First Lady."

"Please, call me Sandy," she said.

"It's such a pleasure to meet you," the lady said.

"What's your name, dear," she asked.

"Ima Saltus." The woman said. "My son's name was Preston."

The whole experience of the Gold Star Mother's meeting was becoming overwhelming to Sandy. She threw her arms around Ima and wondered who was comforting whom. Soon Sandy was called to the podium, as she was the featured speaker.

"I don't know what to say." She started in a faltering manner. "I cannot claim the sacrifice that any of you have laid on the altar of freedom. The child you bore and nurtured to adulthood is no more in this life. Your greatest labor of love is now a memory. Remember! Remember the joys of your child and even the heartaches, for your son or daughter was a unique gift from God.

"Greater love has no man then he lay down his life for a friend. So says the Bible in John 15:13. Your children have laid down their lives for their friends, relatives and even for those whom they did not know. I say this to you if your loved one knew Christ you have not seen them for the last time. They are in a better place and await your arrival. God go with you until you meet again."

Sandy retook her seat as she lost control of her emotions. Tears streamed down her face as those present stood to applaud. There was not a dry eye in the house.

The USS Enterprise and three other carriers cruised into the waters of Cape Horn surrounded by their screening and support vessels. Enterprise headed Task Force Harm. According to the intelligence that the Chinese had been allowed to intercept Task Force Harm was on a mission to seek out and destroy Chinese resupply ships. They had done enough of that to maintain their cover. The Chinese were not worried about the task force as it was mostly out of their supply lanes. They thought their convoys had been screen well enough to fool the U. S. forces. The reason the thousands of Army troops were aboard was kept secret to all but those aboard the ships of the task force.

The first chopper lifted off just before dawn. When the sky was filled with troop transports and gunships Hugh signaled for the whirlybird task force to head for the coast.

"Kill Sevrin," the voice whispered.
"Yes, Dark One," Ora answered.
"Kill Sevrin!" The voice was louder and more vicious.
"Your wish is my command," Ora bowed.
"Kill Sevrin!" Nowthe voice shrieked in an unearthly shrill.
Ora unlocked his gun locker, withdrew his .357 and held it above his head. "For the lord of darkness."

A rancher near the town of El Toribio in southern Argentina had just risen to tend to his livestock. His herd was much smaller than it had been some two years earlier when the Chinese had invaded. They had butchered so many of his cattle that the once rich man was now struggling. His head was down as he headed for his stables, and he barely heard the rush of the air that caused him to look up. He was sure those were helicopters, but they made no sound. Was he hallucinating?

As the first chopper touched down in his pasture, an American with a star on each side of his collar stepped out first and started directing the others. Soldiers were rushing in every direction.

Even though the soldiers paid him no attention, Angelo could not move. The Americans had come! His home would soon be free again!

In less than ten minutes thousands of American troops under the command of General Hugh Smith were landed. In another twenty minutes they had the area secure, and Hugh punched a code into his radiophone.

"Webster."

"Sir, start your landing," Hugh informed his superior.

The MEC lifters had been in low geosynchronous orbit over the landing area as an IPF fighter had patrolled the skies under them. Less than four hours after Hugh Smith's foot had touched the soil of Argentina the entire First Army was inspecting their gear and preparing to move north.

A Chinese Colonel came to attention before General Hu's desk just a few hours after Smith had landed. Hu turned from the computer where he had been working. "Yes, Colonel."

"More disturbing news, sir," the Colonel informed him.

Hu's left eyebrow shot upward. "What?"

"We are receiving reports of attacks from the south, sir."

"I thought we had eliminated the local militias," Hu frowned.

"The reports are that the attacking force is the American First Army, sir."

Hu was on his feet in alarm. "From the south?"

"Yes sir."

The Colonel followed as the General quickly strode to the maps. The Colonel pointed out the area where the fighting was taking place.

"But how could they have landed at Cape Horn?" Hu had looked at the possibilities of that before the invasion and found it impossible even for the most sophisticated landing craft.

"We must assume they have."

"Webster. We must turn the army immediately." Hu's eyes were wide. "If they come very far north, they will interdict our supplies."

"And if they do, we suffer the same fate as our comrades in Mexico."

Hu immediately started planning a rear-guard action by his northern most forces as he planned to send the majority of his forces south.

The army that the Chinese had left in South America was a fraction of what it once was. Even so it took nearly a week to fully turn. Webster had time to attack the Chinese unit by unit instead of having to face the massed Chinese army and did so with devastating effect. The American Air Force had also pounded the enemy troops. Hu's army was now less than two thirds of what it had been before the Americans had landed to the south. Hu still had no choice but to throw his remaining troops into the battle against a dug-in first army because the First Army stood astride the supply lines that Hu had established.

Hu's staff meeting was grim. America's Second and Fourth Armies were pressing them from the north while the Third Army was coming back into the line from a week's R and R. They had tried to press First Army to the south only to have them reinforced by the First and Second Marines as well as forces recruited from the lands the US had driven the Chinese out of.

"Evaluation?" The commanding general looked out a window where he could see the silent bombers swooping in and dropping their ordinance on his troops.

"If we continue, we will be destroyed in detail."

"Can we break through to our supply lines," Hu was grim.

"Doubtful," a General answered. "Even if we do, we cannot hold it."

A Sergeant entered the meeting with a message. Hu read the note. "I've been ordered home by Premier Ho."

Some of the men present laughed while others shook their heads in disbelief.

"Just how does he propose you get there," someone asked.

"He is my premier." Ho said. "He is my god. I will find a way do as he orders."

In one of the most brilliant military moves ever witnessed Hu sent most of his army toward the West Coast of South America, using all its fury to break through the allied lines. Hu stayed behind with what appeared to be a rear action. When most of the American forces had shifted to give chase to the Chinese Army, Hu took his remaining troops and drove to the East Coast. Once at the East Coast Hu and his troops boarded ships in the harbors and sailed for China.

Not far from the coast an American wolf pack came upon the transports. The Americans showed no mercy. Torpedo's streamed toward the enemy ships. Despite being escorted by an Aircraft Carrier and eight destroyers nearly half the troop ships were sunk.

The Chinese soldiers that Hu had ordered toward the West Coast of South America fought valiantly though most of the officers had guessed the mission was futile. They fought their way through to the Argentine Mountains only to find themselves trapped against the Pacific Ocean. After more than two years of dominating the continent, the remaining Chinese forces surrendered. Of all the soldiers that had been in the group that invaded the Americas, less than one in ten survived. The fight for the Americas was over.

"The Western Hemisphere is free again." Will was finishing his fireside chat that was originating from a New York City radio station. The President had other stops to make on Wall Street when the broadcast finished. "Make no mistake we still have much to do. In the parable of the Good Samaritan Christ made all men our neighbors and many of our neighbors still live under tyranny. I will not rest until all peoples can breathe free and I challenge you to fight the good fight with me. We have done much, there is still much to do.

"As we liberate each land the armies of freedom grow. Those whom we have liberated stand ready to liberate other lands. We will train them, we will arm them, and we will fight next to them as we carry the war across the great waters of the Atlantic and Pacific.

"May God go with and yes before the armies of freedom!"

When the technician gave Will the clear sign, he took off his earphones and walked out of the studio where Gordo and Dixon waited. "Where to now?"

"We've just enough time to ring the closing bell at Wall Street." The Chief of Staff was feeling better than he had since the war began. He thought there was definitely reason for optimism. "Also, we are moving the advisors and administrators into South America. Our post war plan is starting to blossom."

Will smile at Gordo. Things were moving the right way and moving quickly. "Good. Good. Maybe we can win the peace."

Kirk pointed at the door as Dixon took his meaning.

"Buck Rogers on the move!" Dixon used the Secret Service code name for the President.

Outside the door Dixon led the way. It was obvious that the word had gotten out as to where the President was broadcasting from as hundreds lined the route from the door to the limo. There had been only a few spectators when the official entourage had arrived.

Dixon spotted him. His hair was dyed a very dark black and he wore black mascara. The crowd had arrived in such numbers and in such a short period of time that his men had been unable to screen them. This guy was trouble. Dixon started toward the suspicious-looking man but realized in an instant that he was too late. The man wearing the black trench coat pulled a satin nickel .357 from beneath his coat and pointed it at the President of the United States.